# Acclaim for THE MAGIKER

"Charles Dennis has taken the psychological thriller and woven into it a time-travel story of history and ritual and the power of love to survive anything—including death. It is a brilliantly researched and wonderful read, especially if you're a romantic. As I am."

—Julian Fellowes, creator of *Downton Abbey*

"*The Magiker* is an exuberantly original thriller, at once hilarious and informative, ingenious, and deftly romantic."

—Nicholas Meyer, author of *The Seven-Per-Cent Solution*

"Mysticism, romance, and humor are all between the covers of this new book by Charles Dennis. Not easy to accomplish all three at the same time, like juggling an apple, a banana, and a fretsaw, but he's done it."

—Michael Lindsay-Hogg, author of *Luck and Circumstance*

"Oy, a sight to behold, *le dernier cri*! That's the story Charles Dennis has offered up to us. He pulls us deeper and deeper into the arcana of Jewish mysticism. With this plunge into the netherworld, Dennis gives us a fascinating story. And if you think you're alone out there, if you don't read this book, you will be."

—Ed Asner, actor

"Charles Dennis is one of my favorite writers. *The Magiker* is partially his tribute to Elmore Leonard, with a healthy portion of Mr. Dennis's own sense of irony and, of course, his distinctive humor."

—Dan Aykroyd, actor and author of *Elwood's Blues*

## ALSO BY CHARLES DENNIS

*Given the Evidence*

*Given the Crime*

*Shar-Li*

*The Dealmakers*

*Bonfire* (published in the U.K. as *Talent*)

*A Divine Case of Murder*

*The Periwinkle Assault*

*This War Is Closed Until Spring*

*Somebody Just Grabbed Annie!*

*The Next-to-Last Train Ride*

*Stoned Cold Soldier*

# THE MAGIKER

July 13/14

## CHARLES DENNIS

For Nicole + Brian,
with gratitude for your
love + wise counsel
in these difficult times.

As ever,

*Charles*

**A/V**

*Asahina & Wallace*
*Los Angeles*
*2013*
www.asahinaandwallace.com

Published in the United States by Asahina & Wallace, Inc.
(www.asahinaandwallace.com)

Library of Congress Control Number: 2013949726

ISBN: 978-1-940412-02-3

For Ethne Dennis
The daughter of a different Magiker

The Talmud? Granted, it is deep and glorious and vast. But it chains you to the earth. Forbids you to attempt the heights. But Kabbalah! It tears your soul away from the earth and lifts you to the realms of the highest heights. Spreads all the Heavens out before your eyes and leads direct to Paradise. Reaches out in the Infinite and raises a great current itself.

—S. Ansky, *The Dybbuk*

# TREE
## *of*
# LIFE

Keter
Crown

Binah
Understanding

Hokhmah
Wisdom

Gevurah
Judgement

Hesed
Mercy

Tiferet
Beauty

Hod
Reverberation

Nezah
Cycles

Yesod
Foundation

Malchut
Kingdom

# THE UNCLE

BY NOW YOU *are doubtless aware of my alleged crime. The story went viral from that first Sunday morning in Vermont when the state troopers led me away in chains through the snow. That was followed by months of endless demented Twitter and Facebook denunciations: "Restore the death penalty!" Sorry! They couldn't find her body, and you can't execute someone without having a body. But when did that ever stop anyone in the land of the free and the home of* Dancing with the Stars? *And, for the record, I've really had it with all those unflattering photographs of me, unshaven and wild eyed, leaping out from the front pages of supermarket tabloids. Not to mention the in-depth, high-definition interviews with her family and the bereaved bridegroom, conducted by the likes of Oprah Winfrey, Barbara Walters, Diane Sawyer, and other TV sob sisters, who described me as both a monster and a madman. And don't forget the unprecedented week Dr. Phil dedicated to me. I have been forced for legal reasons to keep my silence. But now it is time for me to tell you my side of the story. I'm confident—once it's been explained—that you will have a very different opinion of me...*

\* \* \*

Hearing the snowflakes gently thump against the window of my office that first week of the New Year was not a good thing. For if I could hear them, I would soon be able to visualize them, and my mind would be filled with images of Fifth Avenue blanketed in snow and children bundled in Eddie Bauer parkas as they frolicked across the street in Central Park. All of which would mean that I was ignoring my patient, one of the few still paying me 175 non-HMO cash dollars for fifty minutes of my attention.

The patient left, and once again I felt a familiar pain across my shoulders. When was I going to get back to yoga? I had been asking myself that same question for well over a year. I was forty-two years old and suffering from terminal stiffness. On the advice of a patient—talk about crazy—I had sunk all my capital into hedge funds, which had allowed me to purchase a fashionable two-bedroom co-op in Carnegie Hill. But when the aforementioned funds were revealed to be part of an even larger portfolio connected to the dreaded Bernie Madoff, a downward spiral began, which sent my bank account, my marriage, and my practice into free fall.

I walked towards the leaded-glass window and, as I had feared, became entranced by the snow as it continued to drift down on the park. For a moment, I flashed back to my childhood in Evanston, Illinois, and a recurring memory of a girl on a toboggan. What was her name and why was she haunting me so? She sat behind me, clutching my waist tightly as we sped down the hill. ("This is such fun, Harry! Isn't it fun? I wish it could last forever.") She had hot chocolate on her breath and icicles in her hair. Had I really turned around and kissed her on the lips? Or only wished I had? She was Donna Schuman's cousin from Syracuse, and she had come for a visit over the Christmas holidays. I was twelve years old and never saw her again. But the memory of her smiling face had remained with me. That brief moment of intimacy was a revelation; the love I had heard sung about in songs and depicted in old black-and-white movies truly existed.

I forced myself back to my desk—only five minutes left to make notes and clear my mind before the next appointment—when the telephone rang. Evelyn White, my stylish, widowed receptionist, informed me that Robert Ortega was on the phone. The name meant nothing to me.

"Dr. Strider? Dr. Harris Strider?" The voice on the other end of the phone had a slight lilt to it.

"Yes?"

"Robert Ortega. Cambridge Medical. Got a minute?" The lilt had a Spanish Harlem provenance.

"Not really. I have a patient arriving in…"

"This'll only take a second or two, Doctor. I've recently taken over your file, and I'm acquainting myself with your claims."

"I'm sorry. Who are…who did you say you were?"

"Robert Ortega. Cambridge Medical claims adjuster. We handle primary insurance for one of your patients, a Dalton W. Lafferty. Now, according to our records, he's been seeing you for some time."

"That's correct."

"How soon will he be cured?"

"I have no idea. Therapy is a lengthy process."

"Not on my watch. Cambridge can't pay out these claims forever. We want results, Doctor. What's this guy's problem? No CPT code shows up on my computer screen."

"CP what?"

"Current Procedural Terminology…Well? What is it?"

"I have no intention of discussing my patient's confidential conversations with a bookkeeper."

"Climb off your high horse, Doctor. I also have a master's degree in social work. Believe me, I can talk shop with you till the cows come home. So what's the deal?"

Professor Dalton Lafferty, an expatriate Canadian from Alberta and a world-renowned Shakespearean scholar, was a very special patient, indeed. He lectured at Columbia University and had chaired three different presidential commissions on literacy. Initially, he'd come to me to discuss his fears of encroaching technology. You must understand that this was no minor trauma spinning itself out; Lafferty felt society, as it had existed for the previous two millennia, was hopelessly doomed.

"Take every book, every original thought for the past two thousand years and shred them," Lafferty orated in his best King-Lear-railing-on-the-heath voice, as he paced my office as he had the lecture halls of Columbia for decades. Throughout the '70s and '80s, the good professor had lent his name to numerous pacifist and antinuclear causes. But he finally made his peace with the atom when he realized the true enemy—the real double agent—that lurked in every household was digital technology. Cyberspace. The Internet. They were harbingers of the death of self-expression. Lafferty felt we had all become helpless slaves to compartmentalized thinking, staring at dots on a screen, no longer able to connect the dots in our own lives.

But I wasn't prepared to share such privileged and precious information with Robert Ortega. Instead, I hoped to put an end to our fractious conversation with a by-the-book answer that hopefully would silence him: "generalized anxiety disorder."

"So he's medicable," said Ortega.

"I don't recognize that term."

"Why aren't you prescribing Ativan, Doctor? Standard procedure with GAD, isn't it?"

When I reminded the claims adjuster that each patient under my care was different, Ortega glibly responded that Lafferty's condition was "a no-brainer, slam dunk" based on the Psychiatric Association's definition of Axis One. On a roll, he urged me to consult the APA's *Diagnostic and Statistical Manual of Mental Disorders* if I was feeling "a bit rusty."

I could have eaten a bowl of Ortega's brains at that moment and washed it down with a nice Chianti. But I knew that Lafferty and I were both stuck in the trouble bubble. The *DSM* was the guidebook for all insurance companies. Patients whom they deemed Axis Ones (those suffering from depression, anxiety disorders, bipolar disorder, etc.) were beloved by pharmaceutical companies, which could earn billions each year by doping them to the gills. Axis Twos (paranoid personality disorder, schizoid personality disorder, antisocial personality disorder, etc.) had problems that couldn't be solved by medication alone. They were the ones who needed years of treatment—anathema to the insurance boys.

In point of fact, Dalton W. Lafferty was an Axis Two. But if I were to admit to that hothouse category, I knew that the great scholar would be denied even minimal insurance coverage. This was symptomatic of the very "compartmentalized thinking" Lafferty had ranted and raved to me about every week.

Having assumed the professor to be a simple garden-variety Axis One, Ortega now had stumbled onto the possibility that Lafferty was an Axis Two. For the combative claims adjuster this was akin to discovering that his wife was cheating on him.

"Well, which one is it, Dr. Strider?" Ortega asked, relentless in his attack. "I'd hate to think you're treating the old guy as a Two and sneaking him onto my books as a One. We're not real big on collusion here at Cambridge—hello? I know you're still there. I can hear you breathing."

"Tell me, Mr. Ortega. Were your ancestors active in the Spanish Inquisition?"

"There's a lot of unnecessary hostility coming from you, Doctor. Are you aware of that? Hey! I'm on your side. We're in the healing business together. Think of us as partners. So let's make this thing work, okay? Get Rafferty on Ativan ASAP and off my books even faster."

Ortega hung up before I could remind him my patient's name was Lafferty, not Rafferty, and that I had no intention of medicating a man of his stature into a Cambridge-approved state of submission. I hadn't watched *One Flew Over the Cuckoo's Nest* twenty times when I was a kid for nothing. Oh, how I had hated Nurse Ratched! Slamming the receiver down in a blind rage, I asked myself what the hell all this had to do with medicine anymore, much less with healing? Why didn't we just anesthetize the entire population and call it a day?

The clock on the onyx mantle chimed three. Mrs. White buzzed me and said that my next appointment, Sherman Rosenbaum, was in the waiting room. I had no recollection of a patient by that name. Must be a new one, I thought. The door to my private office opened, and an elegantly attired man in his early seventies with a prominent nose, full head of white hair, and pencil-thin white mustache strode into the room. Dressed in a gray worsted Savile Row suit and hand-crafted Lobb shoes, he exuded supreme confidence, coupled with a slight degree of irritation at having to be in my office at all. Had he sported kid gloves and a malacca walking stick, Mr. Rosenbaum would have seemed quite at home in an Edith Wharton novel.

"Dr. Strider?" His hard, nasal tones were all Brooklyn, and in sharp contrast to his sartorial image.

Standing behind my antique oak desk, I gestured with my open palm for Rosenbaum to sit down in the leather chair. He ignored my offer and instead walked around the office, silently appraising the wood-paneled walls and the high vaulted ceiling. Finally he cleared his throat in a Gatling gun rhythm and asked, "Did Irv Weinglass ever have offices here? One senses a certain déjà vu."

"Wineglass?" My attention had drifted again, to somewhere between Ortega's ultimatum and the girl on the toboggan.

"Dr. Irving Weinglass, one of the top endocrinologists in the city. Went to high school together. Erasmus. We were batboys at Ebbets Field. The great Pee Wee Reese came to my bar mitzvah. Oh, the Dodger stories one could tell you! Did all right for myself. Land development. Can't complain. Built a few malls out on the Island. Retired now—my wife said she didn't want to be the richest widow in Bellport—but one still keeps one's hand in. Consulting. You know."

I asked if he'd like to sit down, but Rosenbaum gazed out the leaded-glass window and continued to ignore my questions. Then suddenly he turned to me and announced, "Last year in France, they made me a Chevalier du Tastevin. Know what that is?"

Before I could reply, he whipped out an iPhone from his inside jacket pocket and proceeded to play me the video of his investiture into the venerable Burgundian wine-tasting society. Full of all the pomp and ceremony inherent in the French DNA, it lasted an interminable fifteen minutes.

"Pretty impressive, you've got to admit," he said, not so much as a statement but as a challenge that he dared me to refute.

I told him if we ever went to dinner, I would let him order the wine. This launched us into a spirited argument vis-à-vis the superiority of French grapes to those grown in California.

"Admirable erudition, Doctor. Clearly I came to the right man. Are you Jewish?"

"Beg your pardon?"

"Strider. Knew an Abe Strider—got to be forty years ago—in St. Louis. Dry goods."

When Rosenbaum finally settled into the leather chair, I felt a degree of relief. Actually, I was half Jewish on my mother's side, but neither she nor my father had practiced any form of religion.

"No, I'm not Jewish. Is that a problem for you?"

"Not if it isn't for you," laughed Rosenbaum. "How old are you, Doctor?"

"Mr. Rosenbaum, I can't see what my age or religious affiliation has to do with your problem. Although, frankly, you don't strike me as the sort who has any problems."

"I don't," replied Rosenbaum proudly. "It's my nephew, Gordon Jacobs, my sister's son. Remarkable boy. Handsome. Superb athlete. Shoulders. Top ten in his class at Princeton Law."

"What exactly is Gordon's problem?" I was struggling to remember which of my colleagues I needed to thank for referring the imperious Chevalier to me.

"His fiancée, Barbara Warren."

"You came to see me about your nephew's fiancée?"

"Don't get me wrong, Doctor. Barbara's a beautiful girl. Went to Hampshire College. Comes from a well-to-do New Jersey family. She'd make your head spin."

"What exactly is the problem? With Barbara?"

"She has episodes."

"Episodes?"

"Mental episodes."

"Do you mean seizures? Epilepsy?"

"No, no, no." Rosenbaum impatiently waved my question aside, then shrugged: "Like fits. I know that term is no longer fashionable or medically correct. But there's no other way to describe it. Out of nowhere—with no warning—the girl becomes unhinged. Says crazy things. Dances around. You know."

"No, I don't know, Mr. Rosenbaum. But I cannot…"

"Call me Sherman."

"Mr. Rosenbaum, have you personally witnessed one of these 'episodes'?"

"Not personally per se. But Gordon has a video he can show you. The boy and I are very close. His father died when he was twelve, and I stepped up to the plate as a surrogate. My wife and I have no children, so this has been a fulfilling experience for me—without falling prey to the emotional pitfalls parenthood might otherwise have…"

"Mr. Rosenbaum, who referred you to me?"

"Jack Dorfman. Said you were brilliant."

"That was very kind of Dr. Dorfman. I'm flattered. Truly. But what you're suggesting I do…"

"The wedding," whined Rosenbaum. "They're planning a big wedding. Booked the Primrose Club in Tenafly…six hundred people…forty-piece orchestra…the whole schmear. My little sister's biting her nails right down to the bone. Understandably. There will be all these people: Rudy Giuliani, Donald Trump, relatives coming from San Francisco, Hawaii even. We're talking about a big wedding, Doctor."

"Six hundred people."

"Exactly! We're in synch. And my little sister's been having second thoughts about her son marrying a girl who might be nuts. That's a lot of presents to send back, *si tu comprendes, cher docteur.*"

"But what do you want me to do? What do you think I can do? You're under some misconception about…"

"I want you to get together with Gordon. He's got a very busy calendar, but I know he'll make himself available to you for something as serious as this. Get him to show you the video of the fit. Or whatever fancy name you doctors call it now. Meet Barbara. And once you've sussed her out for yourself…"

"Absolutely not! What you are suggesting, Mr. Rosenbaum, is wholly unethical."

"Relax, Doctor. Relax. It was merely an idea. One must try everything in a crisis. How old did you say you were?"

"I didn't." My mouth relaxed into a smile, ground down by Rosenbaum's relentless charm. "Forty-two."

"Really? Who'd have guessed? Tell you what. You're a man who appreciates good wine. Let me take you to lunch tomorrow, for your trouble."

"There's really no need to…"

"Les Trois Moulins?"

"An excellent restaurant."

"So? Shall I book a table? My treat."

I succumbed yet again to Sherman Rosenbaum. What the hell! He was paying, and I certainly couldn't afford to lunch in a five-star restaurant on my tight budget.

The triumphant Chevalier rose from the chair and asked: "Shall we say noon? Why don't I ask Gordon to join us?" He patted down his pencil-thin white mustache with his right index finger, then added: "And don't forget to send me your bill."

"Don't worry."

"I never do. Until tomorrow, Doctor."

18

\* \* \*

As I walked north on Fifth Avenue, after leaving my office for the day, I began chuckling at the notion of Rosenbaum's investiture as a Chevalier du Tastevin. The snow was starting to fall harder, when I saw a female figure wearing a long, blue woolen overcoat and a gray shawl racing towards me.

"*Ist es ein Traum?*" A petite girl in her late teens with long chestnut hair well past her shoulders stood before me in the moonlight. She had twinkling doe eyes and a face that belonged in another time. She wiped the melting snow off her face and asked: "*Vus machst du hier, Rebbe?*"

I couldn't understand a word she was saying and asked if she spoke English. All the while I couldn't stop looking at her face, which seemed to grow more beautiful the longer I stared at it.

"*Ikh ken nisht farshtayn,*" she said. "*Red Yiddish, Rebbe.*" The girl grabbed hold of my hands and squeezed them.

"I'm sorry," I replied. "I don't know what you're saying. Do you need help? Can I help you?"

"*Helfn? Helfn!*" Her voice was tinged with annoyance and she stared up at the night sky with a simmering fury. "*Hast gehert? Fur eine ganze Yoor, du hast gezugt…*"

She abruptly stopped speaking and snapped her head to one side, like an animal sensing danger nearby. She released my hands and dashed across the street into the park. I watched her disappear, yet another of the city's urban cripples.

# THE WIFE

WHETHER IT WAS my commitment to work and research, or simply a failure to meet the "right" girl, I had remained a bachelor until I was thirty-five. I never bothered to examine my motives for not having married. There had been plenty of women in my past, but none who resurrected the deep and tender emotions I had felt for that long-ago girl on the toboggan. I had never experienced any acute sense of incompleteness, until the evening my friend and mentor Martin Corwin drew me aside at my surprise birthday party and pointed out, rather ominously, that I had just "crossed the meridian" without a mate.

"Some people," he said, as he placed a warm and loving hand on my shoulder, "should never marry. Painfully I include myself as a member of that unfortunate focus group. But you, Harry, of the limpid, Omar Sharif eyes and the abandoned puppy-dog demeanor, were not meant to wander the earth without a life partner. The phrase 'little woman,' no matter what her real size, is a perfect match for you, 'a prize catch.' Seek her out now, kid, if the gods haven't already chosen her for you."

No one had ever addressed me in that manner before. The loneliness I often felt was a constant, a way of life, something one learned to live with like dyslexia or asthma. My parents had never pressured me to find a bride. But then they were odd ducks in their own right. Both were teachers, who'd met as undergraduates at Northwestern. My father, Jason, had grown up on a ranch in Montana where the only literature at hand ran to feed-and-grain catalogs and the *Farmers' Almanac*. My mother, Mitzi, was the only child of Brooklyn Jews, and that was all she ever told me about her background. Where her family had come from, how long they had been in America, and why she had no communication with them was never discussed. I loved my mother dearly and, as it was evident that she had no desire to share details of her past, never pursued the subject. Happiest with their noses buried in scholarly books or literary quarterlies, my parents lived for each other and doled out what residual affection was left to me, their only child, whose academic achievements were a source of great pride to them.

The day after my surprise party, I entered the Barnes & Noble in Astor Place. As I drifted aimlessly through the cooking section, I spotted a willowy Nordic goddess whispering recipes from expensive coffee-table culinary tomes into a Sony IC Recorder. Dazzled by her intensity and impressed by her thrift, I took Marty Corwin's good counsel to heart and allowed for the possibility that this attractive young woman might be the perfect companion with whom to traverse the dreaded meridian.

Posing as a fellow gourmet, I gleaned that Claire Lovborg (the Nordic goddess's name) was the eldest child of a large Iowa brood. A compulsive overachiever, Claire was riding the comet at a white-shoe, Park Avenue law firm, with rumors abounding that she would be the youngest female ever to make partner. She also had a steady boyfriend named Edwin Sheffield. He was a struggling but highly respected composer of classical music, who survived on foundation grants and the patronage of Miss Tilly McIntire, a dotty old woman who had briefly been employed as Leonard Bernstein's secretary in the 1950s. She thought herself the Madame von Meck to Sheffield's Tchaikovsky. Tilly had maintained her connections in the music world (via Bernstein's Rolodex, which she had reproduced by hand) and, through her relentless networking, had been able to obtain commissions for Edwin from far-flung provincial orchestras, whose deadlines the cult composer struggled so pathetically to meet.

Normally, a little detail like Claire's boyfriend would have caused me instantly to retrieve my hat from the ring and replace it firmly on my head. How was I to possibly compete with a composer? Me, who had never played an instrument of any kind, a fact I regretted but never had the courage to act upon. But Marty Corwin's speech continued to reverberate. What if the gods had chosen Claire for me? What if we were predestined to be together? How was I to woo and win her with Edwin Sheffield standing in my way?

Clearly I had to utilize my psychiatric training to observe Claire and Edwin interacting at close (if not intimate) range. But how could I do this? Stalking them was out of the question. Hiring a detective to report on their behavior was unscientific and cost prohibitive. No, a different tack was needed: I would be bold and befriend them—innocent but effective. An invitation to dinner at my place would make an excellent start. After all, were we not both devotees of haute cuisine? What possible harm could there be for Claire if she accepted my invitation? And bring your boyfriend, by all means. She accepted. I had never attempted anything so calculating or competitive in my life, but some unknown force drove me.

I took a gamble on Thai food. Obviously I couldn't prepare it myself, but the kitchen had to look as if I had. Again the gods were on my side: Butri, my former cleaning lady, had once run a Zagat-approved spot on Third Avenue called We Are Siamese, until circumstances forced her into Chapter Eleven and back to cleaning apartments.

When I first hired Butri, I had no notion that she once had owned a four-star Thai restaurant. To me, she was just a tiny, scowling creature who wore her jet-black hair in bangs that covered her forehead. She came once a week to my prewar apartment on West Tenth Street, where she would silently clean for four hours. I paid her; she grunted. That was the sole extent of our relationship. Until the day she walked into the living room where I was bundled up on the couch in sweats and thick socks, having come down with an early-winter cold.

"You drink soup?" Butri asked, glaring at me as if I had just dragged in mud (or worse) on my galoshes.

"Chicken soup?" I asked, not sure if she meant had I tried the ancient Jewish cure-all (which my nonreligious mother swore by for all ailments) or had I been accused of snatching her lunch from the refrigerator and devouring it. "No."

Butri snorted and disappeared into the kitchen. Had she quit? I heard her banging cupboard doors and shrieking aloud, then footsteps and the front door slamming shut behind her. Oh well. Better put an ad on Craigslist for a new cleaning lady.

Half an hour later, Butri returned with a huge bag of groceries from a nearby Asian market. She vanished into the kitchen, once more without saying a word. I went back to my book and shrugged. There was more banging of cupboard doors. Perhaps she'd been hungry, possibly hypoglycemic. That might explain her extreme mood swings.

Suddenly the kitchen door swung open, and the tiny Thai woman emerged carrying a steaming tureen of soup. She set it down on the coffee table by the couch and lifted the lid for me to sniff. The aroma was incredible. Then Butri zipped back inside the kitchen and, with the aplomb of a highly trained professional, came out with a tray that held a bowl, napkin, and large porcelain spoon. She ladled the soup into the bowl, and I drank. And drank. And drank, until the tureen was empty.

"Where did you learn to make soup like that?"

"Feel better?" asked an emotionless Butri.

"Great! My sinuses are open. My blood is racing. I think I'm going to live. That was incredible! Why don't you open a restaurant?"

That was when Butri related what had happened to We Are Siamese. She explained how her elderly American husband—a multi-decorated, extremely deaf Vietnam veteran—had pushed her into the restaurant business, backed by her family's money, and then kept her slaving away day and night in the kitchen, while he used the cash register as his own private piggy bank and the gum-chewing cashier as his own private plaything. The tiny Thai woman awoke one morning to discover she was a hundred thousand dollars in debt, and that her husband had vanished to Costa Rica with the gum-chewing cashier

"Restaurant too big," said Butri at the end of her sad tale. "Little noodle shop better idea. Quick. Fast. Make lotta money. Ham over fist."

She had found the perfect spot on Prince Street in SoHo, which could be up and running in a month for a ten thousand dollar investment. I happened to have that exact sum in my savings account and, being unmarried and unencumbered by debt at the time, became Butri's silent partner in the enterprise.

The noodle shop had been a huge success, and so I had no qualms about asking Butri to prepare a small banquet for Claire and Edwin, which I could claim as my own.

* * *

On the appointed evening, the couple rang my doorbell promptly at seven thirty. In her hands, Claire held a tiny pot of imported lingonberry jam with a huge gold silk bow wrapped around it, which she presented to me with all the pomp of a Nobel Prize. Edwin was far from the frail, tubercular Chopin I had imagined. On the contrary, he was tall, imposing, and corpulent. He wore black horn-rimmed glasses and was elegantly attired, like a Connecticut country squire.

"What are you cooking?" asked Claire, sniffing the air like a Weimaraner in heat as she crossed my threshold. She whipped off her yellow cashmere overcoat before I could move to assist her.

"Thai food," I replied nonchalantly, as I wrested the coat away from her. "Do you like it?"

"My favorite!"

Edwin said nothing.

"Are you all right with spicy?" I asked as I hung her coat in the front hall closet.

"Cast-iron stomach," Claire replied and flashed me a dazzling smile.

Edwin remained silent.

"Claire says you're a composer." I couldn't decide if he was shy, aloof, or a garden-variety narcissist.

"Yes." Surprisingly, Edwin had a voice like a foghorn.

"Are you working on something now?"

"Edwin is always working," Claire said. "Humming away under his breath. Raising his eyes to heaven as the music washes over him. First time he did it, I thought he was an epileptic. But I got used to it. That, and the hours on end when he locks himself away with his Steinway."

"Sorry to be such a trial," Edwin murmured and abruptly began humming under his breath.

Claire took the composer's right hand, raised it to her lips, and kissed his fingertips. "Just teasing. My genius. That's your M.O." She turned back to me and announced proudly: "Edwin has his own orchestra."

"Here in the city?" I swiftly was losing confidence in my dreams of romantic conquest. It was obvious she adored her "genius." How could I possibly compete with a maestro who had his own orchestra?

"It's virtual," said Edwin, executing keyboard movements with his fingers inches away from his face and then, dissatisfied with his work, erasing them all in midair. "Do you have any Baltic water?"

"Volvic?"

"Edwin only drinks water imported from Latvia, Lithuania, or Estonia," explained Claire in hushed, conspiratorial tones. "The mineral content inspires his..."

"Don't make me sound so neurotic, Claire. I do prefer Baltic water but I'll drink Schweppes, if I have to."

"Pellegrino all right?"

"Of course, of course," replied Edwin, resuming the finger work on his invisible keyboard and humming quite loudly.

"Please, sit down." I gestured towards a corner of the living room where I had set up a circular oak table for dinner. Then I produced a small platter of *larb*—spicy chopped pork on a bed of lettuce—as an appetizer. Claire scooped some up

26

like a lettuce-leaf burrito in her long beautiful hand and devoured it, making decidedly orgasmic sounds as her taste buds savored the complex flavors. She opened her eyes and nodded at me with gastronomic approval. Edwin, in turn, stared woefully at the contents of his plate, which remained untouched.

"He doesn't really like spicy," Claire whispered from behind the napkin she was using to daub her lips.

"Oh, dear. I wish you had told me ahead of time. My Thai cuisine tends to be exceedingly piquant. Had I known, I would have made it a shade more bland."

"I'll try it!" boomed Edwin, thrusting the rolled-up *larb* into his mouth and swallowing it in one go. "Delicious!" he pronounced, reaching for another one in a heartbeat.

"Edwin!" cautioned Claire. "Is that a good idea?

"Please, Claire! I have a mother."

"O-kaaay."

Little bit of tension, I thought. Encouraging.

"Forgive my ignorance, Edwin," I said, ladling out *tom kha gai* into the composer's bowl. "But what exactly is a virtual orchestra?"

"We play online," replied Edwin, between spoonfuls of the aromatic coconut soup. "Skype…musicians from all over the world. The entire percussion section is in Bolivia. We get together once a month."

"The cellist is under house arrest in Nepal," said Claire breathlessly, "but the authorities allow him to play unmonitored with Edwin."

"Bhutan."

"Sorry, darling?"

"Paro lives in Bhutan. Not Nepal."

Was that a tear welling up in the corner of Claire's left eye?

"Useless at geography myself," I said to the stricken Claire, as I surreptitiously passed my handkerchief to her under the table. "Took me five years to realize the Hudson wasn't on the east side of Manhattan."

Claire's sparkling laugh was a mixture of delight and gratitude. Daubing her eye quickly with my handkerchief, she mouthed a silent "Thank you."

Suddenly Edwin shot up from the table and asked in a strangled voice for directions to the bathroom. I pointed the way and gave him a heads up about the location of the light switch. The maestro disappeared inside the loo, where he remained for the next thirty minutes.

Claire and I took advantage of Edwin's protracted absence and swapped anecdotes from our respective biographies. In addition to the innate ease and glide of our conversation, we discovered how charming, sympathetic, erudite, amusing, sensitive, and maddeningly attracted we were to each other.

Just as I was on the verge of dispatching a hunting party to search for Edwin, the toilet flushed and he emerged green-gilled and shaky from the bathroom. Begging my pardon, Edwin said he needed to go home. Claire apologized for cutting the evening short as she helped a reeling Edwin with his Norfolk jacket and guided him down the hall towards the elevator. I wished the queasy composer a speedy recovery, knowing all the while that his romantic days with Claire were numbered. And so were my days as a bachelor.

\* \* \*

Once our affair began, I discovered that Claire, while outwardly gregarious, was also given to silent bouts of melancholy that could last an entire evening and could only be relieved by a deep sleep. She would reawaken between three and four in the morning bursting with creative energy, which she would pour into painting, sculpture, collage, or whatever dormant artistic demon had invaded her psyche. Perhaps this behavior counterbalanced days filled with torts, writs, and the minutiae of the law.

With equal unpredictability, she would rouse me from sleep in the middle of the night, desperate to make passionate love. Casting herself in the role of the resolute leader of a Himalayan trek, she would end her silent ascent with a triumphant orgasmic cry, as the previously unreachable summit was conquered and the expedition's flag firmly planted in the icy peak.

We had been together for three months when one evening Claire arrived unannounced at my apartment and dumped her duffel bags onto the living room floor. A year later we decided to get married. We had agreed to a simple civil ceremony at City Hall. No parents, friends, or colleagues were invited. So imagine my surprise when I discovered Edwin Sheffield standing mournfully outside the clerk's office. He nodded at me and then removed an iPod with tiny twin speakers from his Prada shoulder bag. Claire drew me aside, seized both my hands, kissed my fingertips, and begged me to be compassionate. Edwin understood that she no longer loved him as she once had, but he had begged her not to banish him entirely from her life. He had even abandoned work on his long-overdue commission for the Sitka Symphony in order to compose a short piano piece *à la façon de* Felix Mendelssohn to celebrate our nuptials. Pressing the play button on his iPod, Edwin proceeded to duplicate his original finger work in midair while his melodic music played, and the morbidly obese clerk guided us through our marriage vows, in between puffs on his portable oxygen tank.

By this time, Butri had remarried, and her Thai husband had been pressuring me to sell him my shares in the noodle shops—he and his wife had opened four more by then. Fearing that New York's love affair with Thai food might be coming to an end, I finally agreed. The hefty return on my original investment made it possible for me not only to make a sizable down payment on our co-op at Ninety-First and Madison, but to also plow a considerable chunk of change into those accursed hedge funds. Claire and I were riding high in those days: eating at the best restaurants, drinking superb wines, enjoying season tickets for the Met.

Eventually, Claire abandoned the law to pursue art full time. The subject of children was never discussed. A great many things were never discussed over the next few years. Finally my bride discovered weaving and pronounced it her sole raison d'être. Much as Edwin had done so often behind his Steinway, she took refuge in her loom and soon lost herself in her weaving.

Which is how I found Claire, several hours after my first encounter with Sherman Rosenbaum, as I let myself into our Carnegie Hill apartment. She was seated at her loom, adjusting the heddles in order to separate the warp threads.

"Sorry I'm late," I called out with what I hoped was a suitable degree of remorse, removing my Abercrombie & Fitch galoshes and placing them on the rubber pad from Lechter's Housewares next to the front door.

"Marty and I were playing racquetball," I said. "I won, and he insisted on a rematch, which he won. So we went for a best of three, which I won. Which is rare, as you know. Then we took a steam and I completely forgot…"

"You could have texted if you didn't feel like speaking to me," Claire said.

"When have I ever not wanted to?"

With a martyr's wail, Claire exclaimed: "It's ruined now!"

Crossing the floor of the living room in my stocking feet and overpowered by the intensity of the central heating, I gazed in mystification at the loom. "Looks fine to me."

"The dinner, Harris," Claire snarled. "The dinner."

"Oh hell! I'm only twenty minutes late."

"Twenty-eight."

"Must you be so anal?"

"Bastard!"

"What?"

"You promised not to throw that up at me again. My people are Norwegian. Punctuality is a virtue. It's how I am."

"Forgive me, Claire. I was having a good time and…"

"Sorry to have spoiled it for you." One of her famous lone tears rolled down Claire's high-cheekboned face.

When had Claire changed? Or had she always been so— God help me—neurotic? There I said it. Shop talk. Maybe she shouldn't have given up her job. Certainly that extra two hundred thousand a year had made our life together almost luxurious. Now she had far too much time on her hands. Her present career as an artist—excuse me, master weaver—had gone unacknowledged, except by the members of her guild, as big a group of wackos as the five boroughs had ever produced.

And then there was Edwin. You remember how adamant and bitchy he'd been about "already having a mother"? Well, Mrs. Sheffield died abruptly, leaving poor Edwin bereft and in effect making Claire his new mother. We went through several weeks of the tortured composer weeping inconsolably on our living room couch. He couldn't write music; couldn't meet his deadlines; couldn't find a woman to love him. Claire held his hand and assured him that the right woman was just around the corner. I would sit on the other side of the room during these crying jags, nodding my head sympathetically and wondering just when the hell the genius was going to leave so that I could go to bed.

Now, staring at my wife as she sank deeper and deeper into an all-too-familiar Norwegian funk, I finally asked: "Are you sure you're not Jewish?"

In slow, slower, slowest motion, Claire pivoted her head around to gaze at me and, with a previously untapped reservoir of venom, asked: "Marty's been at you again, hasn't he?"

"Beg your pardon?"

"The Jewish thing. It always surfaces after he's been needling you. Otherwise you never talk about it. The man's a sadist."

"Marty?"

"Yes. Marty."

The Pasha—my affectionate nickname for Martin Corwin because of his girth and resemblance to an exotic, bearded potentate in the *Arabian Nights*—had been on my case once again. Not so much for my "secret Jewishness" but for enduring Claire's anal obsessions. When I brusquely replied that my wife had a promptness thing, which I had learned to respect, the Pasha reminded me with his patented twinkle that as board-certified psychiatrists, we had been taught to label such "things" as neuroses.

When I hastily pointed out to the Pasha how truly fond of him Claire was, he asked, "Harry, are you sure you're not more the Hebrew than you let on? It's a very Jewish thing, your attempt to make me feel guilty."

"Why is conveying how my wife feels about you remotely connected with guilt?"

"And you call yourself a therapist," Corwin chuckled, pinching my right cheek affectionately. "Better skedaddle on home, young man, before the little woman has another one of her 'things.'"

"Marty's very fond of you," I said to Claire, who had sunk even deeper into her Norwegian gloom and was oblivious to everything except the loom in front of her.

"Jury's still out on that," Claire said. "By my vote, he's a misogynist."

"Marty? Please! Doesn't he always have a different woman on his arm?"

"As adornments. Accessories. The man is fifty-two years old and incapable of a sustained relationship. What does that really mean, Dr. Strider, once you unshackle your chains of loyalty?"

"Marty thinks the world of you, Claire. Hasn't he always been supportive and encouraging of your work? Has he ever missed one of your gallery openings?"

"What better place to pick up girls? And never pay for drinks. The man patronizes me, Harris. He doesn't really take me seriously as an artist."

"That's not true. But, even if it was, why should it matter to you?"

"So you concede it is possible he feels that way?"

"Weaving isn't...everyone's cup of tea. Oh, please, Claire! I beg you. Let's not get into another Marty Corwin argument. It's not what I had in mind for us. My greatest wish—all day long, I swear to you—was to come home and share a quiet, loving, intimate..."

"Then why were you late?"

"How 'bout a kiss?" I asked shifting gears abruptly in the hope it might alter her mood like a shot of brandy or a sharp slap across the face. "Hmmm? Don't we think a little kissie would help?"

"Don't patronize me as well." That lone tear that had rolled down her face earlier was merely the advance scout for the rivulets now cascading down both cheeks. Pointing toward the kitchen, she jabbed the air with the same index finger she had stuck in the faces of reluctant witnesses back in the day. "I-worked-on-that-dinner-all-afternoon."

"Gosh honey, couldn't we sort of give it the Heimlich maneuver or something?" Kneeling down beside her loom, I held my hands up like puppy dog's paws and attempted to abate her tears with my tongue, whimpering all the while. But Claire was in no mood to be humored and shoved me away so rudely that I fell backwards on my tailbone. "Wait, wait! I've got it! Why don't we call in an exorcist or a shaman with powers to revive the dead?"

Against her will, Claire began giggling. Finally, she took a deep breath and announced: "It'll be soggy but it'll be good."

"Didn't you say that on our wedding night?"

"Harris!"

"Maybe it was one of my patients."

"I doubt that very much," said Claire. "You've never once discussed a patient with me. Ever."

That was true. Even though she relished describing in great detail the legal cases her office had handled, I had made it a cardinal rule from day one to never break the sacred trust my patients had placed in me. Professional and personal lives must be kept separate at all costs. Poor Claire. Gossip was one of her few vices. Reluctantly, she agreed. Little did I suspect, as I tucked into my soggy soufflé, our entente cordiale had flown out the window the day the Chevalier Rosenbaum entered my life.

# THE NEPHEW

THE MAITRE D' at Les Trois Moulins informed me that I was the first in my party to arrive and promptly escorted me to a table. A busboy appeared with a wicker basket, which contained a bountiful selection of Eli's best breads. I chose a slice of seven grain and asked for a small pot of mustard as a substitute for the butter lying so temptingly in front of me. Claire prided herself on the gourmet, nonfattening meals she lovingly prepared for me. Unfortunately the deliriously caramelized desserts that she concocted as curtain calls sabotaged whatever caloric benefits the healthy entrées might have offered.

I was in the middle of smearing a thin patina of Grey Poupon across my bread when I looked up and saw the maitre d' ushering a broad-shouldered, athletic man of thirty, with a hawk nose and red hair, to the table. As he approached, he looked down at me and started speaking in short, dispassionate non-sentences: "Gordon Jacobs. Sorry. Late. Almost canceled. Pissed off."

"Is this an inconvenient time?" I asked the young man, whom I assumed was Sherman Rosenbaum's nephew. "We could change it to some other..."

"Nah," said Gordon, as he pulled out a chair and plopped himself down. "Grownup, right? Can't win 'em all." He proceeded to rotate his neck until it cracked loudly. I winced. "Better. Lawyer. Big case. Lost this morning. Don't like losing."

Don't like talking much either, I thought. Was this how Gordon Jacobs conducted himself in court? Could he possibly win any cases without speaking in complete sentences?

The sommelier arrived at the table with a vintage Bordeaux and poured some into a glass for Gordon to sample. "Your uncle insisted you have this with your lunch, M'sieu Jacobs."

"Bet he did," said Gordon, who took a sip, followed by a big swallow. "Does the trick for me."

The sommelier nodded gratefully and removed himself from the table. Gordon pointed to the mustard on my bread. "Healthy."

"Yes."

Gordon exhaled deeply and said: "Actually a shrink is the perfect person to have a drink with following a total humiliation."

"Perhaps." I was pleased to discover Gordon capable of uttering a full sentence. "I hope nothing's happened to your uncle."

"Like what?" Gordon's face registered concern.

"He doesn't strike me as the type to be late for an appointment."

"Oh, Uncle Sherman's not coming to lunch. Just us."

"I'm sorry, Mr. Jacobs. He obviously misrepresented the situation. There is an ethical—"

"No need to lecture a lawyer on ethics. Uncle Sherm can be a little pushy and a tad pompous, but he's got a heart the size of Yankee Stadium. He worries about me. And Barbara."

"He cares a great deal for both of you. But I did explain to him at length yesterday that I cannot—"

"Was he wearing his Chevalier du Tastevin medal?"

"No. His aura suffices."

"Good one, Doc. I see why Uncle Sherm likes you. He appreciates a keen wit. Now, let me tell you about the first time Barbara flipped out."

"Do you and your uncle moonlight in the steamroller business? Neither one of you takes no for an answer."

"Where does that get you in life? So? Will you listen? Please? Unofficially."

"All right, counselor. But this lunch is strictly off the record. We never discussed anything. Now, when did her first episode occur?"

Gordon flashed a beautiful set of veneers and replied: "Late November. Early December. Is the date important?"

"Right now, it's information. Please, go on."

"We were having dinner at Printemps. Place was packed. Several clients were there. Can't tell you how embarrassed I was by the whole thing."

Gordon retrieved the Bordeaux and poured himself a glass. Then he picked up the menu, perused it quickly, and announced: "Fish is fabulous. Can't go wrong."

"What exactly did she do?" I asked. "How would you describe the nature of her 'fit'?"

"I've asked Uncle Sherm to stop using that term. Frankly it's offensive and reminiscent of a time best forgotten. We've come a long way, don't you think, Doctor?"

"What did she do?" I tried to combine compassion and professionalism in my question.

37

"She…sang," shrugged Gordon. "Songs. Folk songs. But not in English."

"Folk songs?"

"Ever been to a Jewish wedding?"

"Where they step on the lightbulb?"

"They always do that," said Gordon, waving his hand in dismissal, much as his uncle had done the previous day in my office. "But at Orthodox weddings they carry the bride and groom around over their heads on chairs. Up in the air."

"Kind of dangerous, isn't it? Especially after a few glasses of wine."

"Believe me, Doctor. No one's carrying me around on a chair. We're not Orthodox. That's what's so weird. All those songs old people sing at weddings? Barbara started singing them too. And she doesn't know a word of Yiddish. Hell! She works at Condé Nast. And the dancing!"

"Dancing?"

"All around the tables—in Printemps! We waited three months for a reservation, and Barbara started dancing around the tables. I was totally freaked out. We had to leave. Ended up going home and Chinese takeout."

"How did Barbara explain her behavior?"

"She didn't remember a thing … complete blank … thought I'd made it up. It's happened another three or four times since then—when we met with the orchestra leader to choose the songs, and with the caterer."

"Did she remember any of the subsequent episodes?"

"No. Not even when I showed her the video."

"Video? Oh, yes. Your uncle mentioned…"

Gordon whipped an iPhone out of his jacket pocket and proceeded to show me a video. He had shot it surreptitiously in the living room of a New York apartment; the images were jerky and often out of focus. But I could make out a young woman dancing round and round like a dervish and singing.

"Is that Barbara?"

"Yes."

"Have you shown it to her?"

"Once. She said it was someone else. When I pressed the subject, she got really upset. Didn't want to talk about it. Begged me to erase it."

"Why didn't you?"

"The lawyer in me." Gordon shrugged his beefy shoulders. "In case I needed proof someday. Like now."

"Does Barbara drink?"

"Drink? Drink what?"

"Does she have a problem with alcohol?"

"Whoa, Doc! Wrong ballpark! Barbara's a health nut, like me—no cigarettes, no drugs. We work out together."

"Don't take offense, Mr. Jacobs. I am just trying to figure out a logical explanation for her behavior. Before we get into—"

"Cool it," said Gordon, who grabbed my hand in a powerful squeeze that all but cut off my circulation. "Don't tell her you're a doctor."

"Tell who?"

"Barbara. Here she comes." He nodded towards the front of the restaurant.

"Your uncle is absolutely shameless! He bushwhacked me without the least concern for my principles or—"

"Shh! Shh! Barbara has no idea who you are."

And never will, I thought, as I rose from the table. "Please, thank your uncle for a delicious—"

Turning around, I found myself staring into the eyes of Barbara Warren, a petite, chestnut-haired young woman wearing a silver-fox coat. She was probably in her early twenties, but her heavy makeup and heavier jewelry added a decade to her appearance. Gordon pulled me back into my seat.

"Surprised to see me, Gordo?"

Her fiancé leapt to his feet and tried to kiss her on the lips but was offered only her left cheek.

"I just left Georgette Klinger." Barbara sat down at the table without acknowledging my presence. "I'll keep it," she snapped sharply at the waiter, who had tried in vain to relieve her of the silver-fox coat, which she let slip from her shoulders onto the back of her chair. "Like my new dress? Vera Wang."

"How did you know where I was?" Gordon asked.

"Uncle Sherman. He phoned the office and said you'd be here. Oh! I am positively famished."

"Honey, this is…" Gordon paused, realizing he didn't know my first name.

"Harris…Strider. Now, Gordon, I really must be—"

"And this is my fiancée, Barbara Warren."

"Congratulations, Miss Warren."

"Congratulations?"

"The coming nuptials."

"Pleeeze…if you only knew! Honest to God, Gordon, my day has been a total horror. To-tal! That cross-eyed wedding planner is driving me crazy. Duh! My bad! Napkins! Whoever thought napkins would be—" Barbara suddenly shifted gears to examine the beautiful Irish linen folded up inside her water glass. "These are divine. Aren't they divine, Gordo? So why can't we have napkins like these?"

She removed an iPhone from her bag, grabbed hold of the napkin, and ordered Gordon to hold it up to the light. She proceeded to snap photos of the Irish linen from every conceivable angle. Satisfied with the results, she e-mailed the pictures to her assistant, pursed her lips, and perused the menu with a laser-like intensity.

"So? What are you guys eating? Nothing on this menu appeals to me. Oh! And your mother, Gordo, I love her to bits—mwah-mwah-mwah—but her seating demands are, like, straight from the Magic Kingdom. She's got those cousins of yours from St. Louis sitting at table two. Donald Trump is at table two...who are you anyway?"

The last question was directed at me, as I stared at Barbara with rapt fascination. Someone was both lying to me and wasting my time. There was no way this spoiled, self-obsessed brat could have entertained her fellow diners at Printemps with ethnic folk songs. From what I could see—based on this briefest of encounters—she and Gordon were perfect for each other: the well-coiffed bride matching the well-built groom in the cuckoo clock of narcissism that would be their marriage for years to come.

No, Sherman Rosenbaum would have to find another shrink to certify his sister's future daughter-in-law as suitable for marriage

.

# THE EPISODE

WALKING BACK to my office after lunch, I discovered an exhaustive text message on my BlackBerry from Sherman Rosenbaum. The Chevalier offered apologies and hoped I did not mind that he had sprung Barbara on me. He said he felt it best that I meet her spontaneously. Of course one could affect a certain verisimilitude (his word, not mine) in such a situation, but it was never as potent as the real thing.

Verisimilitude? Had he used that sort of language as a Dodger batboy? And how did he have the patience or manual dexterity to type so many words onto a tiny screen?

Evelyn was at the dentist when I returned, so I checked the appointment book and discovered my calendar was open for the rest of the day—another debt I owed the pharmaceutical industry and Ortega's masters at Cambridge Medical. Managed care was doing to psychiatry what Disney had done to Forty-Second Street. With no room left for either the unknown or the exotic, everything was required to fall into a specific, potentially feel-good pigeonhole. And, if "common sense" couldn't straighten out the problem, there were always newer and better drugs coming on the market every day that could, all under the umbrella of Axis One.

But a great many of my patients were Axis Twos. They were deeply troubled individuals, whose thorny path to the present had been strewn with emotional limbs maimed or blown away by long-forgotten weaponry. No Happy Pill was ever going to cure them. These were the patients I was most concerned about: some who no longer met the insurance criteria and couldn't afford to pay for treatment on their own; others who had lied about their conditions in order to benumb, but never banish, their crippling sorrows.

At half past three, I wandered over to Bloomingdale's to see if my gloves were still there. Now, they weren't "my gloves," in that I had lost or misplaced them. In fact, I had never owned them. No, these were ridiculously expensive Italian driving gloves, which I had seen and admired but could never bring myself to purchase. They were luxury items I didn't need and, frankly, could no longer afford, not to mention the fact that I didn't even own a car. Yet I insisted on referring to them as "my gloves," and once a week, I would zigzag east through the Sixties until I reached Lexington Avenue, where I would walk south towards the venerable department store. I was like a stalker, obsessed with a love that could never be, a love my saner self knew was forbidden.

The haberdashery department was presided over by Athol Mokabi, an extremely tall Ugandan possessed of impeccable manners and fascinating tribal scars on his face.

"How may I help you today, sir?" Athol's voice was a deep, velvety rumble that echoed his exquisite diction, clearly the product of British colonial influence. And, if this imposing African salesman recognized me from week to week, he let nothing in his demeanor reflect it.

I perused the glass display case for a glimpse of my be-loved gloves. But they were nowhere in sight. My alarm at their disappearance must have registered, for Athol was at my side in a flash inquiring if something was amiss.

"Yes. Yes, there is something amiss, very much amiss. Where are the gloves? There were gloves on display here last week. Driving gloves...very fine leather...incredibly soft. The stitching was barely visible."

"Ah, yes! The Fratelli Orsinis. Perhaps I might have a pair in the stockroom. Could you wait a moment, please?"

"Perhaps"? Who had purchased the others? Week after week, I had stood in front of the display case admiring the Fratelli Orsinis, touching them, and finally trying them on in a kind of priestly ritual, one at which the scarred Ugandan salesman served as my acolyte. After all that, how could he have blithely sold them without giving me, at least, the right of first refusal?

Mortified, I was forced once again to admit the truth to myself: if Claire's "thing" was promptness, mine was ruminat-ing over my wardrobe. The agonies of the damned preceded my selection of the correct tie for a psychiatric conference. Runes were thrown to determine my choice of black shoes versus brown. "Never trust a therapist who makes snap deci-sions," I would laugh aloud. Privately, I felt ashamed, humili-ated, and, worse, human. How I envied those monks and convicts, whose dress codes were strictly dictated and never varied with the seasons.

"By any chance, were these the ones you meant?" asked Athol, who had returned and was proffering a box with the name Fratelli Orsini embossed on it. He lifted a layer of tissue paper, pursed his lips, and revealed the adored driving gloves within. "Very similar to the ones you liked, wouldn't you say?"

44

"Similar?" I was prepared to swear in court—under oath—that they were the exact same pair.

"Why don't you try them on?" purred Athol.

"Not today."

"Why not? You try them on every week."

"I beg your pardon?"

Athol had blown his cover. He knew exactly who I was but, for whatever private motive, played the game of Greet the New Customer every time I appeared.

"You come in every week," said Athol, "browse a bit, then always end up trying on the Orsinis."

"So they are the same gloves?"

"Of course."

"Then why weren't they on display?"

"I was curious to see what you would do if they weren't here."

"That was very devious."

"I am a student of human nature," said Athol, with a slight shrug of his huge shoulders. "Come on now, why don't you put yourself out of your misery? Clearly you love these gloves. Treat yourself. You deserve them. Buy them today."

"I don't 'love' them. I…I admire them. They're beautifully made."

"And comfortable." Athol held the gloves out to me like the serpent in Eden offering Eve her first bite of the forbidden fruit. "They should fit you like a…well, need one be redundant? Go ahead. Try them on."

"I can't. Please, don't ask me to explain." My agitated hands performed a weird ballet of helplessness.

"Is it the price? Perhaps, if I had a word with my manager, he could…"

"No, no, no. Please! Maybe next week."

"Here," said Athol, holding up the right-hand glove and whispering seductively. "Slip your fingers inside. Go on. You can always bring them back if you're not satisfied. But I know you will be. Why deny yourself the very thing you want? Life is too short."

I was on the verge of succumbing to my wily Ugandan tempter when I became aware of a commotion at the far end of the store. Babbling voices were gaining in volume and intensity. Was it a terrorist attack? No, there were no hysterical screams and no sense of panic. The shoppers were exhibiting the same curiosity New Yorkers display in the presence of some visiting celebrity or head of state.

Mentioning a prior engagement and promising on my honor to return afterward for my gloves, I beat a hasty retreat from Athol's domain and joined a small crowd, which had formed a circle near the store's Third Avenue entrance. I could hear snippets of conversation.

"She must be on drugs."

"Ya think? Maybe she's just crazy."

"Someone should call the cops."

"Don't get involved."

"She might hurt herself."

"That's the store's problem. Stay out of it."

I stood on tiptoe and struggled to catch a glimpse of what was happening. All I could make out were occasional flashes of what seemed to be a dervish spinning deliriously round and round, singing all the while. Finally I managed to squeeze through the crush of winter shoppers and caught sight of what everyone was staring at.

A teenage girl, whose chestnut-colored hair reached down to her shoulders, was the cause of all the commotion. To my embarrassment, she locked eyes with me, stopped singing, and advanced towards me, smiling all the while. I felt as if I were the only person in the world she wanted to see, indeed, as if I were the only person in the world she *could* see. I recognized her as the girl who had accosted me the previous evening on Fifth Avenue and then disappeared into Central Park. Her eyes twinkled as she resumed singing, clapping her hands all the while:

*Sha, shtill*
*Macht nisht kein Geriever*
*Der Rabbi geyt shoyn*
*Tanzen, tanzen wieder*
*Sha, shtill*
*Macht nisht kein Gevalt*
*Der Rabbi geyt shoyn*
*Tanzen bald*

Taking hold of my hands, she attempted to pull me into the circle with her. Trying my hardest to resist, I caught sight of a silver-fox coat lying on the floor. Only then did I realize—as incredible as it seemed—that the dancing girl was Barbara Warren. And that it was she who had accosted me on the street the other evening. My face must have registered shock or disbelief because she burst out laughing, released her grip on me, and began spinning faster and faster until finally she collapsed on the floor in a heap.

I had witnessed another one of the episodes that Gordon Jacobs and his Uncle Sherman had described. Neither had done justice to the intensity and hypnotic power of her possession. Dropping to my knees, I cradled Barbara's head against my chest. The circle of customers crowded around us had swollen by then to almost a hundred, and uniformed security guards were forcing their way through the crowd to make way for the irate store manager. He demanded to know what the hell was going on.

47

I informed him that I was a doctor and the young woman was my patient. Could he please move these people away? He immediately obliged. I scooped the silver-fox coat off the floor, wrapped Barbara in it, lifted her up in my arms, and carried her towards the exit.

The now obsequious manager flagged down a yellow taxi van, handed me his business card, and held the door open while I gently settled Barbara into the backseat. Murmuring thanks, I gave the driver my office address as we sped off.

Barbara lay stretched out on the backseat with her head in my lap deliriously repeating: "Shimon … Shimon … Shimon. Come back!"

When we got back to my office, I stretched the sleeping girl out on the couch and used her silver-fox coat once again as a coverlet. Observing her slow rhythmic breathing, I wondered why I had not taken her to Lenox Hill Hospital. Why had I become involved? She wasn't my patient. Why had I lied about that? I could have walked away from the whole thing. Perhaps it was her beguiling smile. The way it snuck up on me. The vulnerable girl asleep on my couch was the polar opposite of the nattering narcissist I had endured at lunch. I was keen to see this girl's smile again and bask once more in its radiance. And, from a strictly professional point of view, I was fascinated by her behavior—so unlike the humdrum, uninspired neurotics I dealt with on a daily basis.

I sat behind my desk and observed her, as the light outside dimmed and the room grew dark. My mind explored the more obvious solutions to the problem: chemical imbalance, premenstrual stress, epilepsy, alcoholism, or simply wedding jitters. One thing was certain: she had danced and she had sung.

The clock on the onyx mantle chimed six. In the dimness I reached for the telephone and began punching in the first

48

few digits of my home phone number. I had promised Claire that I would be home on time that evening. Now, I had to let her know...

Barbara stirred abruptly at that moment and in a state of panic, sat up and demanded to know where she was. Hanging up the phone, I calmly assured her everything was all right.

"Who are you? Why's it so dark in here?"

"It gets dark quickly in the winter." I switched on my desk lamp, then asked: "How are you feeling, Barbara?"

Barbara stared at me warily and asked, "Do I know you?"

"Harris Strider. We had lunch together this afternoon with Gordon. Remember? You're in my office. On Fifth Avenue."

"How did I get here?" Barbara tried rising from the couch but couldn't quite manage it. "What's going on?"

"I brought you here in a cab after you collapsed. Don't you remember what happened? In Bloomingdale's?"

"What are you talking about?" Barbara stared at me as if I were a raving lunatic.

"Apparently you experienced another of your episodes. I'm a doctor. It was just a coincidence that I was there when you..."

"I don't have fits!" shrieked Barbara. "No matter what the great Sherman Rosenbaum says."

"No one said you did. But I did witness you behaving in...an eccentric manner. You were singing and dancing in a public place. Do you have any recollection of that?"

"Singing and dancing in Bloomies? Like, I don't think so."

"Apparently it's not the first time this has happened."

"It didn't happen, 'kay? Bloomingdale's or anywhere else."

I debated whether or not to mention the video on Gordon's iPhone but realized Barbara was in complete denial about her problem: "Maybe I…get a little faint sometimes. Dehydrated. I try to drink eight glasses a day, but I'm on the go a lot and…have you got a mirror in here?"

"Over the mantle."

Barbara got herself off the couch, picked up her bag, and walked unsteadily to the mirror. She checked the state of her hair and makeup and immediately began putting everything back in place.

"Also…I get a little uptight," Barbara admitted, powdering her face and applying a fresh coat of lipstick. "Probably the pill. Makes me irritable. I've been meaning to see my gynie about an IUD."

I watched her expertly apply her makeup for a moment before I asked: "Who is Shimon?"

"What?"

"On the ride over here, you called out for Shimon. Who is that? Sounded like someone very important to you. There was urgency in your voice. It was as if you desperately wanted him to come back. Where did Shimon go? Who is he?"

Barbara spun around, placed her hands defiantly on her hips, and stared into my eyes: "Look, Doctor, I don't know why you were having lunch with Gordon. I've got my suspicions, 'kay? But I want you and everyone else to leave me the fuck alone. There's nothing wrong with me. Nothing!" With that, she gathered up her silver-fox coat and stormed out of my office

# THE PHONE CALL

THE RADIATORS in my apartment were banging incessantly as I sat at the dining table eating a paper-thin slice of veal marsala and regaling Claire with the tale of my adventure that afternoon. Her blue eyes bore deeper into mine with every twist and turn the story took, while I grew progressively more irritated by the cacophony coming from what sounded like the boiler room on the *Titanic*. Claire clung to my every word like a wirehaired terrier whose teeth were clamped onto a favorite squeaky toy. She wanted to know everything that occurred after Barbara denied having one of her fits.

"That was the end of it," I replied, touching my lips with a linen napkin. "She basically told me to lay off and flounced out of my office. That was a first for me. No patient has ever flounced out of my office before. What exactly determines a flounce? One good thing about it all...I didn't buy those Orsini driving gloves from Athol. That was a fabulous meal, honey, just fabulous. Aren't those radiators driving you crazy? Isn't there something we can do about them? Have you spoken to the super, the Polish guy? What's his name? Stanislaus?"

Claire ignored my questions and stared at me for what seemed an interminable length of time. Finally she broke her silence and asked: "Is she pretty?"

"What does that have to do with anything? Hey! Is this sorrel? Is that what I'm tasting? Your marsala recipe, right? Brilliant! Have you ever considered opening your own restaurant, one of those places where people have to make a reservation a year ahead of time? I'm not exaggerating. Your cooking is that good."

Claire ignored the compliments and answered my first question: "It has to do with the fact that in five years of marriage, plus eighteen months of living together, you have never discussed one of your patients with me. Ever!"

"That can't be."

"Oh, yes, it can! You wrote the law and you created a Pandora's box for our marriage, Harris. 'I cannot and will not discuss my patients. I will not violate their trust in me. Even to my wife.'"

"Well, in all fairness, this girl isn't really my patient. Not technically. She's more like an anecdote. That's it! She's an anecdote, who collapsed in Bloomingdale's."

Claire rose silently from the table and drifted into the living room. When she didn't return for several minutes, I filled two Baccarat Perfection brandy glasses with Armagnac and went in search of her. She was standing in front of the sliding-glass door, staring up at the cloudy, starless night sky.

"It's the winter, isn't it?"

"No," she replied. But I could still feel a cold Iowa wind blowing off the Plains into our living room.

I held a brandy glass out towards her. She took it. We stood together in an interminable silence until I finally asked: "How's the weaving going?"

"It isn't."

"But you're so good at it. Melba says you're the best one in the guild. Melba says..."

"Nella. Her name is Nella. Why can you never get her name straight? She's one of my closest friends." Claire took a sip of brandy then added: "I don't think New York and I are meant for each other."

"New York being a metaphor for me?"

"Why does everything have to be about you, Harris?"

Placing my snifter down on the sideboard, I impetuously moved towards her, grabbed her in my arms and said, "Let's go dancing!"

"I beg your pardon?" She shoved me away as if I were a drunken sailor who had accosted her at a church social.

"We never go dancing anymore."

"We never went dancing at all."

"In Jamaica. Remember? On our honeymoon."

"Once."

A lull descended on the living room. I began singing under my breath:

*There's an Iowa kind of special*
*Chip-on-the-shoulder attitude*

"What is that?" asked Claire, whose emotional thermometer was climbing steadily towards the boiling point. "That song you're singing?"

"Was I singing?"

"Yes, you were. You know you were."

"I'm sorry. I didn't..."

"'Iowa Stubborn.'"

"Io-what?"

"From *The Music Man*. You were singing it purposely to get my goat. You always do that when we quarrel."

"Whoa! Who said we were quarreling? There is no need going to Condition Red. We were having a civilized discussion—at its simplest, a conversation."

"This is not a conversation," snarled Claire. "Don't insult my intelligence!"

Is it a baby? I wondered. Does she want to have a baby? We never talked about children. Surely people have to talk about these things to make them happen. It can't just be telepathy or suppressed anger that propels a husband and wife towards the bed, with a child's creation as the miracle solution to their problems.

"What are you talking about, Claire? Is all this about the song? I truly had no idea I'd been singing aloud."

"Bullshit! You know how much I hate that song. You sing it on purpose to make fun of me. To punish me."

"Oh, Claire! This is ridiculous. You're behaving like an irrational child."

"Thank you, dear husband. Thank you so much for your loyal vote of support. God! I must have been crazy to marry a psychiatrist."

Time for an abrupt gear-shift, I thought to myself; something completely out of left field. "How's Edwin?"

"What?"

"We haven't heard from Edwin lately."

"As if you care!"

"I'm very fond of Edwin. He's a great talent. He doesn't get anywhere near the recognition he deserves. Where has he disappeared to now? Is he up at Yahoo?"

"Yaddo. Yahoo is an Internet company. Yaddo is an artists' colony."

"My bad."

"If you must know, he's gone to Paris with Tilly."

"Who?"

"His patroness. She can't maneuver the subways alone anymore."

"When's he coming back?"

"I don't know. Good night."

"Are you going to sleep? Now? For God's sake, Claire! It's only eight thirty."

"We go to bed early in Iowa. Remember? There are cows to be milked, and the north forty needs plowing. As you never cease to remind me!"

"Once! I made a joke about it once."

"Good night, Harris." Claire turned her back on me and flounced out of the living room.

Two flouncers in less than twenty-four hours had to be some sort of record. What did it all mean? And why had I broken my long-standing rule and discussed Barbara Warren with Claire? I polished off the Armagnac in my snifter and debated pouring myself another. It was a quarter to nine. I couldn't possibly go to bed yet. Not with my dear wife feeling the way she did. What had compelled me to tell her that story? Had there been an unconscious, masochistic desire on my part to seek this confrontation? Winters in New York were hard enough. But winters with Claire!

A call to the Pasha was in order. I wanted to recount the day's bizarre set of events to him, but when I tried his phone, I only got his voicemail. Who else could I call? My parents? No. Not in the middle of the week. Communication with them was restricted to weekends. Breaking the pattern would only make them anxious about my motives. How about watching a movie on Netflix? There was that new Swedish zombie movie everyone was raving about. No. I was determined not to support the zombie craze. Regular broadcast TV would suit me fine. PBS had a documentary about managed health care. After five minutes, I switched it off fearing Robert Ortega might appear on the screen and denounce me.

Finally I closed my eyes, which was a big mistake. When I opened them again, it was midnight. Claire would be asleep by now, convinced that I had dispatched her to dreamland without wanting to patch things up. Of course I could have wakened her to say I was sorry, but she was always so irritable when her sleep was interrupted—another unfortunate legacy of her Iowa upbringing. No, the best thing would be for me to quietly slip into bed next to her and hope the morning would bring Claire a different outlook on life.

The bedroom was freezing. I tiptoed across the parquet floor to close the window and discovered to my horror that it was already shut. Oh, God! Why was it so frigging cold? Was the thermostat a metaphor for my marriage? Reaching under my pillow, I found that my pajamas weren't there. Not wishing to wake Claire, I slid across the floor toward the chest of drawers she and I shared. Where were my pajamas? I didn't dare wake my grim-faced, sleeping wife to ask. Shivering, I whipped off my clothes and in uncharacteristic fashion, let them drop to the floor before I plunged under the covers. Jesus! It was colder inside our bed than out. How was that possible?

Stealthily reaching an arm across my wife, I gently tugged her sleeping body towards me. She let loose a heart-stopping shriek.

"You're like a block of ice!"

"I know. I c-c-can't find my pajamas."

"In the laundry hamper."

"Why's it so c-c-cold?"

"I'm asleep, Harris."

"I'm sorry. Aren't you c-c-cold?"

"Not till you woke me."

"What are you wearing? Is it flannel?"

"Harris, please, don't wake me."

"Sorry."

She rolled over and went back to sleep. I blew on my hands then placed my warm palms on my shoulders. It was a survival game I had taught myself as a child on frosty Illinois nights. Continuing to blow on my hands, I applied the heat to different parts of my body. Before I knew it, I had drifted off.

I awoke to the ringing telephone. From deepest sleep I heard Claire mutter, "Who the hell is that?" Feigning unconsciousness, I prayed it was a wrong number. Or maybe it was Edwin calling from Paris. Claire was bound to be nice to him, and maybe some of that residual affection would rub off on me. She fumbled in the darkness for the receiver. Please, I prayed, let it be Edwin.

"Hello…He's asleep…Just a second." She began shaking me and then angrily thrust the receiver towards my head. "For you."

"Yes?" I croaked into the receiver without opening my eyes. "Hello?"

"Dr. Strider? This is Barbara Warren. I have to see you right away. I just had the most horrible nightmare."

"What…what time is it?"

"Quarter to four," answered Claire angrily.

"Please, honey, go back to sleep." I hoped the reply would inspire and satisfy both women.

"Can't," Barbara said. "I'm afraid to sleep."

"Let's talk about it tomorrow."

"What time?"

"I don't know. My appointment book isn't...Call my office in the morning and we'll see what's available. Good night."

My eyes were still glued shut as I passed the receiver back to Claire.

"Was that her?"

"Who?" I asked innocently.

"The anecdote."

"Go back to sleep, Claire."

"Why did she phone here in the middle of the night?"

"Claire, please! I'm begging you. Go back to sleep!"

"Can't you refer this woman to someone else?"

"She's not my patient."

"Then why did she phone you? How did she get your number if you're not..."

"I'm listed in the phone book, Claire, like everyone else. And you can find me on the Internet. No one has privacy anymore."

"She's obviously a nut."

I chuckled.

"What's so funny?" she asked.

"Most of my patients are."

"Then she is your patient?"

"No, she is not. And tomorrow I will refer her to someone else, okay? Will that make you happy? Tell me it will make you happy."

"Believe it or not, Harris, I'm thinking of you. Not me. I just have a strange feeling about this woman."

# THE MISSING HOUR

BARBARA WARREN was pacing back and forth outside my office door when I arrived at a quarter to nine. Neither Evelyn nor any of the other doctors had arrived yet, and I reminded Ms. Warren that I had asked her to phone first to make an appointment. This mini-rebuke had no affect as she followed me into my private office, griping that she had been unable to go back to bed after we spoke. She seemed to feel that sleep deprivation granted her special consideration. I was impressed that she could plead with me to see her immediately, while still checking the e-mail on her iPhone.

Truth be known, I could have used another patient in those days. With the Great Recession still going strong, the HMO rats were deserting my therapeutic ship in droves, and I was having trouble coming up with my share of the rent for the medical suite. The nitty-gritty had me facing the real possibility that I might have to sell our co-op (although I hadn't breathed a word of this to Claire). But still, I wasn't prepared to roll over and bark for the monetary treat Ms. Warren held in her purse.

Leafing through my appointment book, I screwed my face into a grimace of conflict and determination to try and squeeze Barbara in before my first appointment. I saw no reason to tell her my next two hours were all too available. Two hours! What longtime patients had bailed on me now? Evelyn would break the news to me later.

"Sit down. Please." I gestured towards the leather chair. "You must be exhausted."

"I am." Barbara sat down and crossed her legs.

"What do you do at Condé Nast?"

"Advertising."

"Ah! Would you like some coffee?"

"No. What I'd really like is to sleep."

"Tell me about your dream."

"It was scary. Really freaked me out."

"What happened? Describe it to me."

"This is really difficult for me, you know. Coming here. Really weird." Barbara rose from the chair and began pacing the room. "There was this girl in my high school. Elise Kaplan. She went to a shrink twice a week. We all made fun of her. Crazy Elise. She ended up killing herself.

"Strange part was that we had been, like, best friends in first grade. She'd come over to my house; I'd go to hers. She lived in a mansion, a huge estate with a housekeeper and a maid. The maid would make us exotic sandwiches with, like, rose petals in them. I never saw Elise's mother. But there was a room upstairs at the end of the hall that was always locked, and someone was crying inside. Elise and I were in different classes in second grade so we stopped playing together. I'd completely forgotten we had ever been friends, till I heard she was dead."

"Tell me about your dream, Barbara."

She kneaded her forehead with her fingertips, as if this might help summon up the memory. Then she spoke: "We're walking down a cobbled street. It is steep and winding. Like in Europe somewhere. It is dark out. And we come to a carved door—really thick wood and an old-fashioned brass knocker. We unlock the door and climb the stairs."

"You keep saying 'we.' Are you with Elise?"

"Elise? Why would I be with Elise? No! It's this guy. I don't know who he is. But he's young, good-looking, buff. He's got a full beard. He takes my hand and we climb the stairs, wooden ones that lead to a darkened attic room. I hear chanting. I'm scared. Reminds me of *The Exorcist*. I don't want to climb anymore but he keeps pulling me up those stairs. They creak. We finally reach the room at the top. There are candles lit everywhere, and old men in prayer shawls. They are squeezed in tight under the roof, rocking and chanting on benches. I'm dressed funny. Like, you know, peasant clothes. My hair is long and braided. The men see me, and their faces get all twisted with anger. They try shooing me away, as if they're doing something illegal or forbidden. But the young guy keeps insisting it's all right."

Suddenly Barbara began swaying as she spoke. I thought she was about to faint and reached out a hand to steady her but hastily withdrew it. I was afraid if I touched her, she might stop speaking.

"There's a man seated in a chair at the front of the room. He is gesturing for me to approach him. I don't want to. The chanting grows louder and louder. I'm scared. He's wearing a big hat and has a black beard, but I can't see his eyes. He's holding his hands outstretched to me. What does he want from me? I shake my head no, no. Leave me alone. But the young guy pushes me gently towards him. I'm walking on tiptoe, little short steps like a child. Floorboards creak underneath me. I reach my hands out to the bearded man, who takes hold of them and squeezes them gently. Then he lifts his head up and smiles at me.

"He looks like you."

"Like me?"

"Yes, Rebbe. Except he has a beard."

"What did you call me?"

"Call you?"

"Just now. You called me a name."

"Doctor."

"No, Barbara. You didn't say doctor."

"Yes, I did." Her voice was decidedly peevish.

"Okay, okay. What happened next?"

"I...I don't remember."

"Then why did you phone me in such distress? What frightened you enough to call me in the middle of the night? Granted, it was mysterious but nothing about it warranted..."

"Have you got a cigarette?"

"No. I thought you didn't smoke."

"I don't. I just thought it might...Oh, God!" Barbara flung her head back then forward until her face was in her lap. "What is happening to me? I feel like screaming."

"It's okay. There's no reason to get upset. Take a deep breath. Slowly. Slowly. Are you listening to me?"

"What is Zohar?" she asked, letting the air out abruptly.

"So hard? I don't understand."

"No, no, no. Zohar. The man with the beard, who looks like you, opens an old leather-bound book. I think he calls it Zohar. He takes my hand and makes me touch the pages. I struggle to pull my hand away. And then I faint. That's when I woke up. Weird, isn't it? I woke up by fainting."

"You probably fell to the floor in your dream. That's what woke you up."

Barbara sat on the couch again and buried her face in her hands. Then she murmured: "It started in November."

"What did?"

"Gordon and I went skiing in Vermont. We, like, totally love skiing. What a rush! I wanted to race with Gordon. He hates racing because I always beat him. Anyhow, it was, like, this perfect day. Sun shining. Blue sky. But when we got off the lift, the weather had changed. The sky was gray, almost black. Gordon didn't want to race anymore. Said he was worried about the weather. I called him a wuss who was afraid I'd beat his ass. I even offered to give him a head start. That really pissed him off. He huffed and puffed and got all red in the face. His machismo was offended. He said he didn't need a head start. So we got into racing positions and took off down the hill. The wind was awesome. We were neck and neck for a while but I shot ahead of him like I always do. I skied straight into the woods at the end of the run.

"Gordo shouted after me to come back, but I didn't hear him. He told me about it afterwards. He said he started to, like, totally freak because I wouldn't answer him. The snow was really coming down by then and I couldn't see more than a few inches in front of my face. Gordon was calling out my name, swearing at me, and begging me to come back. He sounded really scared. He didn't know what had happened. Like maybe I'd fallen off a cliff or got buried in a snowdrift. Poor Gordo. He was really upset."

"What actually happened?" I asked.

"Dunno. I skied into the woods and, like, came out an hour later."

"What were you doing in there? You must have been doing something for an hour."

"I don't know! 'Kay? All I remember is going towards the trees. I watched them get closer, closer, and then ... nothing. But Gordon refused to believe me. He thought I was hiding. Duh! Like, I don't think so! It was freezing cold, and the snow was blowing so hard I couldn't see my hand in front of my face. Why the hell would I play games with him?"

"Were you playing games?"

"No! I don't play games. But nobody wants to believe me. I don't know what happened, Doctor. Not a fucking clue! Sorry. My bad. But this thing has driven me nuts for the past two months; an hour of my life that I cannot account for. Gordon, my darling fiancé, still doesn't believe me. I know for sure Uncle Sherman doesn't. That's where you come in, right?"

"Mr. Rosenbaum is understandably concerned about your…"

"My 'fits'?" Did he tell you what happened at Printemps? The dancing? Do you know about the dancing?"

"Gordon showed me the video."

"What? I told that lying SOB to erase it."

"He was worried about you, Barbara. He didn't mean to betray you."

"Why doesn't he just put it on YouTube? Dancing! I don't remember any of that either."

"And what about the other evening on Fifth Avenue?"

"Like, what are you talking about, Doctor?"

"Outside my office. You ran up to me, babbling in some strange tongue. Then you ran into the park."

"Am I dreaming all this? I'm really upset. I never met you before yesterday. What the hell is going on, Doctor?"

"I don't know, Barbara. Without all the information, it is difficult for me to…When you came out of the woods did you have a bump on your head? Any kind of bruising?"

"Like Natasha Richardson? Maybe I ran into a tree? Duh! Don't think so! I'm a fabulous skier, 'kay? Things like that don't happen to me. For the record, I went into the woods and I came out again."

"An hour later."

Barbara burst into tears then blurted out: "What if it's a tumor or something?"

"Is that what you're afraid of? We can put your mind at ease about that soon enough." I thumbed quickly through my Rolodex and found the card for Norm Kaplansky, a radiologist, whose office was two floors below mine. I made a quick call. His nurse told me to send my patient down immediately.

I told Barbara that I was certain there was no neurological disorder, but in light of her past behavior, she should start seeing me regularly. Without hesitation, she agreed.

# THE PASHA

THE SNOW WAS falling heavily once again as I stared out the window. The clock on the onyx mantle chimed five. Evelyn buzzed me from the reception area to tell me she was leaving for the day. The sun was starting to set. I had personally escorted Barbara down to Kaplansky's office that morning, introduced her to the pallid radiologist, then returned upstairs. I had heard nothing since from either of them.

The telephone rang, and I sprang for it like some ravenous leopard, hoping the caller might be Kaplansky. Unfortunately it was Robert Ortega calling again from Cambridge Medical to see if I had put Dalton Lafferty on Ativan yet. When I told him I had no intention of prescribing the drug for the professor, Ortega fired back that the HMO would drop Lafferty immediately.

"The man's a malingerer," said Ortega. "We can't keep picking up the tab for someone who's clearly medicable."

"Wait a minute! Do you have any idea who Professor Lafferty is?"

"Frankly, Doctor, I'm not interested. Okay? To me he's just someone who is costing this company a great deal of money unnecessarily."

"The man is one of the foremost Shakespeare scholars in the United States. Have you never read *The Dragon and His Wrath*?"

"I'm not a big fan of Anglo literature."

"Whoa! Whoa! Is this a cultural thing, Ortega? If I had said he was the foremost authority on Garcia Lorca, would that have made a difference?"

"Hey! Don't try and bait me, Doctor. You want to continue to treat Lafferty, that's your business. Be my guest. But you can't bill Cambridge any longer. Okay?"

No sooner had I slammed the phone down than I heard a loud string of oaths coming from the hallway outside the office. I looked out and saw Marty Corwin, huffing and puffing up the stairs while brushing snow off his un-PC raccoon coat.

"Doesn't your fucking elevator ever work?" asked Corwin, following me inside. He removed his Persian-lamb hat and wiped the perspiration from his bald head. "It's a goddamn blizzard out there." The Pasha continued to shake the snow off his fur coat as he lit a cigar. "What are you staring at, Harry? Never seen an Abominable Snowman before?"

"You look like Rod Steiger in *Doctor Zhivago*. What was the name of that character he played?"

"Victor Komarovsky," replied Corwin, removing his wet galoshes and tossing them in a corner. "A lewd, immoral womanizer and my role model all through medical school. Sort of our relationship in microcosm, don't you think?"

"Me? Dr. Zhivago?"

"Not the first time I've commented on your brooding, Midwestern Omar Sharif persona. I'm sure you had to beat the girls off with a stick in Evanston. Or was it Skokie?"

Martin Corwin was my closest friend. I had attended Stanford Medical School and, when I chose psychiatry as my specialty, was accepted to the program at Columbia University Medical Center. It was there I fell under the spell of Corwin, a mesmerizing lecturer. His brilliant insights and irreverent wit fascinated and entertained me from day one. I still don't know why Corwin chose to befriend me initially but, as a stranger to the city (my mother had forbidden me to set foot in New York before I was eighteen and was subsequently thrilled when I went to school in Northern California), I was honored and touched when he asked me, six months later, to be the best man at his second wedding. The marriage didn't last, but it did produce two beautiful girls, Jessica and Robin, whom the Pasha adored to distraction.

"Did we have a racquetball date, Marty?"

"Relax, Harry. No need to humiliate me on the court twice in one week. I'm having drinks with a sweet young thing at the Plaza, and I'm early. I thought I'd stop in here and kill some time with—what's wrong? You seem upset."

"Have you ever had any phone calls from a Robert Ortega at Cambridge Medical?"

"I refuse to talk to HMOs."

"How can you avoid it?"

"They just know better than to call me. Life's too short."

"Are you serious?"

Corwin's reply was a series of smoke rings blown in my direction. Followed by: "Whatever became of the Chevalier du Tastevin's..."

"Did I tell you about him?"

"The steam room at the club. Remember? Wasn't there a niece or a granddaughter or..."

"Nephew's fiancée. She was here this morning."

"Could we possibly sit down? I'm making a puddle on your expensive carpet. What kind of rent do you pay here?"

"Take your coat off, Pasha."

"Thought you'd never ask."

Corwin hung his coat on a wooden hanger on the back of the door, stretched out on my couch, and resumed blowing smoke rings in the direction of the ceiling. I sat behind my desk and recounted the story Barbara had told me that morning.

"Which one do you believe?" asked Corwin. "The girl or her boyfriend?"

"My patient, of course."

"She might have hidden just to piss him off. Sounds like she has considerable hostility towards him. Speaking of which, how is our Little Weaver these days?"

"Edgy. Barbara phoned me in the middle of the night."

"Barbara? Don't you mean 'the patient'? Let's not lose our professional distance here, Harry."

"Couldn't it be like 'driver's amnesia'?"

"What the hell are you talking about?"

"Have you never done it, Marty? Driven across the George Washington Bridge to New Jersey without any recollection of how you got there?"

"Upper level or lower?"

"I'm serious."

"Okay, Sherlock. Let's rewind the tape. Why didn't the girl have frostbite? Hmm? If she was standing still in the woods for an hour in near zero weather, why didn't she?"

"What's the difference between a rabbi and a rebbe?"

69

"Nothing. One's the English word and the other's Yiddish."

"Barbara had a dream…"

"The patient!" Corwin held up his index finger in a gesture of rebuke, which returned us to our former teacher-student days.

"Okay, okay. The patient dreamt that a strange young man escorted her down a cobblestone street to a mysterious attic. It was somewhere in Eastern Europe, from the way she described it."

"Was this dream in present time?"

"She didn't say. But the details made it sound long ago. Candles lighted the attic. It was full of men wearing prayer shawls and chanting loudly. There was a strong air of secrecy, and they resented her presence."

"Kabbalists. Did she mention the Book of Zohar?"

"Zohar is a book?"

"Yes, the Book of Splendor, the mystical and mysterious bible of Kabbalah. Isaac Luria, the father of the Kabbalistic movement, was born in Jerusalem in 1534 and was a real Messianic character. He was known as *Ha-Ari*, the Lion. Legend has it that the spirit of Elijah the Prophet visited Luria's father and told him that his wife would conceive a child, Isaac, who would deliver Israel from the forces of evil, reveal the mysteries of the Torah, and expound on Zohar.

"As a young man, Isaac lived the life of a recluse for seven years; he devoted himself to silent meditation and only came home to his family for Friday-night meals—just like me. During this ascetic period, Elijah visited him as well and clued him in on the unexplained portions of the Torah. The Lurianic line still exists today. In fact, one of his female descendants is a psychologist in Los Angeles."

"So Zohar is a basic Jewish text?"

"Let's rewind the tape," said Corwin, reveling in the role of teacher. "Quick test: Do you even know what the Torah is?"

"It's a large scroll. Containing the five books of Moses: Genesis, Exodus, Leviticus, Numbers…and Deuteronomy! Jewish boys read from it on their bar mitzvah."

"Do I detect a wee note of regret that you never had a bar mitzvah, Herschel? All those fountain pens that might have been yours. Now, you were correct about the boys reading from the Torah. But…they also read a portion from the Talmud. What do you know about the Talmud?"

"Nothing."

"Okay. The Torah is the written law while the Talmud is a compilation of the oral laws."

"You lost me."

"Which is why we have summer school, *boychik*. No goy left behind. The Torah was transcribed and was the law for the Jewish people for a thousand years. People went to temple every Saturday and heard 'thou shalt…whatever.' The only problem was that there were no details. So a passage in the Torah like 'thou shalt prepare the meals in the manner I have described' is a dead end. There is no description, no appendix, and no glossary. It's easier to assemble a rolltop desk from Ikea. At least they give you a drawing and tell you the number of screws. Not so with the Torah.

"The Lord spoke to Moses and gave him the details. In turn, Moses told Joshua. Nobody else! So for a thousand years the details—the how-to of being a good Jew—were passed down by word of mouth. And, as with anything that isn't written down, it tends to get misinterpreted, corrupted, or turned inside out. Which is why rabbis would argue into the wee hours over the explanation of 'explanation.' Bill Clinton would have been a great rabbi: 'It depends on what the meaning of the word *is* is.'

"So around the second century AD during the Roman occupation of Judea and after the destruction of the Second Temple…"

"Second Temple?"

"Did you never see *Raiders of the Lost Ark?* The ten tribes of Israel were wandering around the desert for years, schlepping that ark everywhere. King Solomon—you've heard of him—finally built a temple in Jerusalem to house it and give the Jewish people a spiritual center. The Babylonians invaded years later and destroyed it. The Temple was rebuilt and destroyed once again during the Roman occupation of what was then called Judaea. To make matters worse, the Muslims later built the Dome of the Rock on the former site of the Temple. If it wasn't bad enough having Holocaust deniers, there are now Temple deniers, who says the Jews were never there at all. "

"Fascinating. But what does this have to…"

"During the Roman occupation, a rabbi named Judah Hanasi—a direct descendant of King David—took up the heroic task of compiling the oral laws into a volume known as the Mishnah. The sixty-three tractates contained therein codify Jewish law and are the basis of…come on, Harry. Stay with me."

"The Talmud."

"Bingo! Now this is important because without a temple in Jerusalem—think no Vatican or no Mecca—the Jews are adrift, both spiritually and legally. They are an exiled people in desperate need of a homeland and a system of belief, which leaves them emotionally vulnerable to mystical overtures. Voilà, the Kabbalah.

"It flourished throughout the Middle Ages, but by the eighteenth century, the era of Haskalah—Jewish enlightenment—began. Suddenly there was a desire to become an integral part of the European community, to embrace secular studies, and interact with non-Jews. All of this meant turning one's back on the medieval mysticism of Zohar and its practitioners. The Kabbalists were forced to go underground."

"Or up in attics," I said. "Like my patient's Rebbe."

"Until the dawn of the twentieth century when Gershom Scholem came along and made it legit again."

"Who was he?"

"A German Jew who emigrated to Palestine in 1923. He became the first professor of Jewish mysticism at the Hebrew University of Jerusalem and wrote a great many books on the subject."

"So it's conceivable my patient could know about all this through Scholem's books?"

"Or just hanging out in metaphysical coffee shops. Red string bracelets, along with crystals and sweat lodges, have been the rage for the past twenty years."

"Frankly, Marty, she doesn't seem the type—diamonds, yes, crystals, no. Oh, wait! There is a part of her dream I left out. I'm not sure what it means."

"But you understand everything else? I'm impressed, Harry. You're a quick study."

"She said that the rabbi conducting the service looked like me. Except he had a beard."

"My God, Harris! What have you done to this girl?"

"Nothing. I've only met her twice. Three times. Actually, four."

"Certainly made a hell of an impression on her."

"Claire says she has a strange feeling about her."

"Ho-ho! I'll bet she does."

"I told the patient I'd continue treatment. For a while."

Corwin swung his legs off the couch and sat up. He looked at his watch, got to his feet, and walked over to the door to fetch his coat.

"Big mistake, Harry, big, big mistake. Your wife sent you a polite warning, and I suggest you pay attention, if you want to keep your marriage intact."

# THE KLEZMER TRIO

THAT SUNDAY MORNING I lay in bed with my eyes glued shut, fantasizing how Claire and I might "rediscover" each other. How seductive the silence can be in Manhattan after a week of—*thud*!

I had either experienced a mild heart attack or had a cinder block fall on my chest. Opening one eye, I recognized the familiar bulk of the Sunday *New York Times*, which Claire had dropped on me from a height of three feet.

"Ouch."

"Sorry," said Claire, grinning down at me. "Did it hurt?"

"Ouch was an understatement. Why are you dressed?"

"Weavers Guild."

"On Sunday? Why? I was kind of hoping we could…"

"How many times did I mention it to you this week? You never listen to me, Harris."

"But, Claire. Wait! Just a second."

I stumbled out of bed and followed Claire into the living room where Nella, an obese, red-faced woman in her mid-thirties, grunted and sweated as she helped pack up Claire's loom. Nella's cheeks turned even more scarlet upon seeing me stark naked. I hadn't expected company.

"We're not alone," murmured Claire, biting her lip to keep from laughing.

"Oh, Jesus!" I dashed back inside the bedroom and re-appeared a second later wearing a Ralph Lauren bathrobe.

"Hi, Melba. How's it going?"

"Nella. Her name is Nella,"

"That's okay," whispered Nella, with a slight lisp.

"Nella, Nella, Nella." I mimed hammering the word into my forehead each time I said it. "So sorry, Nella. Someone cruelly tossed the *Times* on me, and I'm afraid it affected my brain."

"All set," said Claire, heading towards the door.

"When will you be back?"

"By seven."

"At the earliest," lisped Nella.

"There's coffee in the kitchen," said Claire. "It'll give you a new lease on life."

"I was really hoping we could...just..."

"This is important to me." Claire kissed me quickly on the lips, picked up her loom, and left with Nella.

I tried going back to sleep without success. So I got up, showered, shaved, and then spread out the different sections of the newspaper on the glass dining-room table in the vain hope of actually reading the entire paper for once. But I found myself unable to concentrate on any single article past the first three paragraphs. In frustration, I abandoned the project.

It was now eleven o'clock. Not bad, I thought. Claire would be home in eight hours. She would be tired—no hope of rediscovering each other then. But I could surprise her with a candle-lit dinner. It had been years since I had cooked for her. What little gem could I whip up? I needed something romantic, with lots of wine—and garlic. Hmm. Perhaps we would rediscover each other after all.

By noon I had seven different cookbooks open on the kitchen counter and had rejected every recipe inside as too difficult to prepare, shop for, or digest. The recipes only reminded me that I still hadn't had breakfast.

I dressed in my warmest winter clothes and left the building in search of scrambled eggs and a bagel, which I found at a coffee shop on Madison Avenue. Despite the cold, I continued aimlessly west. At Fifth Avenue, I examined the sidewalk art on display in front of the Metropolitan Museum, but as before, nothing could hold my attention for more than a few minutes. Turning right on Seventy-Ninth Street, I bought a large hot chocolate from a sidewalk vendor and entered Central Park.

I soon found myself in the middle of the park, in front of the Delacorte Theater. Were those clarinets I heard—in the dead of winter? Impossible.

Entering at the top of the steeply tiered outdoor theater, where Claire and I had spent so many memorable summer evenings watching Shakespeare, I stared down at the distant stage. Those summers of love seemed long ago. Now, alas, it was the winter of her discontent. And what were three men playing klezmer music doing on stage in the freezing cold? And who was the young girl with them in the long blue overcoat?

The klezmer trio was infused with a wild mystical energy, and the girl, whose beautiful dark hair tumbled down to her shoulders, matched their passion and vitality with her spirited dancing and singing. What a lovely, pitch-perfect voice she had. And her smile! God help the man who fell under its spell!

The men caught sight of me, their lone audience. Bowing deeply in appreciation, they called out in what I assumed was Yiddish and beckoned me to come closer. When I reached the apron of the stage, the musicians resumed their playing and the girl—little more than a teenager—held her arms out in a gesture of welcome. I declined politely with a wave of my hand. The lead clarinetist, who looked like an extremely tall Harpo Marx, clapped a hand to his brow in despair and hissed at me in heavily accented English: "Dance with her!"

I shook my head and improvised excuses on the spot: two left feet, don't know the steps, etc. But the young girl's eyes bewitched and overpowered me. Against my will, I climbed on the stage. She took my hands and began to swing me round and round the empty stage until I felt giddy. All the while, she dazzled me with her smile and her twinkling eyes. There was something familiar about her. Where had I seen her before? Had there been a charity dance recital or some other…Of course, that laugh! It was the girl from Bloomingdale's. How could I have been so dumb? It was Barbara, again without the makeup, the jewelry, or the off-putting affectations. Before me danced a pure, loving creature. How could such a transformation be possible?

I tried to ask her, but she silenced me with a finger to my lips, as if to say: "Don't spoil it." So I continued to spin round and round with her. When the dance was over, I pointed away from the stage, she nodded, and we waved good-bye to the musicians.

Silently we wandered hand in hand through the park. I bought another hot chocolate and held the cup out to her, but she shook her head and gestured for me to hold it while she placed her hands over mine and sipped from the other side. We alternated taking sips, our eyes locked on each other.

A strange transformation had taken place: the girl was no longer my patient, and I was clearly her slave—completely in her power. How had this happened?

Some laughing kids in brightly colored parkas whizzed past us on a toboggan. Suddenly I felt an irresistible urge to recapture that happy memory from my childhood in Evanston, the one on the sled with Donna Schuman's cousin from Syracuse, whose name I still could not remember. I asked the oldest kid if my girlfriend and I could borrow his toboggan for one quick ride. In exchange for the rest of our hot chocolate, he agreed.

Hand in hand, we pulled the toboggan behind us up the steep hill. We still hadn't exchanged a word, but my heart pounded with excitement, both innocent and timeless. I sat at the front of the toboggan to steer, and Barbara sat behind me clutching my waist. Seconds later we were barreling down the hill with the snow spraying in our faces. I was twelve years old again, sailing towards the uncharted shores of that New World called Love. How pure and cleansing it felt, so devoid of cynicism and irony. I could hear Barbara squealing behind me with delight and smell the hot chocolate on her breath. How I wanted that moment to last forever. Then Barbara cried out in alarm. We had hit a large rock buried under the snow and been thrown off the toboggan.

We lay sprawled atop each other in the snow, holding each other's hands tightly and laughing uncontrollably. By some miracle, we had not sprained or broken anything. The young boy came running over to claim his toboggan, cursing me for almost wrecking it. I helped Barbara to her feet and handed the kid a five-dollar bill for his trouble.

Her scarf and overcoat were caked in snow, and I made a futile attempt to clean it off of her. Instead she clung to me; it took all my will power to keep from kissing her deeply, passionately, and gratefully. Barbara had given me back a lost part of my youth that afternoon. Had I died at that moment, it would have been in a state of bliss.

Then reality reared its unpleasant head. What would I say to her the next morning at our session? How could I reconcile my vow never to socialize with my patients with this romp in the snow, like some love-struck adolescent?

As if reading my mind, Barbara stared warmly into my eyes and whispered: "Don't worry." Those were the only words she had spoken all afternoon. She kissed me on the cheek, said good-bye, and hurried away across the park.

# THE MORNING AFTER

IT WAS ALMOST TEN when Claire returned home from her guild meeting. She was filled with the unbridled sense of enthusiasm that intense sisterhood always brought out in her. I was starving; she had eaten dinner with Nella and the other weavers. As I made myself a grilled Brie and Swiss, I pretended to listen while Claire babbled away about wanting to attend the Weavers Guild's spring exhibition in North Carolina. But my guilt-free thoughts were focused wholly on Barbara. Claire had no inkling of this as she snuggled onto my lap and kissed me in an incandescent fashion, which could easily have morphed into the elusive "rediscovery." But I remained immune to such temptation. My mind was filled with the klezmer melodies that accompanied my beloved as she danced over and over in my memory.

Finally breaking my silence—and in the hope of removing the newly kittenish Claire from my lap—I lied about having caught a chill that afternoon. When that ploy failed, I slid out from under her like an affronted virgin set upon by a masher at a movie matinee.

"Where did you go today?" asked Claire, concerned about the fragile turn my health had taken.

"The park."

"The park? Wasn't it cold?"

"How do you think I caught a chill?"

"Then why did you go?"

"I had to get out. Cabin fever. Clearly, I overdid it."

"Didn't you wear a scarf?"

"I'm an adult, Claire. Let me take responsibility for my mistakes. Please, don't cross-examine me. I just want to crawl into bed now, that's all."

* * *

The next morning I was in a buoyant mood. On my way to the office, I stopped off at a Korean market and bought some outrageously priced flowers to brighten up the office. Given sufficient time, I would have hung new wallpaper in advance of Barbara's visit at nine o'clock.

Bounding into the reception area like a man transformed, I dispatched an open-mouthed Evelyn in search of a vase for the dozen red roses I was clutching. Minutes later I was pruning the stems and placing them in the glass carafe she had found gathering dust in the broom closet. Plucking one bloom loose from the arrangement, I clipped it short and placed it in the lapel of my Barney's suit jacket.

I checked myself in the mirror over the onyx mantle and was quite taken with my reflection that morning: intelligent, mature, and slightly dashing. Perhaps there *was* a trace of Omar Sharif. The clock chimed precisely at nine.

Twenty minutes later, I sat behind my desk drumming a nervous tattoo with the fingers of my left hand. Where the hell was she? Had something happened? Maybe Gordon had found out about us and beaten her to a pulp. I swore I would kill the big red-haired palooka if he had harmed her in any…I looked up at the clock. It was nine thirty. She wasn't coming. Maybe she was fine; maybe she just couldn't handle how we felt about each other.

I stared at the rose in my lapel. What a fool I had made of myself! Tearing it loose, I tossed it into the wastebasket. Then I noticed blood dripping down onto my Mark Cross stationary; I had cut my right index finger on one of the thorns.

Just as I had gotten up and gone over to the coffee table to retrieve a tissue, the door flew open and in sailed a breathless Barbara. She was carrying two Bergdorf Goodman shopping bags, apologizing profusely for her tardiness, and feverishly texting on her iPhone.

I stared blankly at the young woman multitasking in front of me. What had happened to my companion from yesterday? Where was the beautiful young girl with the long dark tresses? And who was this bejeweled woman in front of me, wearing full war paint and with her hair pinned high and tight on her head?

"Sorry, sorry, sorry," she repeated, as she collapsed into a chair and dropped her shopping bags on either side. "My bad. Gordon's mom phoned at eight this morning just as I was going out the door, with a heads up on new seating arrangements. Heads up? Heads off! Don't get me wrong. I love the old sweetie—mwah, mwah, mwah—but she's making my life *Nightmare on Elm Street, Part Ten.* Now she's got people coming in from Hong Kong. Hong Kong! What sort of food does she expect me to serve them—Crouching Tiger Quiche? Is it kosher? Ha-ha!" Barbara's iPhone rang. She sighed, fanned her face with her fake red nails, and answered it. Almost as an afterthought she asked: "D'ya mind? I'll keep it short. What happened to your finger? You should put something on it." She turned her attention to the phone. "Gilles? Honey, sweetie, can't talk right now. I'm at the doctor's…Can you do me Saturday? What? You little mutt! Who's more important in the world than me? No, I can't get in after work. Can't! Can't! Can't! Duh! Who's getting married? Remember? Squeeze me in, and I'll get you a hair credit when they run my bridal picture in the *Times*. You're such a little mutt. Love you. Mwah-mwah-mwah." She switched off the phone and dropped it into a shopping bag. "There. No more calls. How's your finger? Why are you staring at me like that?"

"Oh. I didn't realize." I twisted the tissue tourniquet around my wound and continued to stare in confusion. "You looked so different yesterday."

"Yesterday?"

"The park. It was so much fun. I can't remember having such a good time in—"

"What are you talking about, Doctor?"

"Yesterday afternoon. In Central Park."

"I wasn't anywhere near the park."

"Don't tease me, Barbara. We danced onstage at the Delacorte. The klezmer trio was playing? We tobogganed together? The hot chocolate?"

Barbara pushed herself back in the chair and stared at me. "Is this like part of the therapy? Trying to freak me out on purpose? Definitely not cool."

What was going on? Was I dreaming all this? Stop it, Harris! Concentrate. Everything yesterday occurred exactly as you remembered it.

"Where were you yesterday afternoon, Barbara?"

"Chill, doctor, 'kay? Like back way off! My private life is my private life, and I'm, like, really not comfortable with this whole interrogation thing." A patina of perspiration had broken out on Barbara's forehead, and she searched frantically through her bag for a handkerchief.

I passed her the box of tissues and grabbed another one for myself to make a fresh tourniquet. This afforded an excellent opportunity for shifting gears and changing the subject. "So! How are the wedding plans proceeding?"

Barbara leaned in towards me and did her own gear-shift, very much the coconspirator. "Can I, like, ask you something?"

"Of course."

"Which of these do you prefer?" Thrusting a hand into one of her Bergdorf bags, Barbara withdrew two swatches of satin fabric. "Apricot or peach for my bridesmaids? I can't make up my mind. Gordon doesn't want to know."

Barbara spent the remaining few minutes of our session complaining to me ad nauseam about the dressmaker, the caterers, the florist, and the orchestra leader. The bride-to-be prattled on and on in this vein as I sat in mute shock, praying for a glimpse—however brief—of the delightful creature with whom I had spent such a glorious afternoon the day before.

The clock on the onyx mantle finally chimed ten. From the depths of my despair, I whispered that our time was up. Barbara rose cheerfully, straightened out her skirt, and proclaimed what fun it had been. She said she would be back the following Monday; I suggested she make it sooner, possibly Thursday. This posed no problem for her, and on her way out the door, she asked if my wife and I would like to come to the wedding. She could squeeze us in with the Hong Kong guests. Just kidding. Mwah-mwah-mwah. P.S. Did I really prefer the apricot?

Once she'd gone, I raced to the bookshelf and thumbed furiously through my medical textbooks looking for something, anything, to explain the bizarre episode that I just had witnessed. Possible pressure on the temporal lobe came to mind. Recent research had shown such behavior could be sparked by some kind of spiritual awakening, similar to that of people who start speaking in tongues. No, Barbara's problem was far from neuro-theological. Totally frustrated, I abandoned the books and plowed through copies of the *American Journal of Psychiatry*. In desperation, I picked up the phone and speed-dialed the Pasha's office.

Two hours later, my mentor and I sat opposite each other at a window table in E.A.T. on Madison Avenue. Corwin hummed "(I Can't Get No) Satisfaction" as he swabbed a thick coating of butter across the top of his seven-grain bread while I stared at the ceiling, not knowing where to begin.

Corwin stopped humming, popped a chunk of bread in his mouth, and expressed a total lack of interest in any lurid details regarding the dissolution of my marriage. I had no idea what he was talking about. "Having traveled down matrimony's bumpy interstate twice, I feel confident when I say that you and Claire have been driving off the map for quite a while. Now maybe you guys will work it out, or maybe not. *Que sera, sera*. But could you, for Chrissake, try to be a little more discreet in public about your dalliances?"

"What you are you talking about?"

"This was my weekend with the girls. We were walking through the park yesterday afternoon, and Jessica said: 'What's Uncle Harris doing on that toboggan?' I turned my head in time to see you go flying through the air and, once I was convinced you hadn't cracked your skull open, did a one-eighty and steered my little daughters, who I want to believe exist in blissful innocence, toward the skating rink. What the hell were you doing, Harry, rolling around in the snow with that teenager?"

"You saw her?" I could barely contain my excitement and the tremor in my voice. "You actually saw her?"

"Half the city saw her! Claire's detectives definitely saw her."

"What detectives?"

"The ones she may have hired by now, putz! They could have seen her, videoed the whole thing, and posted it on YouTube! Tobogganing! What the hell were you thinking, Harry? The girl's barely older than my Jessica."

"Oh, Marty! Thank you, thank you." I grabbed Corwin's hand and began jerking it up and down like a pump handle. "I thought I was going out of my mind this morning. She was totally adamant about not being there. I only knuckled under to avoid a quarrel, but now I know it really happened."

A bald, skeletal man with a unibrow rapped on the window abruptly. Corwin yelped with surprise at this specter and clutched a hand to his heart. Norm Kaplansky, the radiologist from my building, stood outside wagging a disapproving finger at me. He entered through the front door and moments later stood over our table.

"Where did you disappear to last week?" Kaplansky asked in his surprisingly deep basso. "You brought that girl in for an urgent X-ray and then you never…"

"Is she okay, Norm? Nothing wrong with her, is there?"

"She's fine," said Kaplansky. "But you should start taking it easy." Staring at Corwin's buttered bread, he added: "Both of you." And with that pronouncement, the gloomy radiologist left the restaurant.

"What X-rays?" asked Corwin.

"At first I thought my patient's recurring blackouts might be neurological. But obviously it's more complicated than that. It could be schizophrenia, perhaps even multiple personality. One of her identities definitely made an appearance in the park yesterday."

"That Lolita on the toboggan was your patient? Are you completely *meshugga*?" exploded Corwin. "Maybe you did crack your skull open."

"For God's sake, Marty!" I looked around the upscale Upper East Side eatery in embarrassment. "Keep your voice down."

"What for? You're going to lose your license anyhow."

"Don't be ridiculous!"

Corwin pulled his chair in closer and whispered hoarsely: "You're in way over your head, Harry. She's a patient and she's a minor."

"She's twenty three."

"Bullshit! The girl I saw was a teenager."

"That one, yes. But not the one who comes to my office."

"Get rid of her, Harris. Now! Trust me. This whole thing is bordering on obsession."

I said nothing. What could I say? All I wanted was to see the girl from the park again. Of course I knew I had broken all the rules of my profession, but she had renewed my long overdue membership in the human race. I had ceased to be a detached observer examining everyone under my emotional microscope. Barbara had put me in touch with a part of myself that I had mislaid such a long time ago. I didn't want to lose that feeling. I refused to lose that feeling.

# THE TRIP TO TAHITI

A WEEK LATER I sat submerged in the bathtub, absorbed in a volume on schizophrenia, while Brian Williams on the television kept my wife company in the living room. Without warning, the light went off in the bathroom.

"Claire! Did a fuse just…?"

Backlit from the hallway, an arched bare leg dangled seductively through the half-opened bathroom door. Seconds later, Claire vamped into the room holding a flickering scented candle and wearing a colorful sarong. She was nude from the waist up.

"What's going on, honey?" An image of Norman Bates's mother holding a carving knife behind her back flashed through my mind.

"Not being a fan of the B-word, I'm forced to admit I've behaved like a first-class bitch for the past few weeks. I haven't been happy, and my behavior hasn't made you happy."

"Really, Claire, there's no need for all this…"

"Shhh! We both need a break, Harris. It's been a horrible winter. So…"

Romantic South Seas music drifted in from the stereo in the living room. Claire slid her hand down inside her sarong and withdrew two airline tickets. I watched her in rapt fascination.

"Two weeks for two, Harris. Seriously rekindling our love. In a little grass shack in Tahiti."

I was touched by the trouble and expense she had gone to—with an American Express card that, unbeknownst to her, was perilously close to its limit. Before I could express my appreciation, Claire undid her sarong and let it slip to the floor and sank down next to me in the tub. The tome on schizophrenia dropped onto the tiles, as she reached between my legs and affectionately squeezed my manhood. Her face registered amazement at the speed at which the sleeping sentry awakened and snapped to attention. Shifting her body until she was sitting up on top of me, she leaned down, kissed me passionately, and slid my hardness inside her. Soon bathwater was splashing all over the tiled floor. At long last, we had rediscovered each other.

\* \* \*

Imbued with the afterglow of our intense lovemaking, I set off the next morning for an appointment I had canceled too often. Gilbert Tolson was the manager at my local Citibank branch. Although he claimed that he had never been in analysis himself, Tolson was a great fan of films with psychiatric themes. The diminutive bank manager from Auburn, Maine, spoke with admiration for the various actors he had watched cure people's emotional problems over the years. Lee J. Cobb (*The Three Faces of Eve*) was someone he held in high esteem, as were Herbert Lom (*The Seventh Veil*), Brian Aherne (*The Locket*), and Leo Genn (*The Snake Pit*).

Neither the names of these actors nor the titles of the films in which they had impersonated members of my profession meant anything to me. So, as I was unable to play Screen Shrink with him, we were forced to discuss the issue at hand: my bank overdraft.

"It's become quite hefty," said Tolson in his thick Down East accent. "If we were an airline, we'd have to charge you for excess weight. I hate having conversations of this nature, Dr. Strider."

"Call me Harris." I was attempting to emulate Sherman Rosenbaum's bonhomie, for I hated conversations of this nature even more than Tolson did.

"Are you aware, Harris, that you're forty-eight thousand dollars over your credit line?"

"How is that possible?" I asked, knowing full well the exact amount I owed and wondering why Tolson had left off the additional $731.42.

"Actually," said Tolson, reading my mind. "The exact sum is $48,731.42. Apparently, you haven't managed to reduce this figure at all in the past six months. Citibank frowns on that sort of indifference."

"The market has been very cruel, Mr. Tolson."

"Don't I know it…Gil."

"Harris."

"No, no. Please, call me Gil. We've all taken a bit of a shellacking. The recession simply refuses to end. I've been forbidden to even utter the phrase 'in this economy' at home."

"Ouch!"

"Yes. But what about the noodle shop? It seemed to be doing so well."

"Still is. My partner bought me out a few years ago. That's why I was able to make such a sizable down payment on our co-op. With the profits from my investment." I hoped the words "sizable down payment" and "profits" would remind Tolson that I was not a complete loser when it came to financial matters.

"Aren't there more branches of the business now?"

"Yes, yes, there are." I wanted to add: No need to rub it in, Gil.

"Unfortunate case of bad timing. I wish you had consulted me before you sold, Harris. However that neither negates nor excuses the present situation. You must start paying off your debt. Immediately."

"Would it were that easy, Gil. My income seems to have dropped precipitously. Patients have deserted me. The HMOs have a lot to do with that. The mortgage on our co-op is quite high—stratospheric—and, my God, the maintenance. All within the shadow of the Great Recession."

"Perhaps, Harris, you should consider selling." The bank manager turned his back on me and redirected his attention to his computer screen. Tolson clicked on a website which gave him an instant evaluation of my co-op's worth. "Still got some healthy equity. Enough to sell and find a dandy little place in Brooklyn. It's enjoying quite the renaissance, Brooklyn is. There are a lot of film stars living there these days. No shame in downsizing."

"My wife loves where we live. She decorated the place herself."

"Ah! What about her income? Lawyer, isn't she?"

"She hasn't practiced law for the past two…actually, three years."

"What's she up to now? Do you have children?"

"No. No. She…weaves."

"Ah!"

"Yes."

"Well…perhaps it's time for her to hang out her shingle again. Or is it only doctors who do that?"

"I suppose I could introduce the idea."

"Soon, Harris…the sooner the better."

Thoroughly depressed after my meeting with Tolson, I wandered along Madison wondering how in hell I was going to "introduce" the subject of our impoverished circumstances to Claire. She had no idea how close to the edge we were. We had made so much money on the market. So much! It never dawned on me to strap on my chute and bail until it was too late. And by that time, Bernie Madoff's calumny had been revealed. Yes, I would tell her the truth…after we returned from Tahiti.

My good intentions were put on hold when I found myself confronted on the sidewalk by three elegantly attired women, dripping in furs and jewelry and looking remarkably alike. The youngest took my hand and began addressing me with the intimacy of an old friend, but I had no idea who she was. Then in a flash I regained my composure and found myself shaking hands and exchanging pleasantries with Barbara Warren, her mother, and her older sister, Judy, a painfully thin creature, who had obviously had a great deal of bad cosmetic surgery.

"I can't thank you enough, Doctor," said Mrs. Warren, a petite New Jersey duchess in her late fifties. "My little Barbara is my little Barbara again. Her anxiety is gone. Mine, too. *Oy!* The sleepless nights. Grinding my teeth. Acid reflux. And constipation, Doctor, like you can't imagine. Me, who's been like clockwork all my life. For a while I thought I should become your patient too. Hey! Maybe you can give us a group rate."

"Mother, please!" groaned Barbara, turning to her older sister and rolling her eyes.

"She's just kidding," said Judy. "Our mother should have done stand-up."

"Who's kidding?" asked Mrs. Warren. "A miracle man is a miracle man. The sessions obviously worked. She hasn't had any more of those fits. Don't look at me like that, Judy. Your little sister had fits. Now, they're gone…like acne. And I'm thrilled to death! You did a *mitzvah*, Doctor. Know what that is? A good deed. And I insist you and your wife be at our *simcha*. *Oy!* He doesn't understand what I'm saying. I'm inviting you to Barbara's wedding."

"I already invited him, Mother."

"Terrific! We've got wonderful friends coming from Hong Kong, who I know you'll get a big kick out of. He owns the biggest oyster farm in China and she does feng shui. Did I say it right? Fascinating people. We'll seat you at their table."

"We'd be honored."

"Does Barbara have your home address?"

"I'll get it from you at our next session, Doctor. Thursday, right?"

"Actually, I won't be able to see you for the next few weeks, Barbara. My wife and I are going to Tahiti on a rather spur-of-the-moment vacation."

"What's your home address, Doctor?" asked Judy, whipping an iPad out of her purse and punching in the address I gave her.

"Tahiti?" asked Barbara. "Gordon and I can't decide on Tahiti or Greece."

"My vote is Greece," said Mrs. Warren. "Went with my husband years ago. Have you ever been? The Parthenon! The Acropolis with all those stairs! Gave me a charley horse. And the retsina! Hoo-ha! Thrill of a lifetime! After all, how long can you lie on the floor of a *verkakte* grass shack?"

"Hopefully, two weeks," I replied. "Nice meeting you, ladies. See you at the wedding."

\* \* \*

I took a long lunch at a charming little bistro on Lexington and tried out my rusty French on the waiter in anticipation of my trip to Tahiti. Barbara was Barbara once more. Seeing her with her mother and sister had made that clear. And I need never fantasize about the girl on the toboggan again. Sherman Rosenbaum would, of course, be thrilled. He would get all the credit for her recovery, just as Claire would receive a Presidential Bathtub Seduction Medal for rescuing our drowning marriage. It was almost three when I finally returned to the office. Evelyn gestured for me to approach her desk and whispered: "Professor Lafferty's here."

"Does he have an appointment?"

"No. But he insisted on seeing you. I didn't know what to say…"

"It's okay, Evelyn. Nothing to worry about."

I stepped into my private office and saw Dalton W. Lafferty standing in profile by the window. At seventy years of age, through a regular regimen of Kundalini yoga, the professor had maintained the athletic trim of the semipro hockey player he had been in his youth. His receding white hair was almost shoulder length and offset by thick black eyebrows. With his robust theatrical voice and upright posture, the professor could easily have passed for Zeus traveling incognito. That afternoon Lafferty wore a faded Yankees baseball cap, New Balance sneakers, the jacket and trousers from two different Brooks Brothers suits, and a red-and-yellow plaid shirt, which only added to his mismatched appearance of sartorial indifference. There had not been a Mrs. Lafferty for many years, so the look was probably not intentional.

"What the hell are these?" thundered Lafferty, shaking a fistful of medical bills in my face.

"Unless I'm mistaken," I answered in a stern but calm voice, "you don't have an appointment today, Professor."

"Don't try to change the subject, Doctor." Lafferty stood resolutely rocking back and forth on the balls of his feet.

"Something is clearly upsetting you." Perhaps the time had come to medicate the great man.

"These. These." Lafferty waved the offending bills in my face once more, then recited: "'*When sorrows come, they come* not *single spies but in battalions.*'"

I perused the statements from Cambridge Medical and then sank despondently onto the couch. "I'm so sorry, Professor. I'd been meaning to discuss this with you but the moment has never really..."

"Won't they pay for my visits anymore?" Lafferty's tone had shifted to that of a child who had been informed he now had to pay full fare on the bus.

"No. They...want me to medicate you."

"Stalinists! Would they prefer that I drink hemlock like Socrates? Put pebbles in my pockets like poor Ginny Woolf? Is this not proof positive of what I've been claiming all along? The death of thought itself. Take the Bible, for instance—the Old and New Testaments—plus the Torah, the Koran, and add Aristotle, Plato, Euripides, Chaucer, Shakespeare, Marlowe, Molière, Milton, Pope, Congreve, Sheridan, Shelley, Keats, Dumas père et fils, Hugo, Tolstoy, Dostoevsky, and Chekhov. Nothing! All banished forever into the furthest extremes of cyberspace. And all books will vanish, as well. No need to stain ourselves any longer with the ink of inspiration. The time-tested sensation of holding and savoring the printed word will have disappeared from experience. Guttenberg need not have been born. The desensitization caused by the too-smooth iPad under our fingertips will eventually desensitize our brains. Creative thought will die. Resistance will die. Uninspired survival will be the norm. The Morlocks will have triumphed over the Eloi. H.G. Wells knew more than Christ or the Buddha. And there is no one to listen. To whom am I to address my fears? Rush Limbaugh? Bill O'Reilly? Keith Olbermann? Are these not the opinion makers and fear massagers for the new E-epoch? But I am no longer a celebrity, if I ever truly was. Who is there to listen, Doctor? I've even lost my barber's ear. He thinks Sarah Palin is God's messenger. What are you going to do about it, Strider?"

"Me?"

"Yes! You are the doctor, the healer. All that stands between mortality and eternity. Are you not going to speak out, man?"

"Mr. Ortega and I have clashed several times on the phone already."

"Ortega?"

"Robert Ortega. He's the claims adjuster at Cambridge Medical. He thinks I'm hiding you amidst a crop of garden-variety Axis Ones when he's certain you're a stark raving Axis Two."

"But I am, aren't I?" There was a degree of perverse pride in Lafferty's retort.

Realizing that I had left the door open to the reception area, I closed it and turned my attention back to Lafferty, who now was struggling to maintain the archer pose.

"Shh! For all I know they're bugging my office."

Lafferty, unable to maintain the yogic posture, tumbled onto the carpet. I helped him back to his feet.

"They won't insure an Axis Two," I said, trying to explain the facts of life to him in a soft, urgent voice. "Not that there's anything wrong with you, Professor. Everything you've told me all these years is absolutely true."

97

"Oh, dear! Having a bad day, are we, Doctor? Care to tell me about it?"

I burst out laughing at this unexpected bit of transference. The professor beamed; I stared back at him with undisguised affection and asked: "Can't you pay for your sessions?"

"Of course not. I live in a rent-controlled apartment in the middle of fraternity row. My so-called salary barely keeps me in contraband Cuban cigars. Haven't seen a royalty check since Clinton was impeached."

"I don't know what to suggest, Professor."

"Hmmm. Mind if I smoke? I'll do it by the window."

"Have I ever said no to you?"

Lafferty withdrew one of his cherished Cuban cigars from a pocket humidor and pushed the window open. A patina of snow drifted in and covered the window ledge.

"Do you like books, Doctor? Rare books?"

"Why do you ask?"

"Because I possess several hundred beautifully bound volumes of considerable value. Could we not barter like the Swedes do? I'll remove your gallbladder if you will give me a new Volvo, something like that. I don't think anyone in Stockholm has picked up a check in a hundred years. What do you think?"

"I couldn't see you here."

"Why not?"

"There are two other doctors sharing this suite of offices. We all pay Evelyn's salary. I wouldn't vouch for any of them being bibliophiles. Mickey Mantle's jersey would be a different story altogether."

Evelyn knocked on the door and popped her head in two seconds later, apologizing for the intrusion.

"It's quite all right, Evelyn. What's wrong?"

98

"There's a young woman in reception, Doctor. She insists on seeing you. She doesn't have an appointment."

"No one has an appointment," said Lafferty. "It's that sort of day, Evelyn."

"I've never seen her before," said Evelyn. "But she refuses to leave without…"

I did a double take when I saw the "other" Barbara enter my office carrying a bouquet of assorted flowers. It had only been two hours since I had left her and the rest of her royal family on Madison Avenue. Now here she was sans makeup and jewelry, hair unpinned, and wearing the same blue coat and gray shawl from our initial encounter in Central Park. She lit up the room with her radiant smile, nodded respectfully to Lafferty, and said hello.

"It's okay, Mrs. White. You can leave us." Evelyn stared at me dubiously then left the office.

"Hellooo," said Lafferty, arching one black eyebrow while staring at me in an entirely new light. Pointing to the bouquet, he quoted:

*Here's flowers for you.*
*Hot lavender, mints, savory, marjoram.*
*The marigold, that goes to bed wi' the sun …*

"I didn't mean to interrupt you, Rebbe."
Lafferty held up a warning finger in order to finish:

*And with him rises weeping.*
*Pale primroses*
*That die unmarried ere they can behold*
*Bright Phoebus in his strength.*

"That's beautiful," she sighed. "Did you write it?"

"Would it were so!" Lafferty replied. Then turning to me, he asked: "Who is this delightful creature?"

99

"My name is Leah."

I was momentarily stunned. But then it all made sense. She didn't look like Barbara because she wasn't Barbara. She had created another identity for herself. This girl's name was Leah.

As if reading my thoughts, Lafferty began to recite:

*In my dream, I seemed to see a woman*
*Both young and fair; along a plain she gathered*
*Flowers, and even as she sang, she said:*
*Whoever asks my name, know that I'm Leah,*
*And I apply my lovely hands to fashion*
*A garland of the flowers I have gathered.*

As a postscript, Lafferty added: "Dante wrote that. And now here you are, as if summoned up by…"

Leah—for that was how she wished to be known—held a daffodil up to the professor.

"These were her favorites, weren't they?" asked Leah.

Lafferty was startled, not knowing what to make of the question.

"Don't be sad," said Leah. She took his hands and spoke in a low, intimate voice. "You two were *bashert*."

"*Bashert?*" Lafferty turned to me for an explanation, but I merely shrugged my shoulders. The professor turned back to Leah and stared deeply into her eyes. "The daffodils. How could you have…?" His voice trailed off, and like someone experiencing a tremendous electric shock, he broke loose from her grasp. His humor had become agitation and, to my amazement, he fled the office without saying good-bye to either of us.

"He carries a great sadness," Leah said wistfully. "But it is not necessary." She handed me the bouquet. "These are for you, Rebbe."

"What's the occasion?" I asked.

"You're going away. It makes me very sad. I was hoping you could help me find Shimon."

"Shimon?"

"I know that you know where he is."

"Oh, yes, of course, the Book of Splendor. There's so much more we need to speak—"

"Shh! It's all right, Rebbe. I can be patient till you return."

She handed me the bouquet and hurried out of the office. I thought for a moment about what had just occurred and then followed after her, but she had disappeared from the reception area. I dashed into the hallway; she was nowhere to be seen. Racing down the stairway, I collided with Sherman Rosenbaum, who was climbing up.

"Ah, Doctor! Just on my way up to see you. How's our girl doing?"

"How did she look to you?"

"When?"

"Just now. Didn't you pass her on the stairs?"

"I didn't pass anyone." The disbelief on my face didn't seem to register with the ever-ebullient Chevalier. "So, Doctor? How goes the treatment? Are we making progress? One realizes these things don't happen overnight, but we're up against a deadline. *Le monde se tourne, mon ami.* If the kids postpone the wedding now, they will have to wait months to book the Primrose Club again. And they'll forfeit the deposit."

"To be brutally honest, Sherman, for Gordon to marry Barbara at the present time would be inadvisable and foolhardy."

"Then when might one anticipate…?"

"Nowhere in the foreseeable future."

"Not wishing to offend you," said Rosenbaum, as he paused to pat down his pencil-thin white mustache with his index finger, "but one might prefer a second opinion."

"No offense taken. But, I'm warning you, Sherman, that the young woman is disturbed. Her grip on reality is extremely fragile."

* * *

I kissed the nape of Claire's neck as she stood over the stove that evening preparing a spicy chicken vindaloo. Turning around, she kissed me warmly and then held the wooden spoon up to my lips. Both the kiss and the vindaloo were equally hot and delicious. I suggested she forget about weaving and open the restaurant we had spoken of so often. She countered with the idea of our opening it together in Tahiti and never coming back. At that moment Barbara Warren and her troubled condition were the farthest things from my mind. I finally realized what a rare jewel I possessed in my wife, and that our forthcoming journey to paradise would be the solution to so many problems.

These loving reflections were interrupted by the sound of the doorbell ringing.

Opening the door, I was unprepared for the sight of an incensed Barbara Warren, who exploded through the doorway with all the fury of a New Jersey Gorgon, complete with poisonous snakes writhing in her hair.

"What did you tell Gordon's uncle?" she shrieked. "How fucking dare you interfere with my wedding plans!"

"How dare you barge into my home uninvited! How did you get past the doorman?"

Claire's voice called out from the kitchen: "Who is it, darling?"

"What kind of sadistic prick are you, Strider? Do you know how much work I put into this wedding? How could you, like, spoil everything?"

"Would you please leave my home?" I was bristling with anger and struggling to control my temper. This invasion of privacy had pushed all my submerged buttons. "Now!"

The front door was still ajar, and my elderly neighbors, Irene and Mel Kellerman, who lived across the hall (and whose collection of Balinese masks we had admired on more than one occasion), were in the midst of locking their door, en route to an eight o'clock movie. The Kellermans turned just in time to catch me twisting Barbara's left arm in an attempt to eject her from the apartment.

"Everything okay over there, Doctor?" shouted the slightly deaf, eighty-year-old Irene, who shifted her walker around to get a better view of me struggling with my demented home invader.

"Need any help?" growled eighty-five-year-old Mel, a gruff and burly ex-Marine sergeant, who waved his cane in the air, welcoming any opportunity to prove he was still no one to mess with.

"No problem, Mel. Everything's fine, thank you." I waved good-bye with my free hand to my inquisitive neighbors, who shuffled down the hall towards the elevator. Irene paused once more to gaze over her shoulder at the unusual bit of melodrama unfolding on our doorstep.

Barbara wrenched loose from my grip just as Claire emerged from the kitchen, wiping her hands on an Irish-linen dishtowel.

"What's happening, Harris?" She stared at Barbara in total dismay. "Who is this woman?"

"Like, you don't want to see me happy at all, do you?" asked a tearful Barbara, who had begun pounding on my chest with her fists. "You controlling prick!"

"What I want is for you to leave here now." Grabbing hold of Barbara's wrists, I shoved her away from me, adding the hostile, sarcastic postscript. "Am I, like, making myself clear?"

"What's the matter, Strider? Afraid the neighbors will find out what a meddling quack you really are?"

Claire drew a deep breath, stepped in front of me, and with all the Iowa politeness she could muster, said to our intruder: "Please, leave before we call the police."

"She your wife?" asked Barbara, examining Claire from head to toe. "What's her fucking problem?"

Heedless of snakes or Gorgons, Claire grabbed Barbara by her hair, shoved the shrieking girl out into the hall, and slammed the door in her face. Seconds later, Barbara began pounding on the door, screaming vile obscenities.

"I'm calling the police," said Claire.

"No, no! Don't. She'll go away…eventually."

"When? This sort of incident doesn't sit well with the co-op board, Harris. We had difficulty enough getting into this building. To hell with the circumstances, call the police."

"Shh! Shh! Wait a second. I think she's gone." My body was trembling with rage as I eased the door open a crack to check. No Barbara. I sighed with relief. "And that is it for me. That is the end of it. Once and for all."

"Was that…she? The anecdote?"

"Yes. And I can't tell you how sorry I am to have put you through this, Claire."

"Didn't I warn you?"

"Yes, you did, darling."

"I'm not the I-told-you-so type but…"

"Thank God for that!"

Claire smiled, wrapped her arms around my neck, and stared adoringly into my eyes: "This horrible incident has been a true test of our marriage. And I think we've come through it wonderfully, don't you? I feel closer to you than ever." She began nibbling on my bottom lip. "I'm starving. Let's eat…and other things. Hmm?"

We were hot and heavily into those "other things" an hour later when the telephone on the nightstand rang.

"Don't answer it!" gasped Claire, her long naked torso tangled up between the duvet and the sheets. "So close…so close…"

"Me, too," I gasped. "Answering machine on?"

"Yes."

"Good."

My voice on the outgoing message—crisp, authoritative, and professional—bounced off the walls in my study. Then a beep was heard, and a familiar female voice began to leave a message.

I froze in the midst of our lovemaking. Unable to hear the message clearly from the bedroom, I slid out from under the duvet and grabbed my bathrobe.

"Harris! How can you leave me now? Where are you going?"

By that time, I had entered my study, rewound the message, and was listening carefully to the sweet melodic woman's voice I had so yearned to hear all day.

"Hello, Rebbe. This is Leah. I'm sorry Barbara behaved so dreadfully tonight. Please don't pay any attention to her. She's just used to having her own way all the time. But you mustn't hate her for it. Have a wonderful vacation."

Claire was standing behind me by that time, with the duvet wrapped around her. "What's wrong, Harris? Who was that on the machine?"

I kneaded my forehead with my fingers and made the fateful announcement: "Sorry, honey, but I really can't go to Tahiti with you."

"What?"

"I can't possibly leave my patient now."

"What patient? Not the little bitch I threw out of here! Is that who phoned?"

"She's not what she appears to be. That's the tragedy, Claire, and the fantastic challenge for me. She's in some sort of fugue state. But if I were to go away now for two weeks, she could potentially…"

Claire shook her head in disbelief and said: "I always thought it was a corny joke: All shrinks are nuts. But guess what, Harris? You are really crazy. Completely around the bend."

"Claire, please! Try to understand."

I reached out my arms to embrace her, but she shoved me away violently, stormed into the bedroom, and slammed the door shut.

# THE *SHTETL*

R IGHT UP to the last minute, Claire never gave up hope that I would change my mind and fly with her to Tahiti. But I had always been stubborn and obsessive about my work (two traits she had accepted and even claimed to admire when we first married). She spent the last few nights before her departure sitting cross-legged on our bed, painting her toenails, and weeping softly while I sat hunched over the desk in my study poring over voluminous psychiatric tomes and medical journals.

Finally the departure date arrived, and Nella appeared at the front door in full tropical gear. The second ticket would not be going to waste after all.

It was only after they had left for the airport that I realized what a daunting task I faced: how to lure Barbara back to my office again.

Of course, I could have groveled at the little narcissist's feet and begged her forgiveness. Barbara would have loved that, but ultimately she would have banished me back to the same hole of insignificance out of which I had crawled. Who was there to represent my interests? Gordon? Mulling it over for a moment, I decided I did not have the patience to deal with yet another young narcissist. No. My only hope lay with the esteemed Chevalier du Tastevin.

I placed several phone calls to the Rosenbaum residence on Long Island. Each time I was greeted by voicemail; each time I hung up, not wishing to leave a message. Finally a seemingly inebriated Irish cleaning lady answered and informed me that Mr. Rosenbaum had gone into the city "to have that Chinaman poke needles in him again." Did she, by any chance, know the name of the acupuncturist or where his office might be? No, but Mrs. Rosenbaum probably would. And where might one find her? "At her office, natch."

Hildy Rosenbaum ran a small art gallery on the main street of Bellport, where she represented local artists who all painted identical scenes of Long Island Sound. Clearly Hildy could only take so much of her husband's expansive rhetoric before feeling the need to escape into canvases that displayed their earnest creators' less grandiose visions.

Pretending to be her husband's luncheon companion, who was hopelessly lost in the complex maze of Chinatown, I phoned Mrs. Rosenbaum and asked if she had Doctor What's-his-name's address. You know, the acupuncturist. I must have copied it down incorrectly the first time. Mrs. Rosenbaum promptly gave me the address of Dr. Ellery Fong on Pell Street.

I took the elevator down from my office and walked across the lobby of the building. Pausing to button up my Hugo Boss cashmere overcoat, I was startled to see Edwin Sheffield enter the building from Fifth Avenue. With him was a trembling miniature Whippet, tugging on the end of a leash. The dog was as nattily clad as its owner.

"Hello, Edwin."

"Harris." The composer nodded curtly.

"Your dog?"

"Bizet. I found him wandering outside the Paris Opera House, obviously abandoned. The poor little creature stared at me with those soulful eyes. My heart melted. So I brought him back to America."

"Admirable gesture." Bizet whimpered pitifully. Edwin lifted the miniature Whippet up into his arms, and Bizet licked the composer's face repeatedly. "He's very fond of you."

"Seems to be. I never had a dog before."

"Wonderful companions. Claire will be so pleased for you. She's in Tahiti at the moment."

"Yes, I know. That's not the reason I'm here…Bizet has a problem."

"I don't think there are any veterinarians in this building. Might be one over on Lexington near—"

"We came to see you."

"We?"

"Bizet loves me, unconditionally. This is a completely new experience for me, Harris. Even my mother had issues, and Tilly has as well. But this little fellow…" A solitary tear ran down Edwin's cheek. Had Claire taught him that trick? "It's what makes the problem so painful."

"Edwin, I'm really late for an appoint—"

"He goes to bed every night in love with me. Sleeps on the pillow above my head. But in the morning when I wake, he doesn't seem to know me. He cowers in fright when I go near him and wets the pillow. It takes me hours to win back his confidence again, to reassure him that I love him. By two o'clock, he's fine: leaping into my lap and running up and down the keyboard. I think he's actually composing little doggie sonatas. By the time we go to bed, we're a regular Darby and Joan, happy as clams and similar clichés." Edwin burst into tears. "What do you think is wrong with him, Harris? Brain damage? Are you aware of such a syndrome?"

"I don't treat canines. Have you seen a vet, Edwin?"

"Clearly it's a neurological disorder, Harris. Claire has told me repeatedly how brilliant you are. I can't endure this much longer. All those pillows! I love the little guy, but I can't get any work done. There must be something you can do."

From everything Claire had told me about Edwin, I knew he was a master procrastinator. Bizet, the little Parisian foundling, was his ultimate enabler. What better excuse for not meeting his deadlines than a brain-damaged Whippet, who required round-the-clock attention?

"Maybe you should find him another home," was my brutally honest recommendation.

"Never!" Edwin clutched Bizet to his chest and beat a hasty retreat from my building.

\* \* \*

Thirty minutes later, I trudged up the stairs from the Canal Street subway station and wandered along the crowded sidewalk, past street vendors and open-air fish markets in what had once been Little Italy. I finally located the office of Dr. Ellery Fong on Pell Street and ascended a steep staircase to the third floor.

It didn't take long for me to realize that, as the only non-Chinese in the cramped reception area, I was the oddity. The patients in the room looked at me and whispered to each other, while not paying the slightest attention to the elderly woman holding a live chicken in her lap or the plump teenager with braces, pigtails, and an iPod plugged into her ears, piercingly singing along to one of Lady Gaga's latest hits. Squeezed into the narrow space between these two on the dilapidated office couch, I found myself staring at a poster of a naked man, whose meridians were studded with multicolored plastic tacks. It was at that moment that the chicken leaned over and pecked my recently damaged finger, reopening the wound, which I thought had healed.

Blood dripped onto the floor as I yelped. More from shock than pain, I leapt from the couch and bumped into Sherman Rosenbaum, whom the tall elegant Ellery Fong was escorting past his other patients to the door.

"Sherman!" Hastily I drew a clean handkerchief from my pants pocket and, yet again, fastened a tourniquet around my bleeding finger.

Rosenbaum, carrying a mysterious black attaché case, was startled by my presence in the waiting room.

"Dr. Strider! What are you doing here?" Seeing my wounded finger, he asked: "Are you bleeding?"

"Just a chicken bite."

"Might want to have Dr. Fong examine that. I had no idea you were a patient of his "

"Actually, I'm not."

"Well, you should be. The man's a veritable sorcerer. Forget Viagra." Rosenbaum dropped his voice to a whisper worthy of a CIA agent deep in the Eastern Sector. "A couple of his hot needles—left side, right side—and one could erect a circus tent."

"You are far too kind, Sherman," replied Dr. Fong in a posh British accent. The elegant Chinese physician turned his attention to me, stared deeply into my eyes, and nodded his head. "Sherman is always in excellent spirits when he leaves my office. Are you experiencing erectile dysfunction as well? What is your specialty, Doctor?"

"I'm a psychiatrist."

"Ah! No wonder," sighed Fong. "Strip-mining the human psyche always causes chronic impotence. When would you like to start your treatment?"

"I'm fine!"

"Not what your eyes tell me. Take this young man to lunch, Sherman. Shanghai cuisine."

Threading his left arm fraternally through mine *comme les français*, while clutching the attaché case possessively with his right, the Chevalier du Tastevin led me down the creaking staircase in silence. When we reached the door leading to the street, he confided: "You're wasting your time, Doctor."

"Please, Sherman! Help me. She refuses to return my calls."

"After the way you treated her, who can blame the poor kid? Frankly, I was shocked and disappointed, a man with your reputation carrying on like a Brownsville bum."

"Your niece invaded my home, Sherman. She insulted my wife."

"Who attempted to scalp her." The Chevalier made this pronouncement with all the grandiosity of a man who felt he owned the moral high ground.

"What? How dare she…" I forced myself to keep from spluttering. "That is a lie. She refused to leave after a polite request, and my wife was forced to—"

"Do you like crabs in black bean sauce?" Rosenbaum was a subject-shifter emeritus, and the question from deep left field was clearly the prelude to a peace conference.

"Can we get a decent bottle of white wine to go with them? Or is that asking the impossible in Chinatown?"

"Think I've got the president's secret nuclear codes in there?" Rosenbaum nodded at the black attaché case resting on the floor next to his feet and took me into his confidence. "Two bottles of Châteauneuf-du-Pape. The management decants them into a teapot for me and I pretend they are fragrant oolong."

The wispy-haired Chinese restaurateur with ginger-stained teeth greeted Rosenbaum like a long-lost relative and relieved him of the attaché case, without the slightest nod passing between them.

An hour later, several platters of crab, shrimp, lobster, and scallops in assorted sauces had been devoured, and a second pot of "tea" was brought to our table.

"Tell me the truth, Doctor," said Rosenbaum, daubing his white mustache with the linen napkin. "After your various encounters with Gordon's affianced bride, do you think she might be nuts?"

"Let's just say the poor girl's...not responsible for what she does. Excellent wine, by the way."

"When's your anniversary? I'll send you a case." The sated Chevalier exhaled a sigh for the ages. "It's gonna break my kid sister's heart, you know. She's been a widow for ten years. Gordon's her golden boy, her prince. If they have to cancel the wedding..."

"Don't be such an alarmist, Sherman. There was an 'if' in front of that 'cancel.' This story can still have a happy ending...if I could only see Barbara again."

"That's impossible, Harris."

"Nothing is impossible for a Chevalier du Tastevin."

"You're appealing to my vanity," giggled Rosenbaum, who, having made such a childish noise, produced a few guttural sounds in his throat to suggest that the strange noise had merely been a misguided cough.

"It's your confidence that I need, Sherman. Do I have that?"

"My word as a Chevalier du Tastevin." To emphasize the oath, Rosenbaum drew his shoulders back four inches and rotated his neck several times.

"*Bien compris, mon vieux.* There's a radical therapy I've stumbled upon recently that just might solve her problem."

"But the girl despises you, Harris, like dirt. She never wants to set eyes on you again."

I reached my arm forward, squeezed the Chevalier's hand, stared earnestly into his eyes, and with a degree of pomposity I hoped he'd appreciate, pronounced: "The illness always hates the cure."

Rosenbaum returned my gaze with equal intensity before making his front-page-news pronouncement: "Jack Dorfman was right. You are brilliant. Let me see what I can do."

When the bill arrived, I reached for my wallet only to have my hand smacked by the Chevalier. He promptly withdrew a roll of bills that could have choked a Triple Crown winner and proceeded to peel off three fifties. We said good-bye in front of the restaurant, and I watched him disappear into the throng on Canal Street.

Slightly tipsy, I wandered past vendors hustling their wares and felt extremely guilty. I had lied to Sherman Rosenbaum. I never wanted to see Barbara again. But I was aching inside to be reunited with Leah.

\* \* \*

Late the next afternoon, Barbara swept into my office with all the hauteur of Catherine the Great expecting her courtiers to kneel and kiss her regal foot.

"Thank you for coming, Barbara."

"It wasn't my idea, Doctor. Believe me." She examined her makeup in the mirror over the onyx mantle, then plopped down in the leather chair and crossed her legs. "But Uncle Sherman is a very persuasive man. So, like, what were you so anxious to say to me?"

"I beg your pardon?"

"Don't you have something to say to me? Like, maybe an apology?"

Her behavior was intolerable, and I was determined to put a stop to it immediately. Shock and awe, that's what was needed with this spoiled daughter of the mall. She was examining the polish on her nails when I demanded to know: "Where's Leah?"

"What?"

"You heard me. I want to talk to Leah. Tell her to come out."

"I…I don't know what you're talking about." Barbara rose unsteadily from the chair, her eyes glued to the door, as if she feared it would be gone if she glanced away for even a second. "I'm not going to—"

"Sit down!"

Barbara fell back in her seat. I dropped to one knee beside her and grabbed both arms of her chair so our eyes were level.

"I think you do know. But you're afraid to acknowledge the truth. You're not alone in there. You have a secret companion, don't you? It's okay, Barbara. Leah and I know each other."

"I wanna go home." There was a very scared little girl in that voice. "You can't keep me here."

"Where is Leah?"

"What you're doing to me is, like, illegal. Bet you could, like, lose your license for malpractice. Why are you keeping me here? So many things have to be done today, you know. Like napkins! I still haven't decided which—"

"No, Barbara! No! Stop it! This is the one time you don't get your way. I want to see Leah and I want to talk to her…now!"

Barbara's eyes narrowed to slits and then turned icy cold. Pouting like a spoiled child, she dropped her chin onto her chest, muttering angrily under her breath. My first fear was she might stay this way indefinitely. Then slowly, slowly, she raised her head, and that irresistible twinkle returned to her eyes once again, followed by that dazzling smile.

I struggled to keep some semblance of professional detachment, but my face must have registered amazement and delight at the magical reappearance of this enchanting being who called herself Leah. Laughing, she unpinned her hair and shook it out till the tresses fell to their unfettered length.

"How is it you didn't go away?" Barbara's harsh New Jersey rasp had been replaced by Leah's sweet melodic voice. She threw her arms around my neck and hugged me.

"I just…didn't. I tried but I wanted to stay here with you, Leah."

She broke the embrace and hastily removed her earrings and the jewelry from her fingers and wrists. "I'm glad, Rebbe."

"Why do you call me that?"

"Why won't you tell me where Shimon is?"

"How would I know that?"

"Please, Rebbe, you can trust me, even if I'm only an unworthy woman. Shimon always told me that you were his friend."

"Leah, I'm very confused. I need to know more about you. Who you are and where you come from."

"You know where I come from," she giggled. "Why do you tease me, Rebbe?"

"I don't mean to. Let's pretend this is a game. And I know nothing about you. Okay? Can we please play this game together, Leah?" She nodded enthusiastically. "So, tell me: Where is your home? Where do you live?"

"In Irmunsk. A *shtetl* in the Pale of Settlement." She gig-gled once more, as if this were a game for only the youngest of children.

"The Pale of...? Where is that, Leah?"

She walked over to the leaded-glass window and stared wistfully outside at the snow whirling round and round.

"A long, long way from here," she replied.

For the next hour, I sat enraptured, listening to her tales of another place and time. The details were so vivid I could actually smell the food cooking in the tiny kitchens and feel the fabric of the clothes she described. Curiously, I began to feel as if I had lived in that world as well.

Leah's description of Irmunsk conjured up images of bearded men with forelocks and prayer-shawl fringes pro-truding from their outer garments. They moved guardedly along the unpaved streets as they headed toward their daily prayer services or to such jobs as they were allowed to hold. Women wearing babushkas struggled valiantly to raise chil-dren and run their households with the little money that their husbands managed to eke out.

Against this backdrop, seventeen-year-old Leah first met Shimon, a handsome itinerant stranger, while she was picking berries in the woods on the outskirts of Irmunsk with her little sister, Molly. There was something in the way Shimon looked at her with his kind coal-black eyes that awakened a dormant spirit in Leah. It was the same spirit that had spoken to her when she was younger and asked questions she feared were sacrilegious. What was life? Could there be more to ex-istence than Irmunsk? Was there a world out there other than this one? And why was she not allowed to read, while the less clever boys were? She instinctively felt that Shimon would know the answers to her questions. And, if not, surely he would have asked them as well.

Leah told me how she began to secretly rendezvous with Shimon every day at the same spot where they first had met. These amorous assignations always followed the same ritual. She would race into his arms and he, in turn, would sweep her off her feet and swing her round and round until they both grew quite dizzy. At that moment, they would kiss passionately until she fell into a swoon. On one occasion, Leah playfully confronted Shimon.

"Hiding from me again?" said Leah, as she tousled his mop of black hair. "I saw you peeking out from behind that tree."

"Merely protecting myself. Your beauty is too potent. I'm afraid I will go blind."

She grabbed his face, kissed him over and over, and then forced herself away. Teasing him, she asked: "Can a person die from too much kissing?"

"Oh, I hope not."

"Shimon, I love you! My brain is empty except for thoughts of you. I'm unable to do my household chores anymore. And when I try, I break the dishes."

"What does your mother say?"

"She thinks I'm clumsy."

"Maybe you are," replied Shimon, "and I'm just an excuse."

Leah smacked his arm playfully, then asked: "What are you going to do?"

"Breathe."

"You know what I mean, about my father. You're a…a *luftmensch*, Shimon. You live on air. My father will never permit me to marry you."

"Must we be married?"

Leah gasped and covered her face with her hands. "You're too crazy. This is a real problem, Shimon."

"Come with me tonight."

"Where?"

"To the Magiker."

"I can't. I mustn't...I'm frightened."

# THE SECOND OPINION

I LAY UNCONSCIOUS on the couch in my office. How long had I slept? Was it sleep or a coma? Bathed in perspiration, I awoke to find Leah gone and me fighting for breath. My hands were trembling. The clock on the onyx mantle said 7:30 p.m. What was the violent reaction I was experiencing? What phenomenon had I just witnessed? Multiple personality? Reincarnation? Whatever it was, I had bought every word of it. Barbara had entered my office and Leah had left. When had I collapsed on the couch? Where had she gone? How long would she remain in her Leah state? Had she gone to meet Gordon? And which "she" would he be meeting? Should I have followed her? How could I? What would I have used for legs? The experience left me immobile, incapable of going anywhere. My heart pounded in my chest from sheer excitement. Or was it dread?

I struggled to stand up but was overcome by intense dizziness. I thought I would pass out. Had I been in the tropics, the diagnosis would have been malaria. The present backdrop, though, was not darkest Africa but New York City, deep in a frozen winter.

I managed to push myself off the couch and crawl on all fours to my desk. I pulled myself up onto my chair, grabbed a pen and a stenographer's pad, and furiously scribbled notes of what I could remember from Leah's visit: little Molly, Irmunsk, the Pale of Settlement, the Magiker, Shimon … Shimon. I felt an acute twinge of jealousy as I wrote down my rival's name. How crazy was that—jealous of a fantasy figure? Was I Axis One or Axis Two, Ortega? These were heart-stopping fantasies and traumas, indeed. My forehead felt damp, my pulse continued to race, and my shirt felt clammy. Was I getting the flu? Breathe, Harris. Breathe deeply.

The telephone rang. I didn't want to answer it. Wouldn't Evelyn pick up? No, it was after six. She had left long ago. Why did the phone keep ringing? What was so goddamn important? Everything, if the caller was a patient. You're a healer, Dr. Strider. Remember? You took an oath. Answer the phone!

"Harris? Honey, is that you?"

"Hello, Mom." There was no mistaking my dear mother's Brooklyn accent and, in my mind's eye, I could picture the silver-haired pixie pacing her kitchen in Evanston and nervously winding the phone cord around her fingers. "You sound short of breath."

"Ran up from downstairs when I heard the phone ring." Why was I lying to my own mother? "Took the stairs two at a time."

"Are you doing the breathing exercises I recommended?" My mother had taken early retirement after three decades of teaching English at Northwestern and was enjoying a second career as a yoga instructor. "Your father and I have been a little worried, honey. You haven't phoned us in a while."

"Didn't I phone last Sunday?"

"Not for two weeks."

"That can't be right, Mom. Is Dad okay?"

"Yeah, yeah. The test results came back benign. Knock wood, he'll live forever. We both will. So how are you, honey? Everything okay?"

"Absolutely, Mom. I've just been really, really busy." Go ahead. Tell your sixty-six-year-old mother you just crawled across the office carpet on all fours because you couldn't stand up. See how that makes her feel.

"We called your apartment a few times, honey, but there was never any answer. Is something wrong with your machine?"

"It hasn't been working right, Mom. I spilled coffee on it by accident." Why was I still lying?

"Why don't you get voicemail?"

"If people want me badly enough, Mom, they can always call the office."

"Oh...How's Claire?"

"Fine. Great. She went to Tahiti."

"Alone?"

"No, with a girlfriend, one of her weavers from the guild."

"Why didn't you go?"

"I couldn't. Something came up at the last minute...work. I didn't want to lose my train of thought. I think I'm onto something special, really important."

"Is it a book?" That was the Holy Grail. My parents had always hoped that I might publish a text that would put my name on the psychiatric map. "You know, your father and I have always hoped..."

"What? A book instead of a grandchild?"

"Don't be cruel, Harris."

"Just a joke, Mom."

"Not very funny."

"Sorry. So Dad's okay?"

"Didn't I say it was benign? He can't wait for spring break. Lots of papers to grade."

"Why don't you guys go away somewhere for a change? Somewhere warm."

"Like Tahiti?"

"Not very funny, Mom."

"So? What is it, if it's not a book?"

"A patient. I...I don't know how to explain it to you."

"A woman?"

"A girl...yes...a young woman."

"What? Are you involved with her?"

"Mother, I'm a professional. Insomuch as I'm a healer, yes, I'm involved. Who knows? Maybe there is a book to be written. Certainly it's compelling enough."

"Tell me about it."

"Well, she has lived a previous life."

"Don't tell me. She was a queen in ancient Egypt, right? Shirley MacLaine has a lot to answer for. How come all these past-lifers were nobles? Didn't anyone ever clean the palaces?"

"This girl wasn't royalty at all, far from it. She claims to have lived in a place called the Pale of Settlement, where she fell under the spell of some religious mystics...Mom? Mom, are you still there?"

"Harris?"

"Yes, Mom."

"Harris."

"I'm still here, Mom. Something wrong with your reception?"

"Promise me something and don't question me about it. Can you do that?"

"What's wrong, Mom?"

"Will you promise me?" My mother's tone was deadly serious.

"Did I miss something?"

"Don't see this girl anymore."

"Mom, she's a patient."

"You promised me."

"No. That's not what happened. You asked me to promise but I didn't agree."

"Trust me, Harris. This comes from my heart. Don't ask me to explain. What you're involved in is extremely dangerous."

"Mom, I'm a doctor, and she's my patient. Do you really think I'd jeopardize my career for some kind of dalliance?"

"It's not sex I'm talking about."

"Then what are you...?"

"Trust me. This is so beyond...Just do what I ask. Oh! Your father just pulled into the driveway. Call us on the weekend."

"Will do. Sorry I haven't been—"

"Promise?"

"I promise I'll call, Mom. Okay? Give my love to Dad."

Bewildered and confused, I replaced the receiver on its cradle. What had that conversation been about? My mother had always been a nervous creature, even frightened at times—irrationally so. And I never knew why. It made no sense. Often as a child, I would be awakened by her nightmares and run to her bedroom to see what was wrong. What could I do to help keep the demons at bay? And always there would be my father's soothing voice urging me not to worry. "It's okay, Harry," he'd say. "Go back to sleep."

When I was five or six, people often mistook my adorable, vivacious mother for my older sister. She looked as if she were little more than a teenager. And she was so much fun to be with. We'd play together like children. (Years later I surmised that, unlike most mothers, she was not recreating but rather enjoying a childhood she'd never had.) Then suddenly, without warning, black clouds would appear and hold her hostage. Sometimes they would be triggered by the passing glance of a stranger on the street or an innocent wrong number. She would be overcome with terror, like a slave shackled to an unseen force she dared not disobey. Her chronic trauma eventually spurred me to become a psychiatrist and help others cope with and conquer their irrational fears.

But I wasn't deluding myself. There was a fine line—no, more like a tightrope—I was walking, between infatuation and genuine concern for Leah-Barbara's well-being. One misstep could prove catastrophic, professionally and emotionally. But as long as I kept my balance and didn't look down, I would make it to the far side intact…and to tumultuous applause.

So what the hell was my mother worried about? What detail of my story had she transferred onto her own paranoid fears? I wasn't so far gone as to risk losing my license, even though Corwin was convinced that I was in imminent danger of…of course! Why hadn't I thought of it before? With his encyclopedic knowledge of all things Yiddish, the Pasha would know if there was anything to Leah's fanciful tale of life in Irmunsk. Breathing deeply, I took my pulse. It was almost normal.

\* \* \*

The doorman at Corwin's landmark apartment building on West End Avenue and Ninetieth had known me for years. Despite my disheveled state—my shirt was sweat-stained and my hair unruly—he waved me in without phoning upstairs.

As I neared the Pasha's apartment, I heard the sound of Miles Davis's trumpet spilling out into the hallway. But I was oblivious to the cool vibe as I banged on his front door. Nor was I aware of the passionate female cries over the sound of "My Favorite Things" as I continued pounding with both fists, demanding that Corwin let me in.

Finally, the Pasha opened the door a crack. He had on an undershirt and was hastily zipping up his trousers.

"Not the best time, Harry. Little busy right now."

"Please, Marty! It's important!" To Corwin's amazement, I pushed the door open and barreled inside. "Don't send me away."

I moved deeper into the apartment, clutching my spiral stenographer's notebook to my chest, totally self-absorbed. It hadn't dawned on me that I might be intruding until the Pasha gestured in the direction of a buxom, freckle-faced redhead in her early thirties. She was struggling to put herself back together after a flagrant incident of coitus interruptus on the living-room sofa.

"Maureen Flanagan, this is my colleague and former friend Harris Strider, who appears to have just escaped from a burning stable. What's up, Doc?"

"What's a *shadchen*?" I asked, reading from my notepad. "Is it the same thing as a *shochet*?"

Corwin growled, lit a cigar, and glared at me with undisguised hostility. "What is all this, Harris? Never heard of a dictionary? They sell 'em at the Barnes & Noble on Broadway."

"It's about Leah. Barbara. My patient."

"Oh, boy!" Corwin turned to Maureen and asked: "Do you know how to make coffee?"

"Irish? Spanish?"

"Yiddish. Big cups."

Maureen arched an eyebrow and said: "You missed your chance when you answered the door, Doctor."

Once she'd vanished into the kitchen, Corwin turned on me and snarled: "I could break your fucking neck! That nurse has been shooting decidedly X-rated glances in my direction for the past two months. I risked a potential sexual-harassment suit by inviting her here for a harmless evening of Jeopardy and pizza. Harmless! Alex Trebek hadn't gotten the first question out of his throat before she had her tongue down mine. See the jugs on that girl?"

The Pasha took a deep breath, shook his head, put his hands on his hips, and finally answered my question: "One's a matchmaker, the other's a butcher."

"Ha! I knew you'd have the answer." Flipping excitedly to the next page on my steno pad, I asked. "How about the Pale of Settlement? Is there such a place?"

"Was. It was created by Catherine the Great in the late eighteenth century. Her predecessor, Empress Elizabeth, had tried unsuccessfully to throw all the Jews out of the country unless they converted to Russian Orthodoxy."

"I knew you'd know this. But why did she do that?"

"Did I never tell you about the study commissioned back in the '60s to prove once and for all that Jews weren't smarter than other people? It was hoped the study would finally curb anti-Semitism in America. The problem was that, after every conceivable test, it couldn't be disproved. Needless to say, the study was never published."

"What does that have to do with Empress Elizabeth?"

"The Jews were better businessmen than the Russians. They were making all the money, so she wanted to get rid of them. By the time Catherine assumed the throne, the Jewish population had swelled due to the annexation of the Lithuanian-Polish territories. Suddenly the Russian Empire had five million Jews inside its borders. So the Pale of Settlement was created, and that was the territory in which the Jews were forced to live and from which they were forbidden to move. Basically it made up what are now Lithuania, Poland, Moldova, the Ukraine, and a chunk of western Russia. It ceased to exist after the Bolsheviks took power in 1917."

"What was life like inside the Pale?"

"Awful, a lot worse than *Fiddler on the Roof* made it out to be. The Jews were restricted as to what they could do for a living. Only ten percent of the children were allowed an education. This gave rise to homeschooling and the birth of yeshivas. What else is on your list?"

"Um...*Beis hamidrash*. What is that?"

"House of learning, another word for synagogue. Are you planning another round of Jewish Jeopardy? Because I'm expecting a double-cheese and pepperoni with anchovies any minute, and you're not invited to stay."

"I never encountered anything like this, Marty." I paced the living room, oblivious to the fact that the Pasha was trying to throw me out. "She described to me—in detail—a town at the turn of the century."

"Big deal. This is the turn of the century."

"No! We're talking the previous century: the tastes, textures, smells, sounds, and colors. It was so vivid, Pasha, as if she'd really lived there. Unbelievable!"

"Oh, I believe it. I had a patient once—twenty years ago—told me about his life as a pirate chief in the Caribbean. The man mesmerized me with his detailed descriptions. Smell of blood and gunpowder lingered in my nostrils for weeks. He had me convinced, till I turned on TCM one night and saw the same goddamned story, with Tyrone Power, Maureen O'Hara, and George Sanders."

Marching over to the floor-to-ceiling bookcase on the far wall, I began a frantic search through the oversized volumes. "Got an atlas?"

"Even a Haitian cabbie can find Bellevue."

"Aha!" Whipping a Rand McNally off the bottom shelf, I carried it over to the coffee table and began poring through it. "Trying to find a little town called Irmunsk."

"A *shtetl*?"

"Yes, yes. A *shtetl*. That's precisely what she called it."

"You won't find it. Irmunsk probably ceased to exist by 1920, definitely by 1945."

"Why? What happened?"

"Emigration, Stalinist pogroms, and the end of the Second World War. Poland gobbled up most of what was left."

"What am I going to do, Marty? How am I going to find the answers?"

"Answers? Shmuck! What the hell are the questions?"

\* \* \*

Twenty minutes later I stood alone on West End Avenue, bitterly frustrated. I had failed to win the Pasha over to my cause. There was no way to prove Irmunsk had ever existed. The whole thing could have been a whimsical product of Barbara's imagination. But that seemed impossible. No, the future Mrs. Gordon Jacobs didn't have a whimsical chromosome in, like, her whole DNA. But, if it were true, how could I explain the existence of Leah? And why would Barbara intentionally make her up?

At that moment I heard beautiful choral singing coming from all directions, and before I knew it, I was surround by hundreds of men of all ages wearing yarmulkes. Their Sabbath-eve service over, they were spilling out onto the street from the dozens of synagogues that dotted the Upper West Side.

Standing beneath a streetlamp, I observed the faithful on their way home, with an intensity I had never known. Here were Leah's people, possibly the grandchildren or great-grandchildren of those who had lived in Irmunsk. How or where could I find a survivor of that long-forgotten town? Who among them might know if such a place ever existed?

That was when I noticed two elderly Jewish men with huge beards staring at me. They were a veritable Mutt and Jeff, who managed to study me with fascination while at the same time carrying on a heated argument. I watched as spittle flew out of their mouths and onto each other's beards. Finally the taller Jeff nudged the smaller Mutt in the ribs, and the two approached me. They stopped in front of me and eyed me up and down, as if I had just landed my spacecraft on West End Avenue.

"*Kenst yiddish reden?*" asked Mutt, emphasizing each word by poking me in the chest with his thumb.

"I beg your pardon?"

Jeff pushed his short colleague to one side and with the politeness of a seasoned diplomat, asked in heavily accented English: "Who are your people?"

"*Bist a yid?*" asked Mutt, squeezing between us, his thumb on the attack once again.

"Sorry," I replied with an embarrassed and inadequate shrug. "I…I don't understand you."

"My friend vants to know if you're Jewish," said Jeff.

"My mother is. Was."

Jeff translated for Mutt, who nodded triumphantly, rubbed his hands together, and added: "Aha!"

"Then so are you," replied Jeff with great import, like a mathematician who had solved an unsolvable problem. "*Guten shabbos, Rebbe.*"

Rebbe? That's how Barbara—Leah—always refers to me.

"Why do you call me that?"

"Ask your mother."

My mother? What did she have to do with this? I wandered away from the two old men; their gaze continued to burn into my back as I searched for a cab to take me home.

Try finding a taxi on the Upper West Side on a Friday night when it's freezing. I was almost at the edge of the park when I finally spotted one with its light still on. My body craved sleep, but my mind was filled with more questions about Irmunsk.

Back in my apartment, I powered up my Mac and Googled the name Irmunsk. The search engine instantly asked if I had meant "Murmansk, a city and seaport in the extreme northwest of Russia."

No, I hadn't. But nothing else came up. Maybe the Pasha had been right. Maybe the town had ceased to exist following the Stalinist purges. Or maybe it only existed in the troubled mind of Barbara Warren.

I spent an agonizing weekend alone, obsessing over Leah. Strange dreams of Irmunsk, Shimon, and the Magiker kept me tossing and turning in my sleep. I had been seriously tempted to phone Barbara in the hope that Leah might answer. But why would Leah answer a phone? Did she even know one existed? And what if Gordon answered, or Barbara herself? Leah, Leah, Leah.

# THE REVELATION

EVELYN WHITE ENTERED my office first thing Monday morning, cleared her throat, and told me that the girl who had brought me the flowers the previous week was waiting in reception. Show her in, I replied with undisguised joy. Evelyn gave me a curious look and reminded me that I had a nine o'clock session with Barbara Warren.

So even Evelyn thought that Barbara and Leah were different women. I secretly delighted in that, but knew that some explanation was in order. I lied and said that Barbara had phoned late Friday afternoon and canceled.

"Oh? Oh…And when is your wife coming back?"

"Sorry?"

"Didn't Mrs. Strider go to Tahiti on vacation?"

"Yes, last week. She'll be back this Sunday." At what James M. Cain-inspired conclusion was Evelyn arriving?

"Good."

"What's wrong, Evelyn? Do you think I've done her in?"

"Beg your pardon, Doctor?"

"Let me assure you, Mrs. White. My wife is in Tahiti. She is with her friend Nella. And no, I didn't chop her up and pack her in a steamer trunk."

"No one said that. Are you feeling all right, Doctor?"

"Outstanding. Have the young woman come in."

Leah entered the office, rushed across the room like the heroine in a Verdi opera, and hugged me warmly. I wanted to hold her forever, but she broke the embrace and sat down in the leather chair.

"How was your weekend?"

"Not very pleasant," replied Leah wearily. "She was very busy with her wedding. What a vain creature she is."

"Has she decided on the napkins yet?"

"I pay very little attention to her." Leah's sparkling eyes darted around the room searching for something. "What happened to my flowers?"

"Oh." I hadn't noticed until then that they were gone. "The cleaning lady must have thrown them out before the weekend. They don't last long in winter, you know."

Leah nodded sadly: "I don't know how much time I have left."

"All the time you want. My next appointment isn't till eleven."

"No," smiled Leah. "That's not what I meant. Please don't tease me like that, Rebbe. I must find Shimon before it's too late. Remember what you told me? How little time we had." She removed a folded paper from her coat pocket and handed it to me. "Didn't you draw this for me?"

I stared at a crudely drawn diagram of what looked like a complex molecule. In the center of the page was a row of four vertical circles, and on either side of this central structure was a parallel row containing three more circles. There were what I took to be Hebrew words inside all of the circles, and words and numbers also on the lattice of lines that connected all ten balls. At the bottom of the page was the number 613. I had no idea what any of it signified.

"What is this?"

"Are you testing me, Rebbe?"

"Yes. Yes, Leah. Tell me what it is."

"The Tree of Life," she said. "The *Sefirot*. See? The Ten Fruits."

"And this number, 613? What does it represent?"

"You haven't taught me that yet."

"Yes. Yes. I forgot. May I keep this?"

"Of course. I already memorized it. But why do you need it, Rebbe? Shimon says you know as much as the Baal Shem Tov himself."

"Really?" I had no idea what she was talking about, but I didn't dare ask for fear my ignorance might frighten the Leah persona away. The last thing I wanted was Barbara Warren reappearing. Now that I was an integral part of Leah's fantasy, I had to play my role of the Rebbe and drift back and forth in time as easily as she did. "Did Shimon ever tell you how he and I met?"

"Many times. He sought you out for years and followed your path back and forth between Russia and Prussia. He told me that you were a legend: the Magiker Rebbe who fought the Blood Libel. His greatest wish has always been to serve you."

I nodded, wondering all the while how I would ever manage to remember all these strange names and phrases after Leah left. "Do you mind if I take some notes, Leah?"

"Who am I to question you, Rebbe?"

I nodded, feeling much more confident with the stenographer's pad on my lap and the pen in my hand. "The other day, you mentioned a matchmaker."

"Rayzel the Shadchen." Leah giggled into her fist and then hugged herself. "All the girls in Irmunsk live in dread of her and the terrible husbands she has in store for them. It was she who arranged for me to marry Yochanan Levy."

"Who is he?"

"The son of Isaac Levy, the wealthiest man in Irmunsk. My father, Moishe Littman, has money, but not like Isaac Levy. The marriage would bring their two businesses together. I didn't want to marry Yochanan. 'God has blessed you,' said my father. I folded my arms defiantly across my chest and replied: 'He blessed me with wonderful parents,' hoping that would put an end to the conversation. 'What more could I want?'

"Rayzel looked at me, shook her head and said: 'Cursed with beauty and brains. Thank God, Yochanan doesn't care.' But I cared. Unlike the other girls in Irmunsk, I have a mind of my own. And I am in love with Shimon. From the first moment I set eyes on him. He is funny, smart, and handsome. Shimon has traveled across Europe. On a train! I've never even seen a train. He has relatives in America. With Shimon, there is the hope of escape."

Leah's body was trembling by the end of her passionate outburst, and tears stained her cheeks. As for me, I was utterly fixated. She had made every word sound so real. I handed her a tissue, and she wiped away her tears.

"Did you tell your father how you felt?"

"Are you *meshugga*? My father's a great bull of a man with a big black beard. He picks the dinner table up over his head whenever he's angry. Tell him about Shimon? He'd have wrung his neck like a Shabbos chicken."

"But if you didn't want to marry this Yochanan…"

"What choice did I have? Fathers, not lovers, arrange marriages in Irmunsk. The contract had been drawn up. The date for the wedding set. You were our only hope. Don't you remember that first night he brought me to you?"

"Remind me again. What happened?"

"It was after midnight, and everyone was asleep when I snuck out of the house. Shimon was waiting for me. He took me to the forbidden gentile town where I had never set foot before. The cobblestones under my feet felt so strange. The street was steep and winding, like the serpent in Eden. We went down and down, such a strange sensation. I was afraid of being discovered by the police or by my father. Why were we in such a dangerous place? Shimon squeezed my hand and told me not to worry. The Magiker Rebbe had great powers.

"We came to a door. It was very thick, with a great brass knocker in the middle. Shimon banged on it, loud enough to wake the dead. I heard footsteps coming down the stairs. Finally a thin man, with skin so pale he was almost yellow, opened the door and looked at me in horror, as if I was unclean. He said, 'What possessed you to bring this woman here?' 'The Rebbe knows,' Shimon said. 'I have his permission.'

"We climbed the stairs. Up, up, up until we reached an attic where the air was smoky and filled with a powerful sweet scent. Candles were flickering everywhere. Old men in *tallisim* were rocking back and forth in prayer, all of them squeezed together like baby chicks on benches under this little roof. They turned and saw me. Were they hissing? They certainly didn't want me there. Some flicked at me with their hands as if I were a fly on a piece of honey cake.

"Then a powerful voice spoke out: 'Name the sixth fruit on *Tiferet*, the Tree of Life. Beauty! Would you turn your back on Wisdom, Understanding, Compassion, and Power if they came calling? They are fruits of the Tree as well. Why would you turn Beauty away when it comes to us?'

"I looked up and saw a man seated on a platform in front of the elders. I could see his hat and his beard but not his face. His voice was like lightning against a black stormy sky. The old men bowed their heads and murmured apologies to him.

"Shimon gestured for me to approach. I was terribly frightened. He said there was nothing to fear from the Magiker Rebbe. Then the Rebbe held his hands out to me. Shimon gently pushed me forward. The old men were chanting and clapping. I was like a baby struggling to take its first steps. The floorboards creaked underneath me. I was terrified and exhilarated at the same time. I reached my hands out to the Rebbe. He took them and squeezed. I saw he was smiling. I saw his eyes for the first time. They were your eyes. Those same kind, loving eyes I see before me now. You are the Magiker Rebbe!

"You guided my hands and placed them on the Book of Zohar. You told me of the power that lay in the book. How the power could change my life. That it was surging through me even as I…"

Leah cried out in a wail of religious ecstasy and collapsed on the floor in a dead faint. I stared down in semi-shock at her body, unsure for a moment of what I should do. Wait and see if she came to as Leah? Or step in, and risk reviving Barbara? The doctor in me won out, and I moved to the bookshelf where I always kept a carafe of water. It was empty.

Moving swiftly to the door to ask Evelyn to get me more water, I stepped into the reception area, where I was surprised to discover Marty Corwin. He was sitting on the couch, leafing through a two-year-old copy of *Smithsonian Magazine*.

"Busy tonight, Harry?"

"Why?" I made no attempt to disguise the annoyance in my voice.

"Want to go to a wedding?"

"I have a patient inside, Marty."

"So what are you doing out here?"

"Just getting her some..." A strange sensation came over me, and I popped back inside my office.

As I suspected, Leah had vanished quietly through the door that opened directly to the hall. Disappointed and a little depressed, I returned to the reception room where the Pasha looked at me questioningly.

"Forget it," I said. "She left. What did you say about a wedding?"

"Tonight, in Crown Heights. Can you come with me?"

"I don't think so."

"Come on, Harry! Don't be a party pooper. There's going to be somebody there you're dying to meet."

"Forgive me, Marty, but I'm going to pass."

"Okay. But what are your chances of ever meeting someone again who actually lived in Irmunsk?"

Before I could react to what Corwin had said, a large African-American man in his early fifties walked into the reception area. He wore a fedora and flashed an NYPD detective's shield, which identified him as Fletcher Jones.

Jones turned his attention to Evelyn and said: "I'm looking for a Dr. Harris Strider."

"I'm Dr. Strider."

"Could you please come with me, Doctor?" asked Jones. "Got a car waiting downstairs."

Corwin stared at me with a what-have-you-done-now look.

Ignoring the Pasha, I asked Detective Jones: "What's all this about?"

"Attempted suicide," replied the detective. "Won't talk to nobody but you."

# THE HOSPITAL

AN NYPD SQUAD CAR was parked at the curb outside my
office. A tall, brooding Hispanic woman with a crescent-
shaped scar traversing her left eyebrow stood next to the vehicle on the driver's side, smoking a cigarette down to its fil-
ter. Tossing the butt away, she nodded at Detective Jones,
who muttered: "We got him."

Jones opened the back door for me, and I slid onto the
seat. Then he folded his large muscular body into a smaller
version of himself and got into the front passenger seat next
to his partner. She had gotten in without saying a word to
either of us and sat looking straight ahead, clutching the steering wheel with both hands, wrinkling and smoothing her
brow repeatedly.

"This is my partner, Dolores Ortega. Excuse me. Detective Ortega. She don't talk much. But she drives a helluva lot
better than I do." Jones flashed the biggest, whitest set of
teeth I had ever seen and fastened his seat belt. His partner
ignored him, turned the engine over, and pulled away from
the curb.

"Ortega," I repeated, wondering all the while what the odds were of a connection to my nemesis. "By any chance, do you have a relative who's in the managed care business? Health insurance?"

"Why?" growled Dolores, raising the crescent shaped scar over her eyebrow as she glared at me in the rearview mirror.

"No reason." Shut up, Harris, I thought.

Jones stared at his partner then shook his head, unable to fathom her curt behavior.

We rode along in silence until we reached a red light at Ninety-Sixth Street. Dolores fixed her gaze on my reflection in the mirror once more and asked: "What insurance company?"

"Sorry?"

"Your Ortega."

"Cambridge Medical. He's in claims."

"So you figure all us Ortegas are related? That it?"

"Not at all. Just curious."

"Why?"

"Just making conversation."

"Why?"

"Forget it."

"Leave him alone, Dolores."

"What is it with you?" asked Dolores, ignoring Jones's request. "Is it cuz I'm a woman? Hispanic woman? Think maybe you gonna get lucky? Got some Jennifer Lopez fantasy going on back there? Huh! Figure you'll get my phone number afterwards, and maybe one night when you're bored or your white-bread girlfriend's riding the cotton pony, you'll give me a call. That it? Well listen up, pal. Dolores Ortega's a police detective. Not some little churro you picked up in the Times Square Starbucks, who's gonna wash your socks after you blow a hole in them. They got 1-900 numbers for *turistas* like you. Now, you got something else you wanna say to me?"

"I'm sorry. Truly."

"What, about your Ortega? He rub you the wrong way? Too aggressive, maybe? Latino men can be like that, right?"

"Woo-wee! Kitten with a whip! Wha'd they put in your coffee this morning, woman?" Jones chortled. "Or maybe you got too much animus, huh, Doc? Never seen my partner this riled up or so danged talkative in the two years we've been riding together. I'm telling you the truth."

"Shut up, Fletch!" snarled Dolores. "Just want the Doc here to know he ain't dealing with a fucking stereotype. I am a proud Puerto Rican woman. Now what about your Ortega? Wha'd he do to you?"

"He's giving me a hard time on a claim. Patient of mine is being denied medical coverage." I hoped Dalton Lafferty would appreciate the grilling I was taking on his behalf.

"With good reason?" demanded Dolores.

"No. My patient's nutty as a fruitcake but the man's a genius...like Cervantes."

"Hmm...Cervantes. Hey, Fletch! Why don't you stop by that Korean market on the corner? Maybe the doc'll hop out and buy you a slice of watermelon. He's very interested in different cultures."

I was tired of her needling and finally blew my stack. "What is your problem, Dolores?"

"Don't get familiar with me!"

"Whoa! Am I a suspect here? I've lived in Chicago. Believe me, I know what tough cops are like."

At that moment a text message from Marty Corwin appeared on my BlackBerry: "R U OK?"

"She don't mean nothing," said Jones, readjusting his large frame in the passenger seat. "Trouble at home, that's all."

"What sort of trouble?" My query was a professional knee-jerk reaction, and I regretted it the instant the words had left my lips.

"Oh! You gonna analyze me now?" asked Dolores. "Do I gotta tell my life story to one more jerk-off with a Ph.D.?"

"Were you in therapy, Dolores?" My mind was filled with images of her pistol-whipping the poor shrink.

"Six months!" Dolores all but spat out those two words. "What is it with you people? Huh? With your degrees and your big words and your bullshit about marriage?"

"Was this couple's therapy?"

"Yeah. You married?"

"Yes."

"Happy?"

The question caught me off guard. Claire had been gone for a week and, honestly, I had missed Leah much more than Claire. But Claire was coming back. And I was certain we would straighten out whatever…

"Gotta think about it, huh? Can't be that solid a marriage."

"No relationship is perfect." I realized how pompous and cliché-ridden that sounded the instant it left my lips.

"Especially with two lesbians, right? Or do you just use the rubber stamp what says DOOMED? Isn't that what you fucking Ph.D.s think? That we broke God's commandment and don't deserve no better?"

"Your therapist said that?"

"Him, my priest, my sister, my uncle—they all want me to find a man. What kinda man? Hey, maybe a Ph.D.! They got all the fucking answers, right?"

"There are bad apples in every barrel, Dolores."

"Whoa! Lemme write that one down, Doc. I don't wanna forget that one when my girlfriend comes home. And is that a freebie? Or do I gotta pay for that?"

"You went to the wrong therapist, Dolores. Why take it out on me?"

"Know what this fucking Ph.D. did after he told us how queer we are? He called me up and asked me out!"

"On a date?"

"Sure on a date. He thinks I'm very attractive. How fucked up is that?"

"What is his name? I'll have him investigated."

"No shit!"

"Dolores, it's like a bad cop. He does a disservice to every one else in the profession."

"You think it's bad what he did?"

"Absolutely! He should have his license revoked, for his homophobia and for hitting on you."

Dolores said nothing in reply and retreated into a cone of silence as she drove us north along the eastern edge of Central Park. At 110th Street, she turned left, made her way over to Riverside Drive, and then onto the Henry Hudson Parkway.

"What hospital are we going to?" I finally asked.

"Columbia Presbyterian," answered Jones.

"You came all the way downtown to get me?"

"Door-to-door service," said Jones. "Fascinating man, that Freud. I'm telling you the truth. He and I share a lot in common: both born on May 6 and both born in a caul. That's a thin little membrane that covers a newborn baby's face—it's rare and a sure sign that you are gonna be special. Tell me, Doctor, are you a Freud man? Or did you cast your vote for Jung? Or are you the kind what don't tell?" Jones slapped his huge hand on his knee and roared with laughter. "I'm telling you the truth. Cops and shrinks, we got a lot in common. We spend all our days listening to people's sad-ass stories. Every time you think you heard it all, some crazy motherfucker tells you what he's gone and done with a gerbil, a Dalmatian, and a can of peaches.

"If they got room on the next mission to Mars, count me in. I'm telling you the truth. But when all the votes are tabulated, it still comes down to sex. That's what Brother Freud said. And I'll bear witness to that. I was fifteen years old and doin' the dirty with Miss Gallinger, my tenth-grade English teacher back in West Texas. This was in her apartment, mind you. She said I had a remedial reading problem what needed special after-school attention. Crazy white woman! If it were today, Miss Gallinger would be up on rape charges. But back then, when colored folk still sat up in the balcony for John Wayne movies, my Daddy shoved fifty dollars in my one pocket and a wrinkled Texaco map in the other and said, 'Go north, son,' which I did. But not before I joined the Navy. Oh, looky here! We have arrived. No need to tip the driver." The detective cracked himself up once more with that last remark.

Jones escorted me through the entrance of the hospital's emergency room, while Dolores remained outside smoking another cigarette and brooding over the indignities she was suffering on a moment-to-moment basis. I was almost tempted to give her one of my business cards, but wasn't sure whether or not she thought I, or my opinion, was worth anything.

"How's the patient doing?" The detective had removed the fedora from his head of snowy white hair and was talking to a pink-cheeked nurse in a starched white uniform. She motioned with her hand and escorted us down a hall in the emergency ward. Jones must have been in the Navy for quite a few years; his gait was still that of a sailor making his way across a deck on the high seas.

"What is the patient's name?" I asked.

"We don't know," replied the nurse, in a distinct Scottish brogue. The ID pinned to her uniform read "McNeill."

"We didn't find no ID when we got the suspect off the bridge," explained Jones. "There was just a card with your name on it."

"Suspect?"

"Attempted suicide."

"What bridge?"

"George Washington." Jones pointed a long powerful finger in the general direction of the bridge that linked New York and New Jersey. "Upper level. That's why we're at this hospital. Real convenient."

"We get quite a few every week," piped up Nurse McNeill.

Who could it be, I wondered? My first thought was Barbara. But how could she have possibly traveled all the way up to West 168th Street in such a short a time after leaving my office?

Nurse McNeill pushed open the door to a room on her right. Jones and I followed her inside.

I stared ahead with a mix of surprise and despair at Dalton W. Lafferty. He was sitting up in the bed wearing a hospital gown, with an armed policeman seated in a chair nearby.

Unable to meet my gaze, Lafferty quoted from "Lycidas" by Milton: "'Hence with denial vain and coy excuse.'"

"You know this man?" asked Jones.

"Oh, yes. May I be alone with him, Detective?" I nodded toward the cop seated in the chair.

"You ain't a fan of Dr. Kevorkian, are you?"

"No. You have nothing to worry about. I'll just be a few minutes."

"Take your time, Doc. Dolores is in one of her 'don't-bother-me-when-I'm-thinking moods.' I'm telling you the truth." Jones chuckled loudly and steered Nurse McNeill out the door asking: "Is that accent Irish or Scotch? I know you ain't from around here."

As an afterthought, Jones turned to the uniformed cop and beckoned with a large paw for him to follow. The policeman shot out of the chair and followed the detective and the nurse out of the room.

"Professor, what happened?" I grabbed the chair that the cop had vacated, pulled it closer to Lafferty's bed, and sat down.

"Life. Death. There didn't seem much space between them anymore."

"But the bridge…"

Lafferty turned his gaze toward me and asked: "Do you think it was out of character? Perhaps I should have fallen on my sword, like Brutus. '*This was the noblest scholar of them all.*'"

"Was it Ortega?"

"Who?"

"Cambridge Medical. They refused to insure you anymore."

Lafferty shook his head. "Driven to despair by an HMO? Pshaw, sir! You invest too much power in them, like the credit card companies. I burned all my plastic years ago. What need have I of credit?" He said nothing for the longest time until he finally broke his silence. "Today was my anniversary. Annabel and I would have been married forty-two years today."

In all the years I had known the professor, he had never spoken of his wife.

"How long has she…"

"Fifteen years. She was the love of my life. I never realized it until she was gone. She was my constant companion.
She went on all the protest marches with me, made placards,
and sandwiches, and babies. It was a good life. Then one Friday afternoon, she didn't feel well. By Monday, she was gone.
I railed against the heavens like Lear. What kind of a God
does a thing like that? I kept her dresses in the closet for
years, thinking she might return. But it was as if it had all
been a dream. I would wake every morning and think of
death. How long it would be until I could join her? Oh, to be
with my Annabel once again! I passed my days like a som-
nambulist, sleepwalking through life. My youngest daughter,
who teaches in San Francisco, begged me to come live with
her. Live?

"Then one morning I awoke and didn't think about
death. The weight, the crushing weight that had been on my
chest, was gone. Was the mourning period over? I resumed
my activities with all my familiar fervor. Until one day—in the
middle of a lecture on *Cymbeline*—the weight returned, heavier than before. Unable to speak, I dismissed the class with a
feeble gesture and stumbled back to my apartment. I drew all
the curtains and lay in the darkness. Occasionally I would
hear Annabel's gentle voice call out to me, usually from the
kitchen, near the O'Keefe & Merritt stove. Does this sound
like madness to you, Doctor? To have loved someone so
deeply that even death can not terminate the relationship."

"It's possible, Professor."

"Where is Leah?" The question was so abrupt and unexpected that it startled me.

"Leah?"

"The girl in your office. The one with the flowers."

"Why do you ask?"

"Because she knows."

"I...I don't understand."

"She knows things that...Do you remember when she said the word *bashert*? I didn't know what it meant. I suspected it was Yiddish, so I asked the Little Cantor. He lives upstairs in my building. His real name is Alvin Rabinowitz. He's quite famous and fluent in Yiddish. He told me *bashert* meant a person's soul mate, someone who is predestined to love you. That's how Annabel was to me, Doctor. Leah knew that."

"She is very kind and thoughtful."

"How did she know about the daffodils? She knew they were Annabel's favorite flowers."

"A good guess." I shrugged.

"You're not listening to me, Doctor. When that girl Leah looked into my eyes, I felt she was staring into my soul. How long have you known her? Where did she come from?"

"I can't talk about her, Professor. She's a patient."

"Ah!"

"Tell me, Professor. That crushing weight on your chest, how often do you experience the sensation?"

"There's no real timetable: sometimes every day for a while and sometimes not for months."

"Why did you never tell me about it?"

"Do you have a cure for a broken heart, Doctor? It seemed so much easier to rail against technology."

"So was that all a front to cover your grief?"

"Don't be an idiot!" thundered Lafferty. "The world as we have known it for two millennia has come to an end. The gates were left ajar. The Philistines rushed in and declared eminent domain."

"So what pushed you over the edge this morning?"

"The calendar. It is our anniversary." Lafferty shrugged. "I just couldn't do it anymore. There seemed no purpose. How much more time do I have anyhow? My children are estranged from me. My grandchildren have never met me. Who is there to mourn my passing?"

"I'd miss you."

"Truly?"

"You are a constant in my life."

"Don't you mean a habit? Or, more accurately, a bad habit."

"What about dating?"

Lafferty stared at me in stupefaction and then erupted in what could only be described as Vesuvial laughter. When he finally stopped, he asked, "Is that what they call alternative medicine?"

"At least I got you laughing."

"That you did." The professor smiled and held his hand out to me. I squeezed it warmly.

"Feel better?"

"Actually, yes. I've been holding that in for a long time."

Somehow we managed to steer the conversation to global warming, and within minutes the professor was his combative self once again. We promised to talk next week, and I stepped out into the corridor where Detective Jones was busy charming the starch out of Nurse McNeill's uniform. He interrupted his flirtation to look at me.

"His name is Dalton Lafferty," I said. "Professor Emeritus at Columbia University. He says it was all a misunderstanding. He had no desire to commit suicide."

"Then what was he doing on the bridge?"

"Orating...Shakespeare. He's a celebrated lecturer."

"And he's your patient?"

"Yes."

"He ever discuss suicide with you before?"

"Detective Jones, you know I cannot divulge privileged information."

Just then a tall, olive-skinned doctor walked past us examining a patient's chart. She had gone about five feet when she froze, turned around, and walked slowly towards me with a look of disbelief on her face.

"Harris Strider?" She said my name in an unmistakable Illinois accent. "Are you Harris Strider?"

When I said I was, she broke into a smile and pointed to the ID badge pinned to her chest. It read "D. Schuman, MD."

"Donna Schuman! From Evanston?" I surprised myself by grabbing the physician in a warm embrace. "What are you doing here? Obviously working but...How long have you...? Donna Schuman! Wow! Doctor Schuman!"

"Looks like you two got some catching up to do," said Jones, who seemed in no great rush to leave the hospital.

Donna was on a short break, so we went into the cafeteria for coffee. The smile on her face matched mine as we sat opposite each other for the first time in over twenty years.

"So! How's married life working out for you?" Donna nodded at the gold band on my finger. "I had one of those for a few years. My husband and I were in medical school together. Did our internship here in New York. Then he fell hopelessly in love with a patient. A man."

"I'm sorry."

"Ancient history. What brings you this far north?"

I told Donna as much as I could about Professor Lafferty, gave her my card, and, at the end of her break, said we should keep in touch. As I was getting up from the table, I remembered: "You had a cousin from Syracuse. She came to visit you one winter. A long time ago."

"Suzanne."

"Suzanne?"

"Suzanne Wilson. Her mother was crazy about Leonard Cohen. Played his album over and over during her pregnancy. Why did you bring her up?"

"I think about her sometimes. Remember that Christmas when we all went tobogganing?"

Donna nodded and said: "Suzanne never forgot either. She said you kissed her on the mouth; no boy had ever kissed her like that before. She had such a crush on you for years afterwards. She always wondered why you never wrote or got in touch with her."

"This is unbelievable. I felt the same way about her. Why didn't I act on it? I guess because I was twelve. Does she still live in Syracuse?"

"She died, when she was twenty, of an aneurysm. She was getting married that month too. My aunt and uncle were devastated. They never got over it."

Suddenly I felt as if a gigantic wall had toppled over and buried me alive. I wanted to burst into tears but didn't dare. Who could understand my mourning a girl whom I had only known for a few weeks and whom I hadn't seen in nearly thirty years? What did it all mean? Was I supposed to have loved Suzanne? Would she still be alive now if, young as I was, I had picked up the phone and called her? Was Leah a second chance for that kind of happiness? I saw now that Claire had been a mistake. She wasn't destined to be the one.

"Harris?" Donna reached out an arm and touched my hand. "Are you okay? You've gone pale."

I told Donna nothing was wrong, kissed her cheek, and promised I would call her.

Detective Jones, waiting for me outside the cafeteria, asked: "Ready?" I nodded. Then he floored me with his next question: "How long's he been a widower?"

"Who?"

"Calm down, Doc. I already told you about Freud and me. When I went into the Navy, my grandma sent me a package from Corpus Christi. I opened it up and there was this weird flimsy kinda membrane. It was the caul what covered my head when I was born. I'm telling you the truth. It's a good-luck charm for sailors. And Grandma, she had been saving it for twenty years. It also means you're destined for greatness, and you got psychic powers."

"And which description fits you?"

"Kinda like that little boy with Bruce Willis. Dead people keep turning up in my brain, or thoughts of dead people. Now, you've been thinking about him thinking about a dead woman."

"Do you use this power in your work?" I was fascinated by Fletcher Jones's revelation.

"Not officially. Scares the shit outta my bosses. But it can sometimes help me on a case." Jones began chuckling. "My, oh my! Wish you could see your face, Doc. I'm telling you the truth."

We were on our way out of the hospital when two red-faced ambulance attendants burst through the sliding doors, shouting for everyone to get out of the way. They were wheeling an accident victim on a gurney, which was followed by a distraught woman in what had to be her eighties. She had one of the worst cases of osteoporosis I had ever seen. This human question mark was keening in a manner peculiar to women of Irish descent.

"Heavenly Father! Heavenly Father!" The old lady repeated those two words nonstop, with a thick slice of her native Ireland still in her speech, while staring down at the younger man lying on the gurney as he writhed in agony. "Didn't I beg you to leave the fuckin' dog in Paris?"

"Not now, Tilly. Please!"

Noticing the man's hand gesticulating in midair, my first diagnosis was Parkinson's or some other neurological disorder. When it dawned on me that he was composing in his head and transposing the music onto an invisible keyboard, I knew who the accident victim was. "Edwin!"

The composer struggled to manipulate his head sideways and looked up at me, managing a smile despite his obvious pain. "Harris! How good of you to come." His gratitude sounded so sincere that I didn't want to spoil the moment by telling him my presence was strictly a coincidence.

"Are you Claire's husband?" asked the old woman, who I realized was Edwin's fabled patroness. In order to look at me, she had to contort her body into a pretzel-like posture.

"Dr. Strider, this is Tilly McIntire. I believe you've heard me speak of her often." Edwin's formal introduction was followed by a piercing cry of pain.

"In glowing terms," I added over his cry, hoping that this little white lie might encourage Tilly to remove the silent curse she was clearly invoking on me. She had always hoped Edwin would marry Claire.

"You're a doctor, right?" asked Tilly. "Got any pull in this place? I'm so afraid they'll butcher him like they did me poor father back in Boston. Run over by a milk wagon, he was. Amputated both his legs."

"What happened, Edwin?"

"Bizet," replied Edwin pitifully.

"Should have drowned the creature in the Seine when I had the chance," said Tilly. "Brain the size of a split pea.

What were you thinking, Edwin? Why in the name of Jesus did you take it out of its carrier?"

"We were on our way to see Septimus," said Edwin. "He plays bass fiddle in the virtual orchestra, lives up in Washington Heights, and has a huge flat-screen TV. He had hooked up his computer so I could finally see all my musicians' faces. Aaagh!"

"Maybe you shouldn't speak, Edwin."

"Our taxi pulled up and...aaaagh! Pain! Paaaain!"

Tilly took over the story: "We got outta the taxi. The lyin' cabbie said he didn't have change for a fifty. And the creature was whimpering in its bag, so Edwin let it out to pee. As if it hadn't peed enough all over the Ralph Lauren pillows I'd bought Edwin for Christmas. Well, it didn't pee, did it? Noooo! It ran into the street, and the greatest talent this country has produced since poor Mr. Bernstein—may God forgive him for all those boys he led astray—went runnin' after him, right into the path of an oncoming U.S. Postal truck, what had no business travelin' at such speed on these slippery streets."

"It was a FedEx truck!" wailed Edwin. "Aaaaagh! Can't they give me something for the pain?"

"What happened to Bizet?" I asked. "Where did he go?"

"Hopefully to hell!" spat Tilly.

Jones came to my rescue and reminded me that traffic would soon make it impossible to get back downtown in a reasonable time. I wished Edwin a speedy recovery, and Jones and I walked out of the hospital. A silent and brooding Ortega was waiting for us. Driving south, Jones regaled me with further tales of his childhood in Texas.

He and I exchanged business cards just before the two detectives dropped me off on Fifth Avenue. To my surprise,

Dolores got out and opened the back door for me. She also slipped her card into my hand.

Only after they had driven away did I notice there was something written on the back of the card: "You're okay, Doc. Thanks for understanding. If you need help with the other Ortega, let me know…Dolores."

I have no idea what Dolores did or didn't do regarding Robert Ortega. But after that day, the claims investigator's phone calls to me were marked by a degree of deference that verged on sycophancy. I was sorely tempted on those occasions to ask if he had a relative with the NYPD but I didn't want to push my luck.

# THE WEDDING

I OPENED MY CLOSET door and removed the suit usually reserved for funerals—somber and respectful. The tie, however, would be a problem. Black would be a bit much. After all this was—to use Corwin's word—a *simcha*, a celebration. What about a Versace, with a commedia dell'arte pattern? No, too pagan. Hmmm. Perhaps the Hermès with mermaids? Make up your mind for once, Harris. The Pasha is picking you up in ten minutes.

The telephone rang on the night table.

"Hello?"

"Harris?" Though my mother had lived in Chicago her entire adult life, she never shed her Brooklyn accent, which became quite heavy when she was stressed. This was one of those times.

"Mom! Guess whom I ran into today? Remember Donna Schuman? She lived around the corner from us? I saw her this afternoon. She's a doctor at Columbia Presbyterian."

"And divorced," added my mother. "Very sad, what happened with her and her husband. Donna's mother told me the whole story. You never know what it's going to be like till you get them inside the tent, take my word for it. So what happened to you Sunday?"

"Oh, God! I'm so sorry, Mom. I know I promised to phone but…Well, I just didn't. I'm sorry."

"What's happening to you, Harris? I'm worried."

"Don't be. Nothing to worry about, but I can't talk right now. My friend Marty's picking me up any second, and I've got to finish dressing. We're going to a wedding."

"Anyone I know?"

"Nobody I know actually. It's across the bridge, in Crown Heights."

"Brooklyn?"

"Yeah. Your old stomping grounds."

"A Jewish wedding?"

"I think so."

"Why are you doing this, Harris?"

"Mom, I'm going to be late." I was barely able to hide the annoyance in my voice.

"They're Hasidim, aren't they?"

"I don't know their names, Mom."

"Don't be funny, Harris. Hasidim is a sect."

"You make it sound like a cult."

"Does this have to do with that girl, your patient? I haven't had a single night's sleep since you told me about her. This association will only bring you sorrow, honey. Maybe worse."

"What is it you're not telling me, Mother? Why should you lose sleep over a patient of mine? Someone you've never met."

"I can't believe we're having this conversation."

"Me neither, Mom. There's been a moratorium on Judaism in our family for forty-two years. Now alarm bells go off because I'm attending an Orthodox wedding in Brooklyn. What kind of emotional land mine am I treading on here?"

"What are you talking about, Harris?"

"Okay…itty-bitty steps. Back to square one: religious instruction, or more precisely, my lack of it. Why was that?"

"Now? You want to talk about this now? Weren't you in a big rush two seconds ago?"

"How come you never lit Sabbath candles?" I asked. "Or ever observed Passover or Hanukah, let alone the High Holidays? Why did you abandon your faith?"

"It was personal, my choice. I had my own reasons. What right do you have to question my motives?"

"Because you're Jewish, which under rabbinical law makes me Jewish. Why did you keep me away from it?"

"What is this frantic urgency? You never showed the slightest interest in Judaism before."

"True enough. But that was before people started calling me Rebbe."

"What are you talking about?" My mother's voice grew wary.

"Two old men approached me Friday night outside a synagogue on West End Avenue. They wanted to know who 'my people' were. They called me Rebbe, which I thought was pretty strange. When I asked them why, they told me to ask you. Don't you think that's peculiar? 'Ask your mother,' they said."

"Who…were they?" I could hear fear—real fear—in my mother's voice.

"Something in my background you don't want me to know? You sound like you're afraid of something."

"Don't be ridiculous, Harris. What were these men's names?"

"How would I know? They were complete strangers to me, sort of comical looking, actually, with huge beards. They reminded me of Mutt and Jeff."

"Please, Harris, don't go tonight, as a favor to me!"

"Sorry, Mom. But I'm onto something important here."

"*Yiskadal v'yiskadash shmai raba.*"

"What is that?"

"The Jewish prayer for the dead, okay?" And my mother abruptly hung up on me.

What the hell did that mean? Had I just been disowned? Was she doing something with sackcloth and ashes on the other end of the line? Or was she merely demonstrating knowledge of the Jewish faith she had kept secret from me all my life? What the hell was going on? And what tie was I going to wear? Please, God! Help me pick a tie.

I had finally settled on a cranberry patterned number from Barney's when I heard a voice calling out my name from somewhere in the apartment. Moving cautiously out of the bedroom, clutching a hairbrush to defend myself, I stared in amazement at a deeply tanned and beaming Claire. She was standing in the living room, and she was home a week early.

She raced to me, threw her arms around my neck, and whispered: "You have no idea how much I missed you."

Stunned by her presence, all I could ask was: "Why are you back?"

"Instant replay: 'I missed you.' Aren't you the least bit flattered, Harris? Aren't you touched?" She began taking little bites out of my neck, thinking this might turn me on.

"Of course, of course." I took hold of her wrists, eased her away from me, and looked around the room, sensing something or someone was missing. "Where's Nella? What's happened to Nella?"

"She met a Samoan twice her size. She was smitten beyond belief. Who knows if she's ever coming back!" Claire grabbed my belt buckle, unfastened it, whipped my belt through the loops of my trousers, and tossed it on the bed. "Come on, boy toy, take off your clothes." She took my hand and thrust it up under her skirt. "Moist, huh? I've been fantasizing about this moment all week. Wait till you see what those native girls taught my pelvis to do!"

"Could we put that tutorial on hold for about two hours?" I grabbed my belt from the bed and threaded it back through the loops.

"Oh, no!" Claire grinned and knocked us both down onto the bed. Lying on top of me, she grabbed my crotch with such ferocity that I winced. Shoving her to one side, I leapt up from the bed.

"Where are you going?" Claire was stung as she watched me move towards the front door. "Harris! I've just flown twenty hours—"

"You must be exhausted. Take a nap."

"—to be with you, you bastard! Don't you owe me some kind of explanation for your behavior, your rejection?"

"This isn't rejection, Claire." Pecking her quickly on the cheek, I marched double time towards the front door and opened it. "Welcome home, sweetie. Fabulous tan."

"Don't you dare walk out on me like this, Harris! We need to talk. There's a great deal to discuss."

"And we will." By that time I was in the hallway. "We will. I promise. But I'm really late. Marty's downstairs waiting in his car. Didn't you see him?"

"You're ditching me for Marty?" Claire was framed in the doorway by then, her arms placed defiantly on her hips. "What's so important that you couldn't cancel and spend the evening with—?"

"It's professional, Claire. There's really no time to ex-plain all the…"

Claire stepped into the hallway. "It's that little bitch again, right?"

"No! Yes. Oh, Claire! The most amazing thing has hap-pened. Barbara isn't who you think she is at all. She's—"

Claire slapped my cheek so hard I actually saw those little cartoon birds fluttering in front of my face.

"Good-bye, Harris."

Claire stepped inside the apartment and slammed the door shut. It wasn't until I emerged from the elevator that I realized I had forgotten to tell her about Edwin. No problem, I would tell her later after she calmed down.

* * *

Corwin and I were halfway across the Brooklyn Bridge when his battered 1988 Mercedes started making an ominous death rattle.

"Son of a bitch!" growled Corwin. He slammed his right palm in a staccato rhythm against the steering wheel. "Don't die on me now, you Teutonic piece of shit."

"Why don't you buy a new car, Pasha?"

"Waste of money! I never bought this one; it was a be-quest from an extremely passive-aggressive patient named Merritt Agincourt Jr., who died owing me seven grand for unpaid sessions. It was suicide. Sometimes I think the crazy son of a bitch haunts me under the hood."

"All the more reason to get rid of it."

"Wait, wait! Here we go! Merritt is behaving himself again. Amazing! In death he still exhibits the same passive-aggressive symptoms. So, what was the outcome with the cops today? You really had me worried when that huge black guy carted you off."

"He's psychic, fascinating character. He was born with a caul over his face."

"Just what you needed, another expert opinion. What did he want with you?"

"A patient of mine tried to kill himself...maybe." I was in no mood to discuss Lafferty, or my reunion with Donna. At that moment my mind was focused solely on the mythical Irmunsk and the hope that it really might have existed.

"Ah, those maybes! You can't take them seriously. So, *boychik*, looking forward to our little outing?"

"Very much." The Friday-night traffic was stop-and-go as we exited the bridge on the Brooklyn side. "Can I ask you some questions?"

"About protocol for the evening? First and foremost: don't touch any of the women and don't let them touch you, you irresistible creature."

"Seriously, Marty. Who is the Baal Shem Tov? Did I pronounce that correctly?"

"You have been doing your homework. The Baal Shem Tov was the founder of the modern Hasidic movement, during the early eighteenth century in the Pale of Settlement. Baal Shem Tov means 'Master of the Good Name,' and he was something of a miracle healer. He taught that purity of the heart is more pleasing to God than learning. You give thanks to Hashem, the Lord, through singing and dancing. For the first time, because of the teachings of the Baal Shem Tov, Jews didn't have to be serious scholars in order to connect with the Supreme Being. Hasids were taught to worship and adhere to God's teachings in every facet of their day-to-day life—tooth brushing, texting, whatever—not just formal acts of religious observance. It became the people's faith and spread like wildfire throughout the Diaspora. The young boy and girl getting married tonight are Hasidic Jews."

"What about the Tree of Life?"

"Dabbling in Kabbalah again, are we? Kabbalah is the central framework of the Hasidic movement, the yin and yang of it…mixed in with a little astrology, numerology, and your Aunt Bertha's recipe for goat-cheese blintzes."

"Fascinating. What about the Blood Libel?"

"Who the hell's been debriefing you? Darth Vader? Didn't that apostate mother of yours in Chicago teach you anything about her people's laugh-a-minute history? Anti-Semitism in Eastern Europe was bigger than football is here. Any excuse for a good old-fashioned pogrom. 'So, Yasha, you old Cossack! What're you up to this afternoon?' 'Not much, Igor.' 'Good. Let's go kill some Jews.' The favorite killing season was traditionally Passover, when our hosts claimed the Jews couldn't bake their weird matzohs without using the blood of a freshly murdered gentile child. The psychos in charge would promptly search for a dead kid or have one summarily dispatched to use as evidence."

"How awful!"

"So it was, until a few bold rabbis with brilliant legal minds started going to court and, using logic, proved how blood—anathema in the Jewish faith—was frowned upon in baking, sex, or chartered accountancy. That was one of the reasons the Chief Rabbi of Prague created the Golem. Oops! Have to save that *haymishe* horror story for next week, kid. Sorry, but that's all the time we have left for this week's episode of *Ask Mr. Jew.*"

"One last question?"

"Make it fast."

"Ever heard of someone called the Magiker Rebbe?"

"Was he the one they expelled from Apt? The scandal of the five barren wives."

"Baron's wives?"

"No. Apt was the Yiddish name for Opatow, a town in Poland. And as the story goes, there was a curse on the women of the *shtetl*. They were incapable of conceiving, and the midwives in the village blamed it on 'the evil eye.' That, of course, was the all-purpose excuse for any failure or disaster among the chosen people. Then one day the Magiker Rebbe arrived in Apt and 'conferred' with the barren wives. Miraculously they all conceived and gave birth to healthy babies, who all bore a remarkable resemblance to the Rebbe. He disappeared from Apt and continued to cut a swath through the Pale and other parts of Eastern Europe."

"What happened to him?"

"Who knows if he even existed? For all we know there may have been more than one Magiker Rebbe. Don't forget, our ancestors came to this country with a great gift for fabulism. You know, I just flashed on my Bubbe Esther in Brooklyn, when I was a little boy. We were walking down a street together when she abruptly grabbed hold of my hand and said: 'Walk quickly Moishe! That's where the Magiker Rebbe used to live.' He'd been dead for years, she said, but she was afraid a curse might still be hovering over the building." Corwin turned his head and pointed across the street. "Hey! Does that look like a parking space to you, just up from the bus stop?"

The marriage ceremony moved me deeply. I think it was the Old World garments the bride and groom wore as they stood beneath the wedding canopy taking their vows; the image reminded me of Leah's richly detailed description of life in Irmunsk. I felt I had traveled back in time as I stared at the bearded men with forelocks, long black coats, and wide-brimmed black hats; and the women wearing wigs to cover their shaved heads. The austere clothing stood in stark contrast to the fervent passion the assemblage brought to their singing and dancing, once the couple was officially wed and a klezmer band began to swing.

The groom's father, Bernie Aarons, a huge man with a gray beard and snow-white hair tied back in a ponytail, made his way towards us. A successful kosher butcher, he lifted Corwin off the ground as easily as he would a side of beef and kissed him on both cheeks.

"Thanks for coming, Marty. It means a lot to me."

"Wouldn't have missed it, kiddo. Hope you don't mind that I brought a date unannounced. Take a look at this *punim*, Bernie. Is that a face? Finally, after all these years, I found the real thing—no more women! My hand to God! Harris is the best thing ever happened to me. Plus, he's half Jewish—the half that counts."

My face glowed beet red. "Please! I can assure you, Mr. Aarons, that there is no truth whatsoever…"

"Don't worry, Doctor. Marty's the last of the red-hot kibbitzers. Welcome! You honor us with your presence."

"Did you two really go to school together?"

"English and Hebrew," answered Aarons. "I knew Marty before he left the fold."

I stared at Corwin in a new light and asked in disbelief: "You were a Hasid?"

"Until he deserted us," said Aarons.

"Blame it on Chinese food," said Corwin, shrugging his shoulders. "And shiksas."

"He could speed-read Hebrew," said Aarons proudly. "At his bar mitzvah, not only did he read his portion, but the entire…" The Pasha began singing "Long Ago and Far Away" in a rich baritone. "Oh, dear. It seems I'm embarrassing the poor boy. So, Doctor! Marty tells me you're interested in one of our guests."

"Yes, the one from Irmunsk."

"Zvee Moskowitz, a successful tailor in the neighborhood for many years. He might still try to sell you a double-breasted suit...with two pairs of pants."

The klezmer band played as if they were truly possessed that night. (I had hoped the tall Harpo Marx might be among them, but no luck.) The men danced together in perfect precision—Rockettes with beards—as Bernie Aarons led us towards a table where an elderly man in a frayed pin-striped suit sat. He was leaning on a wooden cane and nodding enthusiastically to the music.

Aarons touched the old man's hunched shoulder and shouted over the din of the klezmer: "Zvee! *Er vill mit dir sprechen.*"

Moskowitz stared up at the groom's father and shouted back: "Can he speak English? It's better for me."

Aarons shook his head and laughed. Then he gestured for me to approach the ancient tailor.

"Hello, Mr. Moskowitz."

The old man looked me up and down several times, as if I were a bolt of cloth he was considering purchasing. Then he licked his cracked lips and asked: "Vat are you? Forty? Forty-two?"

"Forty-two, very impressive. How did you guess?"

"Forty-two long?"

"Sorry?"

"He wants to know your suit size," whispered Aarons.

"Oh. Sorry. I'm a forty, regular."

"Anybody got a tape?" Moskowitz frowned and struggled to get to his feet. "Off the rack?" He clutched his cane firmly with his left hand while fingering the weave of my suit with his right.

"Yes."

"Vat I figured. Tsk, tsk, tsk. Lemme give you a piece of advice about men's clothing, sonny boy. 'In a shop vit no mirrors, everything fits.' *Verstehst?* Ve'll have a fitting. Come back in two veeks. Did I sell you dis suit?"

"No, you didn't." Our exchange was not going well. "So, Mr. Moskowitz, Bernie tells me that you're originally from—"

"Lou Gehrig died."

"I'm sorry?"

"Me, too. He vas a terrific ballplayer. You kinda look like a shortstop. Am I right?"

"No, I'm a doctor. I was hoping we could have a little chat about—"

"Is Sophie Tucker dead?"

"I...I don't know her."

"She died a long time ago, Zvee." Bernie Aarons touched my arm to indicate that we should leave the old man alone, and whispered: "Sorry."

I heaved a deep sigh, rose from my seat, and sat down again, determined to make one last attempt. Filling my lungs to capacity, I asked loudly: "Did you come from Irmunsk?"

Moskowitz shook his head: "Prospect Park. My little granddaughter dropped me off."

"No, no, no, Mr. Moskowitz. Were you born in Irmunsk?"

"Vere's dat?"

I turned to Aarons and Corwin for some much-needed guidance, but the old school chums just shrugged their shoulders. But I still wasn't prepared to quit. "Please! Try hard. Do you have any memories at all of Irmunsk? How about a girl named Leah Littman? Her father was quite wealthy, Moishe Littman? Remember him?"

Moskowitz mouthed the names repeatedly and pondered the questions for a long time. He ran his tongue over his lips several times. Finally his eyes lit up and he replied: "I saw Rockefeller on the street once."

The band started to play "Sha Shtil," and the groom, David Aarons, bounced over to our table with sweat pouring down his face.

"Come dance, Dad."

"Where are your manners, Davie? Have you said hello to Marty? And his boyfriend, Harris, the doctor?"

"Mazel tov, Marty. Always figured you'd have to come out eventually," said David. "Kind of obvious. Too many women for a straight guy."

Corwin's mouth dropped open, and the groom's father burst into a rumble of laughter. "Atta boy, Davie, a direct hit. I always wondered when someone would fly under the radar and zap you, Marty. Come!"

Bernie Aarons kissed his son on the cheek, wrapped a loving arm around his shoulder, and went to join the men on the dance floor.

"Hey! Hey! Hey! Just a second! Vat am I?" demanded Moskowitz. "*Kashe varnishkes?*"

"*Kim shoyn zu mir, boychik*" said Aarons, scurrying back to help the old tailor to his feet and lead him onto the floor.

Corwin whipped out a cigar, sat down next to me, and clapped a hand on my knee. "Sorry, Harry. Bernie should have warned me the old guy was woo-woo. He's a helluva dancer, though. Look at that *alter kocker* make hey-hey in the hayloft."

The wedding guests cleared the floor; they clapped their hands in time to the music and sang the lyrics to the old *shtetl* melody. Moskowitz waved his cane in the air and danced with the Aarons, father and son.

"If only he could have told me something," I said, staring at the old man, who was having the time of his life. "If nothing else, he could have proven that Irmunsk existed. That Barbara—Leah—isn't making it all up."

"And would that have really proven anything?" Corwin paused to blow a series of smoke rings with his cigar. "She could have read about the place years ago, relegated it to a zip file for future use, and forgotten all about it until now. Who knows? Maybe her grandparents came from Irmunsk. Maybe she heard them tell those stories when she was an infant and unconsciously stored them away. Such 'phenomena' have occurred and been documented."

I looked up mournfully and announced abruptly: "Claire came home tonight."

"Yes?"

"She looked fabulous. She threw me down on the bed, grabbed my crotch, and wanted me to make love to her, but…"

"Instead you came here with me? In pursuit of a half-baked, romantic fantasy inspired by some spoiled JAP's pre-marital jitters."

"Is that your professional opinion, Dr. Corwin?"

"Do me a favor, Herschel. Go home to your wife and pick up the pieces before it's too…"

Moskowitz teetered away from the dance floor, gasping for breath. Plopping down in his seat and clutching his cane with both hands, he was still humming the lyrics: "*Tanzen, tanzen, wieder.*" Then he whacked my arm playfully with the back of his hand and spoke: "It just occurred to me, Doctor. Don't know vy I didn't tink of it before, must be getting old. If you vant to know the details about Irmunsk, you should talk to Izzy Friedman's vidow. She's much older than me, but she might remember more. Give it a shot. Vat have you got to lose?"

I stared at Moskowitz in astonishment. Maybe the aerobic affect of the dancing had caused an adrenaline rush of blood to his memory-starved brain. But what did the cause matter? The old tailor had remembered Irmunsk! I was on my feet a second later, pumping his hand. "Thank you, thank you, thank you, Mr. Moskowitz. This means so much to me. How would I go about finding this Mrs. Friedman?"

"Try the phone book. They lived on Central Park Vest for years. Lotta money. Very fancy."

"Thank you again." I started to walk away, when I flashed on something and turned back to the old man with one last question. "What do you know about the Magiker Rebbe?"

Moskowitz stared at me in horror, as if I had removed my mask at the stroke of midnight and revealed my evil identity.

"Vat do you want from me?" he asked in a frail quavering voice.

I leaned in closer. "I only wanted to know if—"

"Get avay from me!" Moskowitz recoiled in terror. "Get avay!"

# THE LITTLE SISTER

THOSE LAST MOMENTS with Zvee Moskowitz had shaken me. On the drive back to Manhattan, the Pasha pointed out that the old man's paranoid behavior was consistent with encroaching dementia. He also urged me to make peace with Claire as soon as I got home, and even stopped at a Korean deli so I could buy her some flowers.

When I unlocked the front door, the apartment was dark, even the bathroom, where my wife always switched on the night-light before retiring. I called out in the darkness and waved the flowers in front of me like a magic wand, guaranteed to insure forgiveness.

Claire was gone. She had emptied out all her drawers and taken whatever she could with her. Three cardboard boxes, with her parents' Des Moines address scrawled in black Magic Marker, were stacked in the middle of the living room. She had certainly been busy in my absence.

On top of the glass dining table was a farewell note with her wedding ring next to it. In shock, I pulled out a chair, sat down at the table, and read what she had written.

*Harris:*

*I had hoped this separation would bring you to your senses. I was wrong. You're a man with too many secrets, and you don't do a very good job of keeping them—like your finances.*

*If you didn't want me to know about them, you shouldn't have left letters from the bank lying around. Did you really think I couldn't handle tough times? I'd have gone back to work in a flash if you had only confided in me. I'd have had a baby (babies) too, if you'd only talked about it. But it's all too late now.*

*I wouldn't worry about Barbara. You're the one who clearly needs help. Get it soon!*

*A carting company will come and pick up my boxes later this week.*

*It didn't have to end this way.*

*Claire*

Talk about conflicted! I felt as if a blend of rage, relief, depression, and delight had been tossed in an emotional Cuisinart and served up to me in a long-stemmed, frosted glass. Babies! She'd never once mentioned babies in the seven years we'd been together. Oh, Claire! Why did you have to come back early? Why couldn't you have been a little more understanding? And what the hell did you do with your loom? Strap it on your back?

Springing from the chair, I raced into the kitchen and began searching for the Manhattan telephone directory. What drawer did she keep it in? Linens, under the linens, right? Where had the linens gone? Had she taken them too? Or were they packed away in those boxes? Those antique linens had been a joint purchase—community property. What else had she taken without asking?

Forget it, Harris. Don't let the trail go cold. What was the old woman's name again? It was Friedman, Mrs. Izzy Friedman on Central Park West. Bingo! There was an Isadore Friedman listed at 101 Central Park West. What time was it? I looked at my watch; it was almost eleven, too late to call now, but first thing in the morning...Please, God! Let this be the answer.

I awoke at six the next morning, filled with all the excitement of the chase. I wanted to phone Mrs. Friedman immediately but forced myself to wait until eight. Speaking with the nurse-caretaker on duty, I muttered some gerontological mumbo jumbo as an excuse for my proposed visit. Then I phoned my office and left a message on the machine for Evelyn, saying I had the flu and would she please cancel my appointments for the day.

The doorman at 101 Central Park West pointed down a long tiled hallway and told me to walk to the end of it, where a beefy Ukrainian elevator operator with a shaved head was waiting to take me up.

"Going to fifteen?" he asked, as I stepped into his car.

"Yes."

"She don't get many visitors."

"Does she get out much?"

"Never. What the hell! She's 103."

A bony woman in her midfifties wearing a starched nurse's uniform opened the front door of the apartment. She introduced herself as Miss Metcalfe and informed me, rather disapprovingly, that Mrs. Friedman was quite excited by the prospect of my visit.

"Excitement is not good for her. It's the last thing in the world she needs," cautioned Miss Metcalfe. "Don't stay too long."

To be capable of excitement at such an advanced age would be a blessing, I thought, as I followed Miss Metcalfe down a long, dark hallway, whose sole illumination were the lights hanging over the museum-quality oil paintings lining the walls. Could that one actually be a Rembrandt? Who had Isadore Friedman been, and what had he done in life to amass such a fortune?

Miss Metcalfe led me into a vast sitting room, filled with priceless Chinese antiques and commanding a magnificent view of Central Park. A minute, shrunken figure dressed in an ornate green-and-orange brocaded Chinese ceremonial robe—looking remarkably like the Dowager Empress herself—stood beside a huge picture window. She was watching the snowflakes swirl about with childish enthusiasm.

"Your visitor is here," Miss Metcalfe all but shouted.

The ancient woman didn't turn around, but dismissed the nurse with a flick of her hand and then spoke imperiously, with the remnants of an Eastern European accent: "Why don't you go watch Hoda and Kathie Lee?"

Stung by the dismissal, Miss Metcalfe turned and left the sitting room.

Mrs. Friedman turned and advanced towards me, using an elegant cherry-wood cane with a carved ivory handle. Her face was wrinkled but her eyes twinkled, like those of a mischievous child. She examined me from head to toe, slowly, as if I were on the auction block and she was debating whether or not to purchase me—if she could get the right price.

"So tell me, Doctor Whatever-Your-Name-Is, have you decided what's wrong with me, besides too long a life?"

"You make it sound like a curse, Mrs. Friedman."

"What else do you call it when everyone you love is dead?" She stared at me, wondering what my response would be. When I said nothing, she asked: "Do you know Willard Scott?"

"Gerontologist?"

"Meteorologist, on the *Today Show*. You never watch Willard, with the bald head and the corny jokes? Never once did he put me on a label of Smucker's jam." When I didn't react, she explained: "You have to be a hundred to get your picture on the label."

"You don't look a day over ninety-nine."

"That's funny," cackled Mrs. Friedman. "Got to remember that one. But whom will I tell it to? Everyone I know is dead. Actually, I'm 103."

"No!"

"Yes. It's not such a big deal anymore, even to Willard Scott, who couldn't care less. So, what do you want from me, Doctor?"

"I was hoping we could have a little chat and share some memories. You are originally from Irmunsk, aren't you?"

Her eyes narrowed suspiciously: "Who told you that?"

"Zvee Moskowitz."

Mrs. Friedman cackled again, then began to cough. "Is that *alter kocker* still alive?"

"He says you're his senior."

"Please! Zvee Moskowitz was born old."

"How long ago did you leave Irmunsk?"

"In the last century. What? You need a date?" She did an adagio with her fingers reminiscent of Edwin's invisible keyboard and came up with the elusive number: "It was 1924, with my first husband."

"Husband? But you were barely in your…"

"I had just turned seventeen. They threw us out of the nest young back then. My marriage was a debt of honor."

Lost in the maze of memory for a moment, she made her way back to the present: "Would you like a cigarette, Doctor?"

"I don't smoke."

"Me neither. I just light them up to get a rise out of people. 'Still smoking at 103? Tsk, tsk, tsk.'" Her veiny, claw-like hands fumbled with an exquisite Chinese cigarette case. She managed to get it open and removed a Gitanes Blondes.

"Have you been to China?" I asked. With fascination, I watched as the centenarian gripped a silver table lighter in the shape of a dragon and with a trembling hand, finally managed to light her cigarette.

"Never," she replied. "But I brought China to me." Her breathing came in flutters, as though the simple act of lighting a cigarette had been a Herculean feat. "So tell me, what possible interest could a good-looking, modern person like yourself have in a little backwater town beyond the Pale? What they used to call a *shtetl*. Are you acquainted with this word?"

"Yes, I am. And fascination with lost cultures is not entirely unique—countless volumes by anthropologists are a testament to that." I was rambling and could see her eyelids start to droop. She was very, very old. "Granted it was the last century, Mrs. Friedman, but..." This was such a long shot. It was over eighty years ago. What if she didn't know or remember anything? What the hell! I had nothing to lose. "Did you ever know or can you remember, when you lived in Irmunsk, a young woman, a girl, named Leah Littman?"

The burning cigarette dropped abruptly from Mrs. Friedman's trembling hand onto the priceless Ch'ing Dynasty carpet. I lunged to retrieve it before the rug started to burn. A second later, I rose and helped steady the tiny ancient woman, whom I had so clearly upset.

"Let me sit down."

"Of course."

Easing her onto a lacquered Dragon Throne, I crouched beside her. "Can I get you some water?"

Mrs. Friedman shook her head, turned her face toward the wall, and in a barely audible whisper said: "Leah Littman...was my sister, my older sister. She died a long, long time ago...in Irmunsk."

My gasp of amazement must have been deafening. Shifting around to face the old woman, I could see tears running down her face and cried aloud: "My God! You're Molly, little Molly. You're still alive! Your father was Moishe, and your mother was Hannah."

"How...how do you know this?" Her hands were clawing at the sleeve of my jacket.

Questions began to tumble out of my mouth like nickels from a slot machine: "Did Leah finally marry Yochanan Levy? What ever happened to Shimon? And what about the Magiker Rebbe?"

Lifting a tiny fist to her mouth to stifle a wail of fear, Molly gazed into my eyes with the same terror that had engulfed Zvee Moskowitz the night before. "These names...so many years ago. How could you know these names? Who are you? How could you ever have known about Shimon?"

"Forgive me, Mrs. Friedman. Please! I never meant to upset you. These people, and their stories, have been racing through my mind for days now. Were they real or not? Was I losing my mind? But it's true, all true. You are Leah's sister."

She pointed a trembling hand in the direction of a priceless Bai-wood liquor cabinet on the other side of the room and gasped: "Please! A whiskey!"

I dashed to the cabinet and returned a moment later with a Waterford decanter filled with Irish whiskey and a matching tumbler. I was about to pour her a shot when I remembered: "Do you have a heart condition?"

"I do now. Better make it a big one, Doctor. Thank you." Mrs. Friedman took the tumbler from me and proceeded to sip the drink slowly. "How is it possible that you could know these things?"

"What if I said Leah told me...everything?"

"Do you know a good psychiatrist?"

"I am a psychiatrist. Molly..."

I took her hands in mine and for the next hour, as she lay stretched out on a mountain of pillows atop an opium bed, told her all the unearthly events that had occurred since Sherman Rosenbaum first appeared in my office.

When I had completed my tale, Molly shook her head, mystified. "And you say all these things really began last November, in Vermont?"

"Yes. Barbara skied into the woods and disappeared."

"In the falling snow, she vanished in the snow. *Vey iz mir*! How could it be possible? And yet it all makes sense."

"What does? Please, tell me, Molly."

Molly sipped her whiskey and began: "It was the day of Leah's wedding. How like a beautiful princess my sister looked, Doctor. Papa had spared no expense to have her bridal gown made. He couldn't lose face, as the Chinese say. Her husband-to-be was the son of the richest man in the *shtetl*. When I told her Yochanan was the luckiest man in the world, she smiled enigmatically and said that in a few hours he might be the unluckiest.

"I told her she was talking poppycock. Papa and Mr. Levy had exchanged signed contracts. They'd already merged their two businesses. Leah raised that stubborn chin of hers and said: 'They haven't merged me.' 'What are you talking about?' I asked. 'Aren't you going to go through with it?'

"Leah didn't answer, but asked me if I loved her. 'Of course,' I said. 'Forever.' Then she asked me to go for a walk with her because she was very nervous. We went through the sitting room where Mama and Papa were dressed in their wedding finery. Leah told Mama she was feeling faint and needed a little fresh air. Mama warned her to be careful not to let Yochanan see her. It was bad luck. 'Don't worry,' said Leah. 'He won't see me.'

"We walked to the edge of woods outside town, and snow began falling. Leah bent down, hugged me, and told me to go home. I stared at the ground and asked her if she was meeting Shimon. She replied that she loved me, said good-bye, and walked alone into the woods. The snow fell thicker and heavier. It was the beginning of a terrible storm. I was afraid to leave her there, Doctor. But I was freezing to death and all I had on was my little bridesmaid's dress. So I returned home with a heavy heart. I never forgave myself."

"Did Shimon turn up?" I had poured myself a glass of Irish by this time and was as engrossed by Molly's tale as I had been by Leah's narrative in my office.

"Who knows?" said Molly. "Perhaps he did. Perhaps they walked past each other in the snowstorm. My father by then was in a rage. He set off after her into the woods. When he finally found her, he dragged her home to be married, snowstorm or not. Leah seemed fine but got sick a week later, right after Purim, and died. Some say it was pneumonia; others, a broken heart."

"And that was the end of it?"

"Not quite. Isaac Levy felt he had been swindled; he wanted the partnership agreement dissolved. My father refused: a deal was a deal. Finally, they went to old Rabbi Himmelman and, after two days of shouting and screaming, they reached a compromise. On my seventeenth birthday, I would marry Yochanan Levy, and the contract would be honored. Which is what happened. And afterward we packed our bags and came to America. Poor Yochanan died two years later in the terrible pandemic. Later I met and married Izzy Friedman. We had sixty wonderful years together."

Molly shut her eyes for a long time, and I was convinced she had gone to sleep when her lids fluttered open once more, and she beckoned me to draw near. "When Leah got sick, she looked horrible—like a dead person. But she insisted I shouldn't worry. Everything was going to be all right. 'How?' I asked. Even on her deathbed Leah whispered to me it was going to be all right. That's when she pressed a piece of paper into my hand. Please, Doctor! Help me down from here."

Gently placing my hand on her spine, I raised Molly into a sitting position and helped her from the opium bed; she seemed almost weightless. Leaning on my arm for support, she tottered toward an apothecary's cabinet. Opening a secret drawer, she withdrew a tattered, faded scrap of paper.

"I kept this ever since. Don't ask me why. Be careful, Doctor. It's fragile, like me."

I unfolded the paper and instantly recognized the drawing on it and the number 613 at the bottom. "This is the Tree of Life."

Molly stared at me in shock: "How could you know that?"

"Barbara—my patient—showed me the same drawing last week. She said the Magiker Rebbe gave it to her. Did you ever meet him?"

"Never." Molly shook her head adamantly. "He was like the Devil. He could make spells, raise people from the dead, and seduce women away from their husbands. He made five women in Apt pregnant at the same time, or so the stories went. Our parents forbade us to ever go near him, although he never set foot inside our *shtetl*. The rabbis forbade him entry, so he lived with his followers among the gentiles."

"The whole thing baffles me, Molly. How can my patient, a vain and vapid creature so unlike your sister, pretend to be Leah and know so much about you and your family?"

Molly leaned on her cherry-wood cane and rocked back and forth. She chose her words carefully before she spoke: "Doctor, have you ever heard of a *dybbuk*, an evil spirit of a dead person that has possessed the body of someone living?"

"Molly, what you're suggesting is impossible."

"Why?"

"Because this is the twenty-first century. Because..."

"A snowstorm is a snowstorm is a snowstorm, plain and simple fact. It's just frozen water, back then or now. It has no supernatural properties. Or does it?"

My mind went back to my first encounter with Leah. The snow was falling that evening on Fifth Avenue, when she came up to me and spoke what I now know to be Yiddish. When did she learn to speak English? Was it when she decided to take up residence inside of Barbara? But could Leah be a *dybbuk*? There didn't seem to be even the slightest thing evil about Leah.

No, that wasn't possible. I didn't believe a word of it. But I knew, in order to move forward, I would have to let go of every bit of science I had ever learned. I would have to acknowledge what that Elizabethan rabbi, William Shakespeare, had written: *"There are more things in heaven and earth..."*

I remembered the word Leah had said to Lafferty in my office, and he to me in the hospital—*bashert*, soul mates. Those years ago in Evanston, had Suzanne and I been *bashert*? And had I taken the wrong path by not pursuing her? Why hadn't I made that extra effort to contact her again? What good had it done me—either of us—to turn our precious moment in time into an aching memory? What was the lesson? What did we learn?

I turned to Molly and spoke as if I were thinking out loud, using logic to solve a problem, only one not of this world: "Barbara disappears into the woods—zooming at great speed—and collides with Leah's soul, which is coming from another dimension."

"See? Not so crazy. You're a psychiatrist, a man of science, but you managed to figure it out." A smile momentarily erased the wrinkles from Molly's face. "Oh, Doctor! I feel as if a great weight has been lifted from my heart, for the first time in ninety years."

"She's trying to find Shimon," I said. "She's come back to find her lost love. Does that really make any sense?"

"Why not?" Molly asked. "He was the love of her life."

"*Bashert?*"

"Yes. Exactly."

"But Shimon is gone—dead. He can't come back."

"Do you know that for certain, Doctor?"

I poured myself another glass of Irish and silently debated the question for a moment. Then I turned to the ancient woman, clutching the faded Tree of Life fragment in her hand, and asked: "Would you like to meet her?"

"What are you saying?"

"Would you like to see your sister again?"

"That such a thing could be possible." Molly shook her head, struggling to accept what her heart secretly prayed for. "I loved Leah more than anything in the world. I worshipped her. Not a day has gone by in over ninety years that I haven't…" Taking my free hand, she kissed it and then looked up at me. "Do it, Doctor. Bring her here to me!"

\* \* \*

Walking out of 101 Central Park West after leaving Molly, I felt a powerful sense of elation. Was this how scientists and mystics felt when they crossed into territories for which the empirical world had no map?

Then I saw Bizet, not the composer but Edwin's dog. It had to be him. How many miniature Whippets would be running around Manhattan wearing Ralph Lauren quilted vests? And how had he made it all the way downtown on his own?

I thought of Edwin lying on the gurney in agony—all for the love of this dog. I had to do something. I called to Bizet. The trembling canine stared at me with a mix of curiosity and fear, as I bolted across the street to retrieve him. A delivery truck driver slammed on his brakes, seconds away from running me over.

"What are you, fuckin' crazy?" shouted the bald, unshaven driver, as he spat out the cigar wedged in the corner of his mouth and jumped down from the truck.

"Sorry. I was trying to…"

"Get yourself killed?"

"No, not at all. My friend's dog has run away, and I was…"

"You're drunk!" said the driver, pointing a finger at me. He turned to the small crowd assembling on the street—one was recording video of me on her smartphone—and repeated: "He's drunk!"

"Don't be ridiculous!"

"You smell of booze, pal! At eleven o'clock in the morning."

I had no comeback, not after two tumblers full of Molly Friedman's Irish whiskey.

"Please, don't!" I said. "There's no need for that."

"You came this close, buddy!" The truck driver held his thumb and index finger a millimeter apart, before he climbed back into his truck and drove away.

By this time, of course, Bizet was gone.

# THE SLIPPERY SLOPE

CONSIDERING MY BRUSH with death moments earlier, I was amazed by my powers of recovery. If anything, I felt renewed by the experience. But why I had tried to rescue Bizet remained a mystery to me. Had it really been my responsibility to return the poor, addled Whippet to its equally addled master? Perhaps the whole thing was a metaphor: You can't save everyone, Harris. Heal yourself first. But what was wrong with me? Nothing. Here I was on the verge of an extraordinary mystical, medical, and scientific breakthrough that could potentially benefit mankind.

As I walked along Amsterdam Avenue, I readied my acceptance speech for the ceremony in Oslo—wouldn't Claire regret walking out on a future Nobel Prize winner—when my reverie was interrupted by a fist rapping from inside the window of a Thai restaurant. What a wonderful surprise! It was Butri, whom I hadn't seen in ages. Was this a fifth noodle shop? Oh, why had I sold my interest in the business?

"When did you open this one?" I said, hoping Butri wouldn't notice the envy in my voice as I entered the establishment. We embraced, and she settled me into a corner booth.

"This old!" Butri replied dismissively. "Gotta be maybe eighteen month. You want soup?"

"Perfect."

"How you wife?"

"She went to Tahiti."

"Without you?" Butri frowned. "No good."

"I couldn't go. Too much work."

"You got other woman?" Butri eyed me suspiciously.

"Of course not. I love my wife."

Butri fixed me with a look that only a woman who had been cheated on could give a man.

"I bring soup." There was an element of disgust in her voice as she walked away from my booth.

This chance encounter with my former cleaning lady dampened the euphoria I had felt earlier. Maybe I wouldn't win the Nobel Prize after all...

Back at the office, Evelyn recited what seemed to be an endless list of woeful messages from the patients whose appointments I had canceled at the last minute. And she presented me with three messages from Martin Corwin. "Urgent" was underlined three times on the final one.

"Is this underlining your editorializing or his?" I asked, holding up the pink memo to a clearly disapproving Evelyn.

"Please, Dr. Strider. Call him back."

The word "hello" had barely floated out of my mouth when Corwin laced into me. "Where the hell have you been all day?"

"A meeting outside the office."

"Evelyn said you had canceled all your appointments with less than twenty-four hours notice."

"What's with the irate tone, Marty? It's the patients who have to give us a day's notice."

"Don't you have a responsibility to them, as well, Doctor? Haven't they been waiting all week to see you? Hmm? To unburden their traumas and terrors on a supposedly sympathetic listener and, hopefully, a guide to their recovery?"

"Was that little speech for real?"

"Yes! Does it come as a surprise to you? I take my responsibilities as a doctor very seriously."

"Are you suggesting I don't? What's this all about?"

"Meet me at the Boathouse in Central Park—fifteen minutes."

"It's freezing outside, Marty. Could we possibly grab a coffee somewhere instead?"

"The Boathouse."

The wind on Fifth Avenue chilled me to the bone as soon as I left the building. I was ravenous and still a little drunk from the two glasses of whiskey I had downed so quickly at Molly Friedman's apartment.

A street vendor stood outside the Seventy-Ninth Street entrance to the park, selling steaming hot dogs. I counted out my change with trembling hands and then lathered the dog with a generous combination of mustard and ketchup. I had barely set foot inside the park when I tripped on a crack in the pavement and spilled everything down the front of my Hugo Boss cashmere overcoat.

Watching my al fresco lunch lying pitifully on the ground, I waited for a moment to see if Bizet would suddenly appear and devour it. Don't ask me why; perhaps I thought that a minor miracle would lead to a major one. My efforts to wipe the large yellow and red stains from my coat, while waiting for the miniature Whippet to appear, merely succeeded in driving the condiments deeper into the expensive fabric.

As I approached Corwin at the Boathouse, I must have looked like a total reprobate, with filthy stains on my coat and whiskey on my breath.

"Jesus, Harris!" The Pasha was repelled by my appearance. "What's happening to you?"

"I dropped my hot dog." My response was more pitiful than I had meant it to sound.

"Are you drunk?"

"What's all the mystery, Marty?" I pointedly ignored his reference to alcohol. "Why have you dragged me out here in the cold like this?"

Corwin threaded his arm through mine and steered me away from the Boathouse toward the frozen lake. Walking in silence past the huge bronze statue of Hans Christian Andersen and his immortal Ugly Duckling, the Pasha finally spoke. "There was a visitor waiting for me when I got home last night."

"Nurse Flanagan?"

"No, your wife. She was standing outside my building like the original orphan of the storm. Totally bereft."

"Did she have her loom with her?"

"It's not funny, Harris."

"I'm not trying to be. Her loom was missing when I got home and I couldn't imagine Claire carting the damned thing around on her back."

"Have you been self-medicating?"

"Where did she stay?"

"Who?"

"The orphan of the storm. Claire."

"On my couch. Okay? She wanted to go to a hotel but she didn't have a reservation anywhere, so I insisted…"

"I bet you did."

"Knock it off, Harris. Maureen was with me. I felt sorry for Claire, okay? She was never my favorite, as you know, but she deserved better treatment from you than she got last night."

"Sorry she enmeshed you in our domestic differences but…"

"She did no such thing. If nothing else, Claire is a realist. She knows the marriage is over, but amazingly—or masochistically—the woman still cares for you. She's also convinced you've taken leave of your senses."

"What do you think, Marty?"

By that time we'd walked the circumference of the lake and were standing in front of the bronze statues depicting Alice, the Mad Hatter, and the March Hare.

"The past month has brought an extraordinary change in your behavior, Harris. Maybe it's early midlife crisis, maybe the seven-year itch. But the relentless professional gravity of yours, which I so often teased you about but secretly admired, has been replaced by an irresponsible sense of frivolity and recklessness." Corwin had chosen his words succinctly, as if he were on the record (or wearing a wire).

"Thank you, Marty. At least you had the good grace not to mention my 'all-consuming obsession.'"

Corwin stared at me, took a deep breath and shook his head in despair. "Have you stopped for a moment to examine your behavior? Or are you just spinning around on this chaotic emotional carousel? Need I remind you, Harry, what a slippery slope you're careening down?"

"Oh, Marty, stop mixing metaphors! Are you so jaded that the possibility of a true medical and scientific breakthrough can't excite you? Imagine being on the brink of a discovery that could change the cold, clinical face of psychiatry as we've known it!"

"Am I to assume such a soul-changing experience has happened to you?"

"Yes!" I bobbed my head up and down like a dime-store dachshund and clutched Corwin's sleeve. In hushed tones I confided: "I've brought someone back from the dead."

"Vincent Price couldn't get away with a line like that! What the hell are you talking about?"

"She's a *dybbuk*."

"Oh, Harry, Harry, Harry! Do you even know what a *dybbuk* is? You've gone overboard as a Hasidic groupie. You'll be growing *payot* and a beard next."

"This isn't a joke, Marty. I've met her sister."

"Whose sister?"

"Leah's."

"Is she dead, too?"

"No! She lives over there." I raised my right hand and pointed gleefully in the direction of Central Park West.

Corwin froze on the spot, shook his head, and nodded at the huge bronzes of Alice and the Mad Tea Party gang. "See those statues?"

"Of course."

"Do you think those creatures really exist?"

I laughed. "It's not the same thing."

"It fucking well is! You've created this *shtetl* fantasy for your own inexplicable—"

"I didn't make up Irmunsk! Or Leah!"

"Tell me something, Harris. Does your patient visit you as Leah all the time now?"

"Yes."

"Never as Barbara?"

"No."

"Uh-huh. Where does she change her clothes? Is there some mystic phone booth near your office where she switches to her secret identity? And how does she go home? As Leah or Barbara?"

"I don't know."

"Don't you care about that detail, Dr. Strider? Or are you as caught up in this little game of *amour fou* as she is—*Last Tango on Fifth Avenue.* No sex involved, right? Hello, did you hear me? Oh, please, tell me you haven't *shtupped* her. Have you? I know the temptation, kiddo. I came close to nailing a few of mine on the carpet a couple of times, but I knew Hippocrates and the New York State Licensing Board wouldn't approve."

"Believe me, Marty. It's not what you think. I love her. I want to marry her. We're *bashert!*"

"*Bashert?* You're crazy!"

"Why? Is it the age thing? Every other man on the East Side is married to a trophy wife, twenty years his junior."

"That's not what I'm talking about. How do you expect to marry a woman who's engaged to someone else?"

"Oh, Marty. You still don't get it." I shook my head sadly. "I don't want to marry Barbara."

"How are you planning to get around that problem?"

"What problem?"

"The girl you claim you're in love with lives in Barbara's body. How are you planning to have her evicted?"

"There are ways," I said, "to stop them from sharing the same body."

Corwin held his breath for what seemed an eternity, exhaled, and kneaded his eyebrows with his fingers. Then he said: "This game isn't fun anymore, okay? Why don't we forget the notion of midlife crisis and just blame it on the asbestos in your building? How about that? Whatever works. But I'm begging you, Harris, take a break—from your practice, from New York, and from her. "

# THE REUNION

For the rest of the week, I callously and haphazardly canceled regular appointments and insulted and belittled those patients who had the bad fortune to discuss their foibles and neuroses with me. Barbara's failure to appear didn't help my disposition. No phone calls from her. No messages. To make matters worse, Molly Friedman phoned Thursday morning demanding to know why I had led her on.

"Coming to my house like you did, under false pretenses, with some cockamamie fairy tale about my poor dead sister. Promising you could make her materialize. What kind of sick monster are you? Toying with a lonely old woman's precious memories. Do you think I'm some kind of greenie fresh off the boat that you can swindle with a séance scam? Mrs. Isadore Friedman still has some powerful friends in this city; they could have you up on charges and your license revoked. Prison even!"

"Please, Mrs. Friedman! Molly! No one is toying with you. I'm no swindler. Everything is the truth. Please! Be patient a little longer. I'll find the girl and bring her to you."

At the end of my rope, I made a desperate phone call to the offices of Condé Nast. Barbara's assistant hemmed and hawed before informing me (off the record) that her boss had an appointment at Maison Gilles. I grabbed my newly dry-cleaned Hugo Boss overcoat (they'd charged me a fortune to remove the mustard and ketchup stains) from the closet and hailed a cab outside.

Ten minutes later I stormed into the trendy hair salon on Lexington Avenue in the upper Sixties.

"Got an appointment?" A pasty-faced Israeli girl with green-and-purple hair sat at the reception desk. She so outrageously mangled her vowels that I could barely understand a word she said.

"Is Barbara Warren here?"

"She's in the back with Gilles. But he can't be disturbed when—hey, wait a minute! Where are you going? Didn't you hear me?"

The future Mrs. Gordon Jacobs was seated in a station at the rear of the shop and staring adoringly at herself in the floor-to-ceiling mirror. She howled with laughter as an elfin creature with dyed blond hair and a long droopy nose—dressed in skintight black jeans and a black T-shirt—danced around her, snipping bits of hair and whispering bits of outrageous gossip.

"Hi, Doctor! Do you get your hair styled here too? What's with the long face? Oh-oh! Bet I'm on the naughty list, huh? Sor-ry. I should have phoned. My bad."

"Therapy can't be interrupted so blithely, Barbara. It's a lengthy and serious process."

"Oh!" squealed the hair stylist in a high-pitched, unidentifiable European accent. "Is this the shrink you were telling me about?"

"May I speak with you alone, Barbara?"

"Can't it wait till after the wedding? I'm really tied up for the next little while, 'kay?"

"When is the wedding?"

"Didn't you get your invitation? It's next week."

"How is that possible?"

"Time flies, huh?"

"Would it offend you, Doctor, if I finished what I started?" Gilles stood with his elfin fists grinding into his hips.

"Say good-bye, Mr. Snips." I growled, struggling to keep my temper under control.

"What did he call me?"

"Gilles, sweetie honey, chill. Mwah-mwah-mwah. I'll handle this."

The hair stylist bared his upper lip over his teeth; in what he must have thought was a threatening pose. Finally he sashayed towards the front of the salon.

"Okay. I'm busted. Put me in the stocks. Get out ye old ducking stool. My bad, little Barbara did it again. But, what the hey! A girl only gets married once—knock wood. Like, you've been a doll, Dr. Strider. I'm sleeping better, feeling better. Gordo and I are just *sooo* grateful for all the things you've ..."

I seized her rigidly by the shoulders and struggled to make eye contact. But she stubbornly averted my gaze.

"Leah!" I sounded like a dog trainer reprimanding his prize bitch. "Look at me!"

"What do you...?"

"I want you to come out, Leah. Please, don't hide from me."

"You're acting weird, Doctor."

"Are you angry with me, Leah? Did I say something to upset you?"

"Who the hell is Leah? You're scaring me."

Barbara shook loose from my grip and backed away, looking around desperately for something with which to defend herself. I advanced and seized both her wrists in a tight grip.

"Let go of me, Doctor! This is so uncool. You're, like, cutting off my circulation. Wanna hear me scream the place down? Gordon's coming to pick me up any minute and he'll...he'll..."

Her angry energy dissipated like a balloon with a slow leak, and she started to fall forward. I caught her just in time. Once she steadied herself, she brushed her hair off her face with her hand and gazed into my eyes. "Hello, Rebbe." She smiled and gave me the fullness of those incredible eyes.

"Hello, Leah."

"Where are we?" Leah stared around the brightly lit hair salon.

"Shh! Shh! Don't worry. We're going to visit someone very special."

Wrapping my arm around her shoulder, I led her toward the front of the salon. Gilles stepped forward in a last-ditch attempt to stop me, but I shoved him to one side and continued out the front door onto Lexington.

"Is she on drugs or something?" asked the purple-and-green-haired receptionist.

Gilles followed us out onto the street from a safe distance, held up his cell phone, and videoed me as I ushered his client into the back of a taxi. Then I saw him talking on his phone—presumably to Gordon Jacobs.

Leah held my hand tightly in the backseat, like a child on a surprise outing with her father. I felt lightheaded at the proximity to my beloved and the prospect of what was waiting for us on Central Park West.

A no-nonsense West Indian woman named Violet opened the front door of the Friedman apartment. I asked what had happened to Miss Metcalfe and was informed curtly: "She be gone." Having experienced Molly Friedman's wrath firsthand, I wondered with what degree of frequency she replaced her nurse-caretakers, and how long it would take before Violet "be gone" too.

Leah paused to admire the priceless paintings and ran her fingers along the expensive flocked wallpaper. "Such beautiful things," she whispered.

Calling out for Molly, I led Leah into the Chinese throne room and announced, "Here's someone special come to visit!" Leah moved gingerly about the spacious room, admiring and examining the priceless objets d'art, tapestries, and mementos. Perched on her lacquered Dragon Throne, Molly watched the enchanted girl's every movement like a hawk waiting for its prey to make the foolish move that would cost it its life. Standing next to the attentive centenarian, I beamed with delight at the incredible human drama unfolding before my eyes.

Molly tugged on my jacket sleeve, and I looked down at her questioningly.

"So, Doctor?" she asked. "Where's Leah?"

"Don't you recognize her?"

Molly glared up at me with disdain. "That's not my sister. Leah looked nothing like her."

"Not physically, of course, but her soul, Molly…her soul."

"What! Are you starting up again, Dr. Fast Talker? Think I didn't work Coney Island as a kid? There were better hustlers than you on the boardwalk: two dimes for a nickel. I meant what I said on the phone. You try to pull a fast one on me, and I'll—"

Her harangue was interrupted by a faint cry from Leah, who had been examining a collection of silver-framed photos on top of the apothecary's cabinet a few feet away. I rushed to her side. With a trembling hand, she showed me an ornate oval frame that held a faded tintype of an elderly couple, obviously posed in a photographer's studio.

"Do you know who these people are?" I pointed to the shrunken, gray-bearded man and his frail wisp of a wife.

"Mama and Papa but…they're so old here. Papa's beard was black like coal."

Molly struggled to her feet and with difficulty navigated her way toward the cabinet. Leah was examining another framed photograph, with even greater confusion than the previous one: a girl in her late teens aboard the Staten Island Ferry. She was standing next to a thin, anemic-looking man in his late twenties.

"Recognize them?" asked Molly suspiciously.

"She looks a little like my sister Molly, but older. How can this be? Molly is only ten. What kind of magic is this?"

"And the man?" asked Molly, whose voice was barely a whisper. "Do you know who he is?"

"Of course." Leah giggled. "That's Yochanan Levy. Poor Yochanan." She turned to stare into Molly's eyes, and for a moment, their thoughts both returned to that unforgettable wedding night in the winter of 1912.

Everyone in Irmunsk was crammed into Moishe Littman's house to celebrate his daughter's wedding. A klezmer trio played joyously in a corner as the guests pumped the hand and slapped the back of skinny, acne-ridden Yochanan Levy. His top hat seemed in constant danger of toppling from his head with all the vibrations his frail body was absorbing.

Rayzel the Shadchen wandered through the party, pausing to congratulate herself, when kudos weren't forthcoming, for the splendid match she had so skillfully engineered. Molly and the other children gorged themselves on rugelach and sugar-studded honey cookies, until a five-year-old boy named Zvee Moskowitz warned: "Better save some for Rabbi Himmelman. They're his favorites." Molly stuck her tongue out at Zvee in reply.

Every smiling face at the wedding party shone with happiness and goodwill, except Leah's. Finally Moishe Littman, unable to tolerate his daughter's behavior another second, steered her off into the busy kitchen and berated her.

"Would it kill you to smile a little? Everyone is talking about your *farbisinna punim*."

"Let them talk."

"This is a *simcha*, daughter, not a shiva. It is meant to be a joyous occasion. What's wrong with you?"

"I don't love him, Papa," Leah answered defiantly.

"You married him. The love will grow."

"How? Look at him, so pale and fragile."

"Yochanan is a nice boy," said her father. "A good provider, not like that *luftmensch* I chased away."

"Shimon? What did you do to Shimon?"

"It was made clear to him that he had no place in your future, what with his poetry and his mysticism. He's under the spell of that Magiker, the Devil's disciple, who lives among the gentiles. He is the same degenerate they drove out of Apt for impregnating all those married women. What kind of a life would you have with an outcast like that? So I sent your Shimon away and paid him well to go."

"Shimon took money from you?"

"No! He threw the money in my face. " Littman snorted. "An even bigger fool than I thought."

Leah began sobbing. Littman's face turned beet red with embarrassment.

"Stop it! Stop it at once! Do you hear me? I won't have you ruin this wedding for some nobody from nowhere."

The wedding guests began a rhythmic clapping of hands. Yochanan Levy was hoisted aloft on a wooden chair and carried round the sitting room. Seconds later the guests began chanting "Leah! Leah! Leah!"

Rayzel dashed into the kitchen searching for Leah. Mistaking her tears of sorrow for those of joy, she seized her hand. "Come! Come! Your husband's waiting." She dragged the unsmiling bride into the sitting room, where the circle of merrymakers awaited her.

The reluctant Leah was placed onto another chair and hoisted off the ground to join her new husband. Yochanan reached out a hand to hold hers, reproving her at the same time. "Smile! Smile! It's our wedding day."

But Yochanan had reached out too far in his attempt to grab hold of his rebellious bride. He lost his balance and tumbled off his chair onto to the floor. The guests gasped in unison. Leah burst out laughing.

Almost a century later, the spirit of Leah Littman was still alive and laughing inside the body of Barbara Warren. She struggled to control her mirth at the distant memory but failed.

"Yochanan the Yutz!" Leah inhaled deeply; she tried to control herself but merely burst into deeper gales of laughter. "He fell on top of a wineglass and spent his wedding night with the town doctor pulling little shards of glass out of his *tuchus*."

"It's true. It's true," whispered Molly, nodding her head up and down. "He had a little scar on his right buttock until the day he died."

Leah turned to Molly in amazement and asked: "How do you know that?"

"Shouldn't I know where my husband had such a scar?"

"Your husband?"

"I'm Molly." The old woman was bubbling over with joy. "Doctor, forgive me. Everything you told me was true. How else could these things be known?" She turned her attention back to Leah. "I am Molly. And you are my beloved sister. God has sent you back to me. It's a miracle. All those years ago…the Tree of Life…that's what you were trying to tell me, wasn't it, Doctor? *Meine schwester*, my big sister, God has sent you back to me." She extended her frail bony arms to the young woman.

"Molly!" Leah stared in horror at the old woman gazing at her so adoringly. "What are you saying? How could you be Molly? She's only six years old. What kind of a game are you playing?" She turned to me, hoping I could explain the nightmare. "Rebbe? What does this mean?"

"Please, don't be frightened," I said, struggling to find words that might reassure her. "There's no easy explanation for all this. But, try to understand that by some…some unexplained phenomenon, a miracle like Molly says, you've come back to us, Leah."

"It's true! It's true!" Molly impetuously threw her arms around Leah at that moment. She panicked and violently shoved the old lady away.

"Where am I?" Barbara Warren was back inside her own body now and looking around the Chinese room in terror and confusion. "What the hell is this place? How did I get here?"

Molly had banged her arm against a giant stone Buddha and fell on the carpet whimpering. "I just wanted to hug you, Leah. So many years since we were together."

"What the hell's she talking about?" Cold and pitiless Barbara looked past the injured old woman and asked. "Why did you bring me here, Doctor?"

"Relax, Leah. Everything's—"

"Don't start with that Leah shit again, 'kay? What's going on? Like, who is this old woman?"

"I'm your sister," wailed Molly. "Don't you know me?"

"She's crazy!" shrieked Barbara. "You both are!"

"Calm down, Leah."

"Stop calling me that! Get me the hell out of here! Right now! Do you hear me? I mean it. Get me out, or I'll scream the fucking place down!"

I reached out a hand to calm her down. Barbara leapt back as if she'd touched an exposed electric wire and ran screaming for help from the room.

Violet emerged from the library to investigate the commotion and tried blocking the corridor with her considerable girth.

"What you done to my Mrs. Molly?"

"Get out of my way!" screamed Barbara.

"Where you running to, missy? You ain't goin' nowhere."

Violet grabbed hold of the hysterical girl in her beefy arms. Barbara, in turn, whipped the Jimmy Choo pump off her right foot and brought the stiletto heel down on the nurse-caretaker's left forearm. Violet howled in pain and released her grip on Barbara, who took advantage of the moment to escape out the front door.

I raced out of the building in pursuit, just as Gordon Jacobs was assisting his weeping and hysterical fiancée into a taxi.

"Barbara! Barbara, please wait!" I dashed across the street to try and stop them.

Gordon saw the look of terror on his fiancée's face as I drew closer. Grabbing me by the lapels of my overcoat, he lifted me off the ground and hissed: "Stay away from her! Do you understand?"

"Trust me, Gordon. It's…it's not what you think. No way would I ever put Barbara in danger, I assure you."

"And I assure you, Strider, if you ever come near her again, I'll have your license, your teeth, and your legs."

# THE OBSESSION

L EAH. LEAH. LEAH. Where was she? I desperately needed to see her again. Things couldn't be left the way they had been on Central Park West. What time did Condé Nast open? My bedside clock read 10:00 a.m. I had been asleep for eleven hours. How was that possible? Was it emotional exhaustion or post-traumatic stress? I kept reliving that horrible nightmare scene at Molly's apartment, followed by Gordon threatening me on the street with such obvious relish.

I grabbed the phone and called Condé Nast. A robotic automated voice told me to press 318 to speak to Barbara's assistant, who informed me that Ms. Warren wouldn't be in all day. Anything wrong? I asked. Some health issue? When the assistant asked who was calling, I hung up. What was Barbara's home number? Evelyn would have it on file.

"Where are you?" Evelyn sounded unusually suspicious after I announced myself with the formal "Harris Strider here."

"At home. Why? Is something wrong?"

"Bronson Maynard is in your office. He's not happy. He took the train down from Rhinebeck and isn't planning to leave until—"

"'Until he jolly well gets here.'" Bronson Maynard was a not very talented novelist and closeted homosexual. His oeuvre was intellectual bodice rippers, set in the court of Charles II and devoid of any historical accuracy—or interesting sex. "Tell him I can't make it."

"He's threatening to report you to the Psychiatric Board," whispered Evelyn.

"Oh! I'm going to go poopie in my pants. Tell Bronnie that what he's really feeling is misdirected anger towards his highly successful and abusive father. I wrote a paper on a similar case five years ago. Check the files, scan it, and e-mail it to him. He'll hate being a cliché, but it'll snap him right out of it."

"I'm worried about you, Doctor."

"Aren't you sweet, Evelyn! That's so thoughtful. Have I ever told you how much I really appreciate you? No? Let me take a moment now and—"

"The police phoned here this morning."

"What did they want?" My frivolous mood collapsed to earth like the Hindenburg over New Jersey.

"They wanted to know if you were presently attending a Mrs. Isadore Friedman. I told them there was no such patient on your books."

"Has something happened to her? This Mrs. Friedman?"

A wave of nausea seeped over me like an oil spill. I was so intent on intercepting Barbara that I had neglected to check on Molly's condition after she had banged into the stone Buddha. It had only been her arm. But at 103 that was the equivalent of a hit-and-run collision. Dear God, let her be all right!

"They didn't say. Do you know this Mrs. Friedman?"

Ignoring the question, I asked: "Have we got a home number for Barbara Warren?"

Evelyn gave me the number and I dialed it a second later. A recorded message from Verizon informed me that the number was no longer in service, and there was no new number. Oh-oh! They were on to me. How could I contact her? Who could be my emissary? Of course...

The Chevalier Rosenbaum was at his home in Bellport, but that was the only positive thing to report about my phone call.

"Please, Doctor, don't attempt to communicate with me again," said Rosenbaum, his voice a distilled blend of distaste and regret. "You managed to hoodwink me, albeit briefly, but that's the end of it. My nephew has taken out an order of protection against you. If you dare come within one mile of Barbara, he will have the police arrest you and your medical license revoked."

"Sherman! I'm shocked. What did Gordon tell you? What devious lies did he concoct that make you so willing, after all our time together, to throw me to the wolves, without even listening to my side? We haven't even tried hypnosis with Barbara yet; it might do the trick."

"Don't! Don't! Please, don't! You're a very clever and devious young man. One realizes now just how much. I'm truly embarrassed that I ever dragged my family into your web of perversion."

"Please, Sherman, please! Aren't we friends? Our lunch in Chinatown holds a treasured place in my—"

"Take my advice, Dr. Strider. Get some help before it's too late, from someone more clever than yourself." And with that he hung up.

Even as I listened to the harsh sound of the dial tone, I knew deep down that the "cure" I sought for Barbara would not be realized through simple hypnosis. No, to liberate Leah from Barbara and confront the *dybbuk* to which Molly referred, I would have to summon up the supernatural.

\* \* \*

I walked up the steep steps of the beaux arts structure at the corner of Fifth Avenue and Forty-Second Street. Formerly known as the main branch of the New York Public Library, it was now called the Stephen A. Schwarzman Building, because of the one hundred million dollars the billionaire financier had given to the library in 2008. A building dedicated to a Jew, with a pair of huge stone lions guarding the entrance, seemed like an excellent omen for someone about to deal with a *dybbuk*.

The librarian at the reference desk referred me to the Dorot Jewish Division in room 111, where I would find an extensive collection of Hebraica and Judaica. Pausing for a moment to stare up at the towering coffered ceiling painted in gold leaf, I moved excitedly across the floor.

"We encourage you to plan your visit," said the officious librarian behind the desk in room 111. "It takes time for us to locate the texts you're looking for."

"Sorry," I replied. "I'm a psychiatrist and it involves a patient. It's somewhat of a medical emergency, very unorthodox…or perhaps very Orthodox." I laughed at my unintentional joke. The librarian didn't appreciate my levity.

"Even if you had planned ahead," said the librarian, "the books you are interested in are already in use."

"By whom?"

"By her."

The librarian pointed across the room to where a Benedictine nun sat at a wooden table. She was poring over numerous rare volumes spread out in front of her.

"Excuse me, Sister," I said, standing over the nun, who was scribbling copious notes on a yellow legal pad.

"What's up?" she asked, in a voice that bore the traces of one of the city's less-glamorous boroughs. She didn't raise her head but continued her transcription.

"I'm sorry to interrupt but—"

"I'm on a deadline here, buddy."

"So am I. There is a soul in peril."

"Now you've got my attention." The nun put down her pen and stared up at me with the most piercing blue eyes I had ever seen. "How can I help?"

"These books on Jewish mysticism..."

"For my thesis. I've had three extensions already. What is it you need to know about?"

"Exorcism. Jewish exorcism."

"The soul in peril?" she asked.

"A patient of mine."

"You an MD?" The nun's blue eyes blazed up at me. Why were they so familiar? I knew them from somewhere. A wimple encased her hair, neck, and chin, but I could tell by her face that she was in her early sixties.

"I'm a psychiatrist. My name is Harris Strider."

"Sister Aurelia." We shook hands. She had quite a grip. "What are we talking about here, Doctor?"

"A *dybbuk*, I believe."

"Really!" She arched her eyebrows. "You've piqued my interest. How much do you know about Kabbalah, Dr. Strider?"

"I've barely got my feet wet, Sister."

"'It tears your soul away from the earth and lifts you to the realms of the highest heights.' That's from Ansky's play *The Dybbuk*. Have you ever seen it?"

"No."

"Read it! Fascinating!" Sister Aurelia's blue eyes were afire with enthusiasm. Why were they haunting me so? "Let me ask you a few questions first. What do you know about Gematria?"

"Is it a place?"

"No!" Sister Aurelia laughed. "Gematria is the science of numerology and the key to understanding Kabbalah. Every letter in the Hebrew alphabet corresponds to a number. Aleph, the first letter, is the number one. Bet, the second letter, is two. Got it? Now, to show you how it works, the word for life in Hebrew is *chai*. The two letters that spell *chai* correspond to the numbers ten and eight and total eighteen. And the number eighteen is a very lucky to the Jewish people. Now, when you got your toes wet in Kabbalah, did you learn about the Tree of Life?"

"May I?" I picked up Sister Aurelia's pen and drew the ten balls from memory that I had seen on Leah and Molly's scraps of paper. "Have I got it right?"

"Very good, Doctor. Those balls are the fruits of the tree and they are called the Ten *Sefirot*. Seven of the *Sefirot* deal with emotions. Seven times seven equals…?"

"Forty-nine."

"Exactly. And there are forty-nine days between Passover and Shavuot."

"What is Shavuot?"

"The Jewish holiday commemorating the giving of the law to Moses on Mount Sinai. It's all in the numbers. You look confused."

"How does all this lead to *dybbuks* and possession?"

"Patience, Doctor. Patience. In my past life, I had to learn that the hard way."

"Are you talking about reincarnation?"

"No!" Sister Aurelia burst out laughing. The librarian glared at her from the other side of the room. "I'm talking about before I took my vows. Wow! That was a long time ago. Your bringing up reincarnation is funny though. It's called *gilgul* in Hebrew. The word is not mentioned anywhere in the Torah or the Talmud, but it's a big deal in Kabbalah. Are you Jewish, by the way?"

"Half. The part that knows nothing about Judaism."

"Yeah. You remind me of a guy I dated in college— before you were born."

College! That was it! I had bought a vintage '60s poster at a head shop in San Francisco and pinned it over the bed in my dorm at Stanford. It was a picture of a girl in a crowd at an outdoor rock concert, and she was sitting on her boy-friend's shoulders, naked from the waist up, her bare breasts covered by her long blond hair. She was making the peace sign with her right hand as she stared defiantly at the camera with her penetrating blue eyes. I must have stared at that poster for hours in med school, fantasizing about the stunning girl and wondering what had become of her.

Now those same blue eyes were staring at me, and there was an obvious look of recognition on my face.

"The poster, right?" Sister Aurelia asked. I nodded, too embarrassed to speak. "I'd know that look anywhere. Can you believe how that picture haunts me after all these years? I don't even know when it was taken or on whose shoulders I was sitting. I got stoned in 1966 and stayed that way for five years. Then one morning, I woke up and had an epiphany: the life I was leading was going to kill me sooner rather than later.

210

"When I was little, I used to daydream about being a nun, a Hollywood nun like Ingrid Bergman or Loretta Young. They seemed to love God and have a lot of fun, especially when Bing Crosby turned up and sang. But I didn't want to sing; I wanted to disappear. And that led me to the Benedictines. Growing up on Staten Island, I'd been a real high-school princess: head cheerleader and queen of the senior prom. So when it came time to take my vows, I chose my name after Sister Aurelia of Strasbourg. She'd been a princess, too, who gave it all up to devote her life to God...But let's get back to reincarnation, okay? Now, the purpose of reincarnation in Kabbalah is to fulfill the 613 *mitzvot*, which..."

"Did you say 613?" I all but shouted the question. "That was the number on the drawing Leah showed me."

"Who's Leah?"

I debated whether or not to take Sister Aurelia into my confidence. But with Marty Corwin unlikely to indulge me in my quest for knowledge, the nun from Staten Island was my only source of invaluable information. I did a quick recap of the whole Barbara-Leah story then asked her what the 613 *mitzvot* were.

"Commandments, more like good deeds. And why is it 613? Come on, Harris? Mind if I call you Harris?"

"Wait, wait. Gematria! And you can call me Harry."

"Okay, Harry. Like I said, it's all in the numbers. The word Torah in Hebrew adds up to 611."

"But..."

"Patience, Harry, patience! To that number we add the first two of the Ten Commandments—don't ask me why—for a grand total of 613. Now, know what a *tallis* is?"

"A prayer shawl."

"And *tzitzit*? No? They're little knotted tassels hanging down from the *tallis*. But they're not just there for decoration.

No. Back we go to Gematria. The letters spelling the word *tzitzit* in Hebrew add up to six hundred. And each tassel has eight threads and five knots for—six hundred plus eight plus five—a grand total of 613. You can't get away from that number."

"And what are these 613 commandments?"

Sister Aurelia reached for a volume on the table and began searching through it. "Here we go. The first dozen are obvious: there is a God, you should love Him, fear Him, and sanctify His name. Twenty-seven through forty-two deal with idolatry and all the no-nos. Then around sixty-four we get into things like not contacting the dead, or sixty-seven, which prohibits performing acts of magic."

"The sort of things the Magiker Rebbe was dabbling in," I suggested. "Maybe that's why he was living in the gentile part of town."

"Maybe. But there are a lot of laws that are more than a little arcane today, like 491. 'Break the neck of a calf by the river valley following an unsolved murder.' Sounds like an episode of *Criminal Minds*."

"And why was Zohar forbidden, if it contained these 613 commandments?"

"Because of the erotic terminology."

"Sister Aurelia, I'm shocked!"

The nun gave me a reproving punch in the arm, which hurt, then spoke. "Only men over the age of forty were allowed to read Zohar, because they were considered mature enough to deal with the notion of the Torah being a bride."

"What?"

"Because in the style in which Zohar was written, the Torah is a very sexy woman. 'She is something that you enter with love.' She is the King's daughter given in marriage. That's why a non-Jew reading the Torah is said to have 'violated the bride.' I wonder what those ancient Kabbalists would have made of a shiksa like me dipping into the Book of Splendor?"

"Why are you doing your doctorate on Jewish mysticism?"

"I don't know how much you keep up on Catholic Church news, Harry, but it's been pretty tough being an American nun these last few years. What with Cardinal Ratzinger—I could never bring myself to call him Holy Father—reading us the riot act for our support of abortion and gay marriage. We are bad girls and 've aren't obeying orders!' What were they thinking when they elected an ex-Nazi as Pope? So I've started thinking about my backup plan: getting a doctorate and jumping ship if the day ever comes when I stop getting myself to a nunnery."

"But what about reincarnation?" I had given up any hope of learning about the *dybbuk*. "Where does 613 come into that?"

"There's very little chance that someone can achieve 613 *mitzvot* in a lifetime. It can take a soul several *gilgulim*— reincarnations—to reach that magic number. To achieve *tik-kun olam*." Off my inquiring look, she translated: "Amends. What others might think of as karma."

"So Leah may be a *gilgul* inside of Barbara."

"No, because Leah wasn't inside her from birth as a reincarnated being."

"So that's where the *dybbuk* comes in?"

"Not a *dybbuk*," said Sister Aurelia. "A *dybbuk* is an evil spirit and from everything you told me about Leah, she's a sweetie. No. What you're dealing with is an *ibbur*."

"An *ibbur*?"

"Here." Sister Aurelia began thumbing through a book, found what she was looking for, and thrust the volume to me. "Read."

"*Ibbur* is the most positive form of possession," I read aloud, "and the most complicated. It manifests itself when a righteous soul decides to occupy a living person's body for a time. *Ibbur* is always temporary, and the living person may or may not know that it has taken place. The reason for the presence of an *ibbur* is always benevolent—the departed soul wishes to complete an important task, to fulfill a promise, or to perform a *mitzvah* that can only be accomplished in the flesh."

"Sounds like your Leah," said Sister Aurelia. "I'm jealous."

"Of Leah?"

"No! Of you having this experience. But I would love to meet her."

"That's not a good idea," I replied, with far too much speed and ardor. I hastily added, "Barbara wants nothing to do with Leah—let alone a Benedictine nun."

Sister Aurelia stared at me for the longest time with those piercing blue eyes, and I had to struggle to banish the image of her with bared breasts, sitting defiantly on her boyfriend's shoulders. Finally she asked me: "What about the exorcism? Now that you know it is not a *dybbuk*, do you still want to separate the souls?"

"Not if Leah's going to leave eventually like the good *ibbur* she is."

"But this constant switching back and forth can't be good for either one, physically or emotionally."

"So who can perform this exorcism?" I had tried to sound as casual and matter-of-fact as I could.

"The Bible tells us that David drove the evil spirit out of King Saul by playing on a lyre. Do you play twelve-string, Harry? There are a couple of cool Joni Mitchell songs…just kidding. What you need is a *tzadik*, a righteous man."

"A rebbe?"

"Exactly. Someone versed in Kabbalah, who has had a degree of experience with exorcisms. Do you know any Hasidim?"

"Yes! Yes, I do, in Brooklyn. And what is the name of the man I'm looking for again?"

"A *tzadik*."

"Thank you, Sister. Thank you so much."

"Harry?"

"Yes, Sister?"

"You're not in love with Leah, are you?"

"Of course not," I lied. "She's my patient."

Sister Aurelia drew a deep breath and sighed. "God help you, if you are."

\* \* \*

Two hours later, I entered Bernie Aarons's store in Crown Heights, where I found the kosher butcher wearing a yarmulke and a bloodstained apron and standing behind the counter weighing a tiny chicken on a scale. He wrapped it in pink paper, rang it up on the vintage cash register, and wished the old lady with the red wheelie cart who took it from him "*a guten Shabbos.*"

"Hi, Bernie." I smiled after the old woman had wheeled her cart out of the shop. "Remember me?"

"Sure. How's it going, Doc? Where's Marty? Parking the car?"

"No. I'm on my own actually. So…how are the newlyweds doing?"

"Still in love."

"Marvelous! And the amazing Mr. Moskowitz?"

"I haven't seen him since the wedding."

"Quite the character. I enjoyed meeting him. Although he seemed unusually rattled by the end of our encounter."

"Hey! Who knows what we'll be like at that age? *Alevai.* So! What can I do for you, Doctor? Looking for a chicken? Got some nice brisket today. Knishes? Kishke? Try a little piece of kishke. I'll warm it up in the—"

"No thanks, Bernie." I paused for a moment, uncertain as to how to segue into the reason for my visit. Finally I took the plunge feetfirst. "I've been doing some research lately. I don't know if Marty mentioned it to you…the Book of Zohar and the Tree of Life."

"Kabbalah."

"Exactly."

"Madonna made it pretty trendy stuff a few years ago. All those *roite bindeles* on people's wrists."

"What are they?"

"Red strings. They ward off the evil eye. It's what we call *segulah*, a charm that supersedes logic. All those Hollywood types opened the floodgates to gentiles. There are a couple of websites on it now, I'm told."

"Really? I had no idea. Are you a believer?"

"Tell me, Doctor, did you really cross the East River on a Friday afternoon to have a theological debate? It's not the best time for me; the sun's going down in a few hours."

"Shabbos! Yes, of course, how foolish of me. You can't work after sundown. It's just that…" Unable to maintain a semblance of social niceties for another second, I blurted out: "Do you know anyone who could perform an exorcism? A Jewish exorcism, of course."

"Is someone you know possessed by a *dybbuk*, Doctor?"

"No, not at all. Actually, it's an *ibbur*."

Aarons stared at me curiously for the longest time before he spoke: "There was a rabbi. Some name like Zalman or Kalman. Whatever. I heard he did things like that about fifteen years ago."

"Where would I find him, this Zalman or Kalman fellow? Is he still around?" I could barely conceal the excitement in my voice.

The butcher shrugged. "He got bounced out of the *shul* by his congregation. They didn't approve of his dabbling in the occult. Who knows if he's still alive?"

"He must be. He has to be." Did the desperation in my voice make me seem a little less than rational? "Could you possibly make inquiries for me?" I handed Aarons my business card. "I'd be very grateful. It's for my research."

\* \* \*

The sun was sinking rapidly as I inserted the key into my front door. The phone was ringing. I prayed it was Leah. Perhaps—somehow—she'd managed to overpower Barbara and was reading my thoughts. Dashing for the phone, I answered it breathlessly.

"Hello?"

"Dr. Strider? Bernie Aarons. I've got to make this a fast call; there's only a few seconds till sundown."

"Yes, yes, of course. You can't use the telephone after that, can you? I appreciate your calling back so quickly. What did you find out?"

"Rabbi Kalman is in Manhattan. He's agreed to see you after services tonight."

"Where? Where do I go?"

"A tiny *shul* on Ninety-First Street, between West End and Riverside. Good luck."

Gazing out the window, the sky had abruptly gone dark, as if God had switched off all the lights. What time did Sabbath services end?

Taking the crosstown bus on Ninety-Sixth Street, I got off at West End and then walked south to Ninety-First Street. I marched in frustration up and down the block without seeing any building that remotely resembled a synagogue or temple. Had Aarons made a mistake? Then I remembered, he had said a tiny *shul*. How tiny was tiny? Wait a minute! There it was, wedged between two brownstones. The diminutive building looked like something out of a Lewis Carroll story, if Lewis Carroll had been Jewish; through the little door with Hebrew letters painted over the top, I half expected to find the White Rabbit as the *shammes* and the Mad Hatter as the cantor. From the street I could hear the hive-like din of the congregation praying ardently inside. I had chosen the same suit I had worn to the wedding in Crown Heights and was grateful to discover that the yarmulke was still in the jacket pocket.

With the skullcap perched precariously on the back of my head, I entered the synagogue just as the service was ending. The men wished each other a good Sabbath and filed out of the building, after which the *shammes* switched off the lights.

Seconds later, I stood alone in darkness, except for the eternal flame aglow over the ark that housed the Torah. Only then did I notice a solitary man with his back to me, hunched over in the front row of pews.

"Rabbi Kalman?" I walked down the center aisle to the front row. "Excuse my intrusion, sir. Would you happen to be Rabbi Kalman?"

The man rose, turned to face me, and asked: "What are you up to now, Harry?" It was Marty Corwin.

"Where's Rabbi Kalman?" Bewildered, I looked around the tiny *shul* for the man I had come to meet. "Bernie Aarons told me Rabbi Kalman would be…"

"Bernie fibbed, okay? It was for a good cause. When you walked into his shop this afternoon looking for an exorcist, all his alarm bells went off and he called me. Your condition has deteriorated, Harry. This *mishegas* has to stop once and for all."

"There is no 'condition,' Marty. Okay? And even if there was, this is none of your goddamn business."

"I'm making it my business. And do not curse in the House of God. The Psych Board called me this afternoon; Barbara's parents have filed formal charges against you. And an old woman named Molly Friedman is in the hospital. She had a bad fall and is not in good shape. Her conservators are holding you responsible. On top of all that, Evelyn phoned to tell me your patients are up in arms. These are all excellent reasons to be concerned. Got a good lawyer?"

"Evelyn had no business phoning you."

"She cares about you, Harris. So do I. This is a one-man intervention, whether you like it or not. You've hit bottom and you need help."

"There's nothing wrong with me!" Tears were streaming down my face. "I love her, Marty. And she won't talk to me anymore. I don't even know how to reach her."

Corwin stepped forward and wrapped a brotherly arm around my shoulder. "Maybe she's gone back where she came from."

"No, no. She's an *ibbur*, Marty. She's here to perform a *mitzvah*. I am the *mitzvah*. She's here to save my life."

"An *ibbur*! Where the hell did you come up with that? Who is telling you this stuff?"

"An amazing nun I met at the library. Actually, I've known her for twenty years but didn't really know her, just her eyes. You'd love this story, Marty. Sister Aurelia of Strasbourg. She's writing her doctorate on Jewish mysticism and she knew all about *gilgulim* and 613 and—"

"Harry, stop it! You're babbling."

"It's not fair, Marty! I've been alone for so long, even these years with Claire. We've been like satellites circling each other but never really touching. She wasn't Suzanne, the girl on the toboggan. But Leah—from the moment I set eyes on her—opened up something dormant in me, and now I feel it's closing again. I was a...a cold fish before I met her. I was cold and passionless. Just another ironic, arrogant yuppie...What does it all mean, Pasha?"

"What do you think it means, Harry?"

"Don't you dare play shrink with me!" I broke loose from his embrace. "I want an answer. Why did this happen?"

"Where do we go when we die, Harry?"

"I don't know."

"That's the answer."

"No! No way...too facile. You don't believe any of this, do you? You think it's because of stress and overwork and Bernie Madoff. But this is real! The first real thing that ever happened to me."

"Please, come with me, Harry!"

"Where? Some place 'medicable'? Is there a safe house where they send burnt-out shrinks to recover? Forget it, Marty. You think I'm out there, don't you? Well, I'm not. She's out there. And I'm going to find her."

As I turned to leave, the Pasha grabbed me by the sleeve of my overcoat. "Harris, listen closely to me. I wouldn't say this if I didn't love you and respect you: You're delusional. It's not safe for you to be—"

Wrenching my arm loose, I screamed at my friend and mentor: "Keep your hands off me! You're jealous. Yes, you are. I'm talking about real love. Something a satyr like you could never understand. Don't you dare give me that patented pitying look of yours, you patronizing fraud. I'm going to find my happiness and you can't stop me!"

# THE UNEXPECTED GUEST

MY HEAD WAS pounding as I burst out onto the street. I was gripped with pain, excruciating pain unlike anything I had known before. Never had I felt so friendless and alone. Things would never be the same again with Corwin, not after the awful things I had said to him. No more racquetball. No more lunches. No more Harry and the Pasha. And it was I, Harris Strider, who had emerged from our confrontation the loser.

Corwin would always have his daughters, friends like Bernie Aarons, his Nurse Flanagans, and innumerable colleagues in the profession, who would admire his wit and skill. But in the final accounting, whom did I have, except for my aging parents? My wife had left me. Suzanne was dead. I had no children, no siblings, and no real friends, except the Pasha, and now I had even lost him. I had led a sheltered life with my parents in Chicago and never made friends a priority. It was always just the three of us, our heads buried in books, reading voraciously and exchanging ideas. Our only trips, every summer, were to visit my father's family out west in Montana. They were fair-haired, blue-eyed people—cowboys strong and stoic—unlike my mother and me. I was close to none of them.

Smoke was rising above Second Avenue as I drew near my building. Fire engines raced through the streets toward the blaze, their blaring sirens only compounding the unbearable pressure on my brain. Where was my beloved Leah? Why had she disappeared again? And why had she sought me out in the first place? Could it be that we were truly *bashert*? Destined to be together forever? It had to be more than coincidence that she was in Bloomingdale's that day; I was meant to rescue her. A Supreme Being, a Higher Power had ordained it. I felt as if I were a finely tuned instrument, being played by a supernatural, all-powerful virtuoso.

I entered the lobby of my building where Cosmo, the burly night doorman, greeted me in thick Bronx tones and stopped me as I moved towards the elevator.

"Hey, Doc! Hope youse ain't gonna be annoyed 'bout this. Just wasn't the right thing to do. Know what I mean?"

"No. What do you mean, Cosmo?"

"She didn't mind waitin' here in the lobby for youse. But after an hour, I just felt it ain't right, y'know? What with her sacked out on the couch there. So I took her upstairs and let her into youse's apartment. She looked real tired."

"Who did you let into my apartment?" My heart was racing again. Had my prayers been answered? Was my beloved Leah waiting for me upstairs?

"Your mother! She said youse wasn't really spectin' her, but she'd flown all the way from Chicago. Through a terrible snowstorm."

"My mother's upstairs now?"

"Yeah. She's a real cutie."

"Thanks, Cosmo."

"Hey! I gotsa mother too y'know."

What had brought my mother to New York so unexpectedly? The city was anathema to her. Was my father dead? No, she wouldn't have come without phoning first to break the news.

I unlocked the door of my apartment and called out: "Mom?"

As I silently entered the living room, I felt my heart warm at the sight of my mother asleep on the couch. She was wearing a plaid flannel shirt and faded jeans—the eternal grad student—and her knapsack, a half-eaten bag of Hain mini rice cakes, and a bottle of Volvic water rested on the floor beside her. With a copy of Rilke's poems clutched in her balled fist, she looked like a sleeping child, obstinately defying the Sandman's order to surrender her favorite toy.

Gently, I shook her shoulder. She opened her eyes and smiled at me. She rose from the couch and stood on tiptoe to hug me. "You look terrible, honey. Hope you don't mind me saying that."

"Is Dad okay?"

"Why shouldn't he be? Ever known him to be sick a day in his life? And, if he were, would he tell anyone?"

"So why are you here? Traveling on a whim through a snowstorm?"

"Come on, honey." My mother clutched her knapsack as she walked towards the kitchen. "Let's go make some tea."

"I don't think I have any."

"Your mother always comes prepared," she said, slapping her bulging knapsack. "I could go to Shanghai with this bag. Do you like raspberry hibiscus? My own blend."

I stared with awe and affection at my five-foot-nothing mother, still the pixie at age sixty-six, with her cropped silver hair and an almost Asian caste to her gray eyes, as she marched into my kitchen and put the kettle on to boil.

"I had a visitor the other day," she said, standing on tip-toe to reach the overhead shelves and pull down some mugs. "My daughter-in-law. Or soon-to-be-ex-daughter-in-law, from what she told me."

"Why don't you just say Claire? I can't believe she went all the way to Chicago to—"

"Be kind, Harris! She stopped off to see us on her way to Des Moines. She was very sad and still very worried about you. Do you have any idea what kind of dynamite you're playing with, the lethal Pandora's box you've opened?"

"Did you fly all the way from Chicago in a snowstorm to tell me that?"

"Nope." My mother climbed onto a tall wooden stool, her legs dangling down likes a child's. "I came to tell you about me. And who I really am. Phone calls weren't getting us anywhere."

"So? What's the drill?" I sat down at the kitchen table and stared at her perched on the stool. "Do I take notes or..."

"Just listen, Mr. Smart Guy. First, what's my name?"

"Mitzi Strider."

"Wrong! My birth name was Miriam Hannah Gelbschein. Later on it was changed to Goldstein, or Gold, or Stein. For various reasons my father found it necessary to employ different names on different occasions. Are you planning to listen with your mouth open the whole time?"

"Sorry. The history of your life has been such a well-guarded secret from me. Now, suddenly you're..."

"You outed me, okay? What options did I have? But you were always a sucker for a good story, Harris. Probably why you became a psychiatrist. Quite the whistle on that kettle."

I rose from the table to get the tea, staring in amazement at my mother all the while. "Just keep talking, Mom."

As I poured the boiling water into the two mugs, my mother continued her revelation.

"I never knew my mother. I have no idea what she looked like. Stories varied about her: some say she died tragically giving birth to me, others say my father was never married to my mother and took me to raise after the woman vanished. No one would ever tell me the truth, if indeed anyone really knew. My father was a legendary philanderer. Rumors were that he had bastard children scattered across Europe and up and down the Eastern seaboard of our great republic."

My mind was spinning. At some point—probably in my teens—I created a fantasy of two lower-middle-class Jewish immigrants banishing their feisty daughter for marrying outside the faith. But this hot-off-the-presses autobiographical account was totally unexpected. My grandfather was a philanderer with multiple aliases...maybe even a criminal. Was his another name I would have to Google in the dead of night? I asked warily: "What did your father do for a living?"

"Meyer Gelbschein was a mystic, a Jewish faith healer. It was said—but only in the faintest of whispers—he had the power to raise the dead. Actually that line was an exact quote from his obituary in the *Jewish Forward*. He once claimed to have been a rabbi, although I never saw a framed certificate from any seminary hanging on the wall. But then, a Jew in Europe a century ago could arrive in a *shtetl*, declare himself a rabbi, and who was there to blow the whistle on him? Try the tea. Good combination, huh?"

I took a sip and nodded appreciatively. "Go on, Mom. Please."

"Your grandfather was a charismatic figure, and to a certain lunatic fringe in Brooklyn, a Messianic one. They thought he walked on water. He was a one-man Supreme Court, who settled claims about marriages, businesses, and legacies.

"I was 'the child of his old age.' He was in his late sixties when my mother gave birth to me. I became the heir apparent. More precisely, I became the mother-to-be of the heir apparent. For his followers, I was the vessel that would deliver his successor, the next Magiker Rebbe...*you*."

My mug of raspberry-hibiscus dropped from my hand and shattered on the parquet floor.

"Have you got a sponge or a mop?" My mother leapt down from the stool in a flash.

"Don't move!"

"But, honey, the tea…"

"Sit down, Mom! I've been through a great deal of mind-boggling, inexplicable phenomena the last few weeks, real hocus-pocus that—"

"Didn't I warn you? When you start tampering with—"

"Please, Mom! Let me finish. This is the ultimate mind-boggler for me, okay? Are you telling me that your father was the Magiker Rebbe? The one who settled all the Blood Libels in the Pale of Settlement? The one they drove out of Apt for 'curing' the barren women?"

My mother's jaw dropped and she asked: "How on earth could you know all that?"

"Not on earth, Mom. Believe me. The tapestry of my life becomes more intricate every day. A patient of mine thinks I am the Magiker Rebbe."

"It's that girl, right?"

"Yes."

My mother inhaled deeply, puffed her cheeks out, and blew out a big gust of air. "Tell me everything, from the beginning."

I recounted the tale, starting with Sherman Rosenbaum's first appearance in my office and ending with the fiasco at Molly Friedman's apartment. I purposely omitted the details about Gordon Jacobs's threats and the legal actions I was facing.

"Do you know about *tikkun olam*, Harris?"

"Yes, it's like Jewish karma."

My mother stared at me sorrowfully. "I wanted to spare you all this, to keep you as far away from it as possible. But the Man Upstairs dictates our fate; we don't. It wasn't easy growing up being told that your father is God's CEO. A child should never be shown the deference I was, just because someday she might bring a boy into the world who would carry on a great mystical tradition. You have to understand that our brownstone in Brooklyn had nothing to do with the United States, or even the twentieth century. Not a soul came to visit who could speak English. My father was like Marlon Brando in *The Godfather*. People made pilgrimages to our building. They waited in line on the street for hours—stammering and stuttering—in his exalted presence, hoping that he would bestow the smallest kernel of his wisdom on them.

"But there were nights—oh, so many nights—when I would awaken frightened and hear chanting from the kitchen—dark, magical incantations, desperate cries and pathetic wailing. Try growing up with that din instead of lullabies. When I was three, maybe four, I wandered down the hall to the kitchen in the middle of the night. My father was holding a baby in the air by its legs and gliding a candle up and down its spine. The child was dead, but the parents were begging him, pleading with him, to bring her back to life."

"And did he?" I was hanging on my mother's every word.

"Who knows? Maybe the whole thing was a dream. I had a predilection toward nightmares in those early years. But by the time I was fifteen, I vowed to escape my preordained destiny. I wanted a normal life. When my father finally died, I was eighteen, and had just received my letter of acceptance to Northwestern. When I announced my plans to move to Chicago, his followers were appalled. How dare I desert them? Suitors were being imported for me from all over the world. I'd just seen *Roman Holiday* for the first time and identified like crazy with Audrey Hepburn. But unlike her, I didn't go back to my responsibilities in the end. I took what little money was left me after my father died and caught a bus to Chicago.

"Then the Man Upstairs put Jason Strider in my path and we fell in love. That long drink of water was as far removed from Brooklyn and the Magiker Hasidim as I could imagine. If your father had asked me to go back home to Montana with him, I'd have bought boots and a saddle. But we'd not only fallen in love with each other but with Chicago. I could be safe there. And I was, for years afterward, until you were born. How the Magiker's disciples found us I never knew. They probably had us under surveillance all those years; they are better than the FBI. For them, your arrival on this planet was akin to a new Dalai Lama. The spirit of the Magiker Rebbe lived on in you, and they were determined to get you back.

"Of course, they wouldn't actually kidnap you—that crazy they weren't. But they waged a war of nerves with me. There were phone calls in the middle of the night, and people passing me on the street whispering, 'Give him back. He's ours.' But I would never have given you up. And I so wanted you to have a normal life."

"Oh, Mom!" My face burned with shame and guilt. "I just never understood."

"What was there to understand? What's wrong?"

"All those phone calls, the strangers on the street, the way you behaved. The things I thought. I'm so sorry. So ashamed."

"What, honey? Did you think I was crazy?"

"Yes! It's why I became a psychiatrist. Maybe I could help other people with the same…What else was I supposed to think? I was a little kid. It made no sense to me."

"Oh, honey! Oh, my poor baby." My mother held her arms out, and I allowed her to embrace me, a child once again. "All those years in Chicago I tried to hide you away from them, until they were, hopefully, all dead, and the Magiker movement dead with them. Now, your patient has found out. Somehow this crazy girl has learned the truth about who you are."

"Not crazy, Mom. Possessed. She has no idea of my connection to your father. She thinks I am the Magiker Rebbe. What fantastic promises could he have made to her that she is drawn back to him from another dimension?"

"Who knows? My father—*alav ha-shalom*—could never resist a pretty face…such a tragic flaw. At first he was famous for his dazzling legal mind. Every Jew in Eastern Europe accused of murdering a gentile child prayed for the Magiker Rebbe to defend them and to discredit the anti-Semitic prosecutors. But he ended up believing his own press—that he had power over life, death…and women. Not many résumés these days list 'resurrectionist' as a major skill."

"Do you know anything about Leah Littman, Mom? Did he ever mention her name or a town called Irmunsk? Did he teach you about Kabbalah and *gilgulim*?"

"Let me explain something, honey. My dear Daddy never told me anything, not a thing. He never shared a word, only demanded. 'What's for dinner?' and 'Did you wash the dishes?' were his two favorite questions. I was a slave in that household. What other job could an unworthy female have?"

"I'm sorry."

"Please, there's no need for that. I escaped, and I have no regrets. But if you really want to learn about the man…here." My mother reached into her knapsack and removed a battered leather-bound book. "His housekeeper gave me his journal after he died. My first instinct was to burn it. Who knows why I didn't or why I held on to it all these years? Maybe there's something about your Leah in there."

"I hope so."

"This is really important to you, isn't it, Harris?"

"More now than ever, Mom. Several times in the past weeks, I thought my sanity was at risk. This volume could explain everything." Reverently, I glided my hand along the cracked leather cover that encased my long-dead grandfather's journal. Up until that moment, I had always associated the word grandfather with a gnarled old cowboy, sitting on a corral fence in rural Montana, twirling a lariat and rolling his own cigarettes. Now that image had been replaced by a brooding, bearded mystic, who had authored the book that I planned to sit up all night reading.

Opening the book to the first page, my heart sank. I flipped through page after page after page. It was all the same. His journal was entirely in Hebrew.

# THE LITTLE CANTOR

IT WAS NOON the next day, and I awoke to discover my mother on the phone in the kitchen, booking a return flight to Chicago for that afternoon. I protested such a brief visit, but she insisted her mission was accomplished. She also warned me about the contents of her father's journal.

"Be careful with what you find in there," she said. "They didn't call him Magiker for nothing."

"Did you miss speaking Yiddish all these years?"

"What are you talking about?"

"Growing up in Chicago, I never once heard you sigh with anything less than WASP-certified fatigue. But since you've arrived here, every intonation and gesture is…"

"Like a Second Avenue tummler? Yiddish was my mother tongue for the first eighteen years of my life. I never heard my father speak a word of English. For all I know he had total command of the language, but being the vain and arrogant creature he was, his ego could never have tolerated being branded a greenie for the way he sounded."

"Do I look like him?"

"Hard to say. He was well past sixty when I was born, which was old back then. But you do have the same mesmerizing eyes."

I took her for a late lunch at Sarabeth's on Madison, and then put her into a limousine bound for LaGuardia. My mother's visit had been a profound revelation and a highly emotional reunion. Now, I had a new challenge: find a translator for my grandfather's journal.

The obvious choice was no longer a possibility. Even if I could repair the schism between the Pasha and me, I doubted if I could endure his blistering scorn when I produced the journal as potential evidence to prove my story. No, some other scholar would have to be brought on board. I thought of Sister Aurelia for a moment, but she had been opposed to my involvement with Leah. No, the man I needed would have to be a true romantic.

* * *

It was half past four that afternoon as I sat with my feet propped up on a threadbare ottoman, sipping Courvoisier from a snifter and smoking a fat, contraband Cuban cigar in Dalton W. Lafferty's cluttered apartment near Columbia University.

I hadn't seen the professor since our meeting at the hospital. Not only was he his old gregarious self, but also he presented a sense of peace and acceptance that I had never seen. Was another therapist treating him? Was he medicated? He answered no to both questions.

"Nice brandy, huh?" asked Lafferty. "One of the great joys of being beloved by successful former students. They send me such generous gifts at Christmas. Pity I never taught anyone from Havana. I don't suppose Mr. Obama will end the boycott anytime soon. A colleague of mine tried persuading me Dominican cigars were on a par with Cubans. Benighted fool! Have I ever shown you my first edition of *The Mill on the Floss*? Of course I haven't; you've never been up here before."

"My loss, Professor," I replied. "Old books have always held a fascination for me." It was my cue to reach for the canvas Metropolitan Museum tote bag, in which I had transported the Magiker's journal. This was it. I prayed Lafferty didn't turn out to be another traitor like Bernie Aarons, jollying me along with more brandy then sneaking off to phone the bully boys at Bellevue, who would come and fetch the demented soul camped out in his living room.

"I don't pretend for a moment to have a fraction of your knowledge, Professor. But I did come across a rare volume the other day—a private journal from the early part of the century, the last century—with an unusual binding. I wondered if you might take a look at it."

"Certainly. Bring it round next time you—"

"Actually, I happen to have it here with me." Had I been too gung ho, as I withdrew the journal and handed it to him? Would he be suspicious of my motives?

"European," said Lafferty, examining the outer binding with professional expertise. "Czech. Possibly Polish." He'd opened the journal by this time. "Hmmm…Hebrew."

"Do you read Hebrew?" Did I sound too anxious?

"I had a smattering of Greek and Hebrew under my belt back in college…wouldn't even pretend to know what it says now."

"Do you know anyone who might? I'm curious about the contents, all the diagrams and such. Perhaps the author was a physicist or…"

"Alchemist?" asked Lafferty.

"Why do you say that?" Paranoia, get thee behind me!

"These peculiar marginal drawings. They're reminiscent of medieval texts. Hmmm. I'll wager the Little Cantor might be of help on this."

"Who?"

"The neighbor of mine I told you about, Alvin Rabinowitz, the one who explained to me the concept of *bashert*. He's a fellow cigar aficionado, with a glorious voice. He dreamt of being an opera singer for years but was deemed too short to command the stage. A great career cut down by inches. So he found another outlet for his vocal talent. Known as 'The Little Cantor with the Big Voice,' he has a considerable reputation in his field. Shall I give him a call?"

The professor thumbed through his address book, dialed the number on his rotary phone, and then boomed into the handset: "Lafferty here! Up for a smoke and some brandy? Excellent! I've got someone I'd like you to meet." Replacing the handset in its cradle, he turned to me and grinned. "'*I drink the air before me.*' You'll like Rabinowitz—a student of Shakespeare and the Talmud."

Minutes later an extremely short, balding man in his early forties came through the door, wearing jeans, a mock turtleneck, and a tweed sports coat. He was carrying a pink bakery box tied with string, which he held reverently from the bottom.

"*Alors mon professeur,*" said Rabinowitz, his large blue eyes twinkling with great warmth. "My mother made these expressly for you. From scratch." He pronounced the last two words with a thick Yiddish accent.

"What about my cholesterol?" Lafferty asked warily.

"Know what my grandfather said on his deathbed?" replied Rabinowitz. "'They'll never take me alive.'" Lafferty chuckled, undid the string, and licked his lips at the tiny raspberry-apple pastries inside the box.

"Ah! Rugelach." He introduced me to the cantor and pointed to the journal on the coffee table. "What do you make of that, Alvin?"

The Little Cantor picked it up, gave the contents a cursory glance, and said: "Yiddish."

"Ah!" said Lafferty. "We thought it might be Hebrew."

"Same characters, but the similarity ends there. Hebrew is a Middle Eastern language. Yiddish is corrupted German, with a dash of Hebrew, a splash of English, and a lot of show biz thrown in. Where exactly did you obtain this, Doctor?"

"It came into my possession yesterday." I didn't want to reveal my connection to the source.

"Dr. Strider hoped to find someone who might be able to translate the text for him," said Lafferty. "My thoughts sprang to you immediately, Alvin.

"Thank you," said Rabinowitz, as he continued to peruse the handwritten script. "Do you know what this is, Doctor?"

"Some sort of journal?"

"Uh-huh. And what hopes or dreams do you have for it, for want of a better expression?"

I considered his answer for a few seconds. "If it is of any social or historical value, I thought the Jewish Museum on Fifth Avenue might want it for their permanent collection."

Rabinowitz nodded. "An admirable thought. Would you be at all resistant if I held onto it for a brief time, perhaps overnight? The text's considerable length will take at least a few hours to examine properly. The professor can, hopefully, vouch for my honesty."

"He's never stolen one of my books," laughed Lafferty.

"Sure." I shrugged, trying my best to play the good sport. "Perhaps you might find a recipe in there for your mother." I handed Rabinowitz a business card, then snatched it back a beat later and scribbled my home phone number on the reverse side.

Tucking the journal under his arm, Rabinowitz walked toward the front door and snapped a jaunty salute. "Let me start work on this right away."

Late that night, I was in a deep sleep when the telephone rang. Was the answering machine turned on? I dreaded knowing the time. The ringing continued. I turned onto my left side and barely opened one eyelid. Half past two. Closing my eye again, I groped in the darkness for the telephone.

"Yes?"

"Dr. Strider?" A man on the other end sounded extremely excited.

"Who's this?"

"Sorry to wake you. It's Alvin Rabinowitz."

"Something wrong, Alvin?"

"Tell me the truth, Doctor. Do you know what this journal is or not?"

"Why?" Both of my eyes popped open.

"Does the name Meyer Gelbschein mean anything to you?"

"Not really." Had I lied convincingly? What had the Little Cantor discovered in the journal? Did the name mean anything to him?

"I see. And what about the Magiker Rebbe? Does that mean nothing to you either?"

There was an interminable pause before I finally answered: "Can we meet, Alvin? Now?"

Rabinowitz gave me the name and address of a diner on the Upper West Side, and I hastily scribbled the information on the back of an apricot-colored envelope I had grabbed from a hefty pile of unopened mail on my bedside table.

# THE TRANSLATION

IT WAS BITTERLY COLD as I entered the all-night Greek din-er on Ninety-Sixth Street, between Broadway and Amster-dam, for my meeting with the Little Cantor. No taxis had been cruising the East Side at that ungodly hour, and visions of hot chocolate with a shot of ouzo were all that kept me going before I finally found a cab on Fifth willing to take me across the Park. My teeth were still chattering as I spotted Alvin Rabinowitz. He was waving to me from a booth near the rear of the diner, while a hunchbacked waiter shuffled off with his order. The waiter was hastily recalled—cursing under his breath in Greek—to fetch me a hot chocolate.

"This better be good." I kept my Hugo Boss overcoat on as I slid into the booth opposite the Little Cantor. Immedi-ately I noticed something was missing from the table. "Where's the journal?" My voice was decidedly edgy.

"Relax." Rabinowitz unzipped his green Eddie Bauer parka and produced the book from under his polar-fleece Patagonia sweater. "It's a heartbeat away. See?" He laid the treasured journal on the table between us and glided his hand lovingly over the cover.

"How much have you read?" I asked, struggling to gauge what the Little Cantor might have gleaned from the text.

"Enough to know it's what I've been searching for these past ten years," Rabinowitz answered breathlessly. "And much more."

"How on earth could you possibly have known about this journal?"

"Don't let me mislead you, Dr. Strider. I had no knowledge of its existence before last night. I'd always prayed there'd be some kind of documentation, monograph, or something that pertained to Gelbschein. But other than his obituary in the *Jewish Forward*—that's the Yiddish-language newspaper—the man left no footprint. Nothing exists about him on Google or Wikipedia. What I found in this journal is beyond my wildest dreams. This document is my Dead Sea scroll. You think I'm crazy, don't you?" Rabinowitz was babbling by this time.

"As a psychiatrist, I'd need a few more years before I made any snap judgments."

Rabinowitz laughed then asked: "Are you Jewish?"

"Yes." I was amazed at the knee-jerk response I'd given, for the first time in my life.

"I couldn't tell at first. But your sense of humor is a dead giveaway."

"Like the journal, I can assure you, it's something I only came into possession of recently."

"Could have fooled me. Okay...we obviously have to dance around each other a little bit more. *Bien compris.* How much did the professor tell you about me?"

"That you have a wonderful voice, and when your original ambitions weren't realized, you were astute enough to figure out a tenor's public is wherever he chooses to take his curtain calls."

"Good one, Doctor, very good, indeed. I see now why the professor holds you in such high esteem. You have an innate ability to handle opera singers, certainly frustrated ones. But I still have dreams and aspirations. I don't want to be remembered just for being the Judy Garland of the High Holy Days."

"Judy Garland?"

"'The Little Cantor with the Big Voice'? That will teach me to sing 'Kol Nidre' in the West Village. No, there's so much more to me than that. I'm also a frustrated composer— lush, epic, Romantic music. I've started and abandoned so many operas because they all seemed so derivative and uninspired. I wanted to create something that would be mine and mine alone. Then one day I remembered some stories my grandmother had told me as a child. I was born and raised in Paterson, New Jersey, but my bubbe lived in Brooklyn. When I was little, I'd often sleep over at her place and she'd tell me bedtime stories—fantastic tales about a Jewish wizard called the Magiker Rebbe, who could put curses on people, fly over tenement roofs, and even raise the dead. Do you know Menotti's *The Medium*? That's the sort of modern opera I envisioned writing. It would be set in Brooklyn during the Depression. But in the end, I realized that I had a great central character without a plot.

"Then God finally answered my e-mail. Professor Lafferty phoned and asked me to come down and meet someone. It was as if you and I were *bashert*. Do you know the term?"

"Yes, I do." I hoped my response hadn't sounded too ironic.

Rabinowitz opened the journal to the first page and read aloud: "'*Ich bin ein Magiker*.' I am a magician. Simple enough declaration, don't you think? Right up there with Chaim Melville's 'Call me Ishmael.' When I first read this line in the professor's apartment, my knees started to buckle; I prayed neither one of you would notice. So, fasten your seat belts, *kinder*, it's gonna be a bumpy night.

"The first thirty or so pages deal with some intriguing legal defenses the Magiker performed all across Europe in the early 1900s. Jews falsely accused of ritual murders hired Gelbschein to get them off using Talmudic logic. It is fascinating at first but wears a bit thin by page forty. The same 'brilliant' defense is described over and over again, in Minsk, Pinsk, Vilna, and Lodz. Eventually, the self-congratulatory tone evolves into pure megalomania. We are talking narcissism run amok! Not long after that, Gelbschein deviates from Kabbalah and the Book of Zohar, as he starts to experience Messianic visions and revelations. An 'unseen hand' begins guiding him in his writings. Today we would call such guidance 'channeling.'"

The Little Cantor was telling me nothing I hadn't already learned from Leah or my mother. But his recitative did confirm the legitimacy of the journal. What I wanted now were revelations: deep background, for-your-eyes-only, maximum-security clearance, and insider dish.

"Next, we get another fifty pages of minor 'miracles,' for which Gelbschein takes full credit," said Rabinowitz. He was now flipping through the pages of the journal. "Frankly, a lot of the stuff in here struck me as auto-suggestion on a collision course with hypochondria. The Magiker was very big on shouting at the top of his lungs, pounding on tables, and generally mauling the afflicted. My beloved grandmother's tales to the contrary, there are no accounts of Gelbschein flying through the night sky or putting curses on Russian landowners."

"Then why the impassioned search for the past ten years?" I was growing weary of the Little Cantor's criticism.

"Wait! He hasn't arrived in Irmunsk yet."

"Irmunsk?" The hairs on the back of my neck stood up. Stay calm, I warned myself; it might not be anything. "What's that?"

"A *shtetl* in the Pale of Settlement, and also the opening scene of my opera." Rabinowitz kissed his fingertips and flung them up into the air. "Leonard Bernstein—*alav ha-shalom*—would have killed for a libretto like this. And I've got it!" The Little Cantor growled the last sentence. "Thanks to you."

"Tell me your plot. Please."

"Don't credit me. The Magiker Rebbe wrote it. He lived it, poor tortured bastard. By the way, what do you think of 'The Magiker' as a title? Too ethnic?"

"The plot, Alvin!"

"Right! There's this passionate kid named Shimon. He's like a Magiker groupie. He wants to be Gelbschein's acolyte and follows him slavishly from town to town. The problem is that the kid falls head over heels in love with a rich man's daughter, a gorgeous young thing named Leah Littman. Don't you just love it? Conflict right off the top, but with twists, incredible twists."

"Is this of your invention?"

"No! It's all in Gelbschein's journal. Here! I'll read you a bit of it. Leah's father has arranged for her to marry the nerdy son of the *shtetl*'s wealthiest merchant."

"Yochanan," I murmured.

"What did you say?"

"Nothing, please go on."

"Leah's desperately beside herself. Doesn't know what to do. Shimon says he'll take her to meet Gelbschein. The

Magiker has set up shop not in Irmunsk, but among the gentiles in a nearby town. Can you imagine? By living there, he thumbed his nose at his fellow Jews and all but invited the authorities to bring him in for questioning, if not torture. But that's what makes him the Magiker Rebbe. Those unbroken court victories have inflated his ego to outlandish proportions. Where's the part I'm looking for? Wait...here it is. '*Sie kimmt in der Zimmer wie Esther Hamalka. Sehst! Der Gang. Der Sprach. Die Stimme. Der Personality...*' Oops, sorry, Doctor. Let me translate: 'She came into the room like Queen Esther. Look at her! Her walk. Her voice. Her carriage. Her personality. A natural beauty unlike any I had ever seen before. What was she doing wasting her time and affections with a boy like this Shimon? Instantly, I found myself consumed by an overwhelming need and desire to possess her. I wanted her for my own. No matter what the cost. No matter who or what stood in my way.' Do you see? The man is lost, besotted, doomed. How's that for an Act One curtain?"

My God, I thought, history was repeating itself. What was the term my mother had used? *Tikkun olam.* Was it my karma to fall in love with the same girl as my grandfather? A beautiful girl promised to another? "Then what happens...Alvin?"

His focus had abruptly shifted to the front of the coffee shop. "Now there's a postcoital couple if ever I saw one. Wait a minute! I know that guy. Why do I know him? Oh, wow! It's my sister Paula's old fiancé." The Little Cantor stood up and waved impulsively.

Turning around in annoyance, I caught sight of Martin Corwin in his raccoon coat. He was ushering Maureen Flanagan in from the cold; the couple was laughing and kissing like love-drunk teenagers. Part of me was delighted to see my best friend again; I had missed him. The other part feared an angry and contentious reunion. I turned back in my seat and watched the drama unfold in the mirrored back wall of the diner. I prayed that Rabinowitz was not waving at the Pasha.

Maureen tapped Corwin on the shoulder and nodded toward the diminutive man who was waving his arms over his head windmill fashion, like some overly enthusiastic fan at a Village People concert. The Pasha stared blankly in his direction, shrugged, and steered his buxom paramour to two seats at the front counter.

Unable to control himself, Rabinowitz cupped his hands like a megaphone and shouted: "Excuse me! Aren't you Marty Corwin?"

Slumping down in the booth, I prayed that the earth might open up and swallow me. Shutting my eyes, I whispered: "Why did you do that?"

"I love this guy!" replied Rabinowitz. "I haven't seen him in years."

Seconds later, a familiar voice behind me asked: "Do I know you from somewhere?"

"Thirty years ago," replied the Little Cantor. "You were engaged to my sister, Paula Rabinowitz. Remember? Weren't you the canoeing instructor at Camp Aviv?"

"Yes, I was the canoeing instructor. And no, I wasn't engaged to your sister. We merely dated."

"She told my mother you were engaged."

"Probably covering up for the debauched weekend we spent loaded on Quaaludes at a rock concert in Toronto—at the Maple Leaf Gardens, I believe. And your name—just a second—is Alvin. Correct? You had more hair then, but so did I. And you sang. How you sang! Maureen, this man sang like an angel. Still does, if I'm not mistaken. 'The Little Cantor with the Big Voice.' Correct?"

"One hundred percent."

"May I presume to ask you a question, Alvin?"

"Sure."

"What are you doing with Harris Strider, and why is he curled up in the booth pretending he doesn't know me?"

I craned my neck and stared up at Corwin. "Hello, Marty." I readjusted myself in my seat. "Would you care to sit down?"

"Maureen, you remember crazy Dr. Strider?" Corwin squeezed into the booth next to the Little Cantor, and his oversexed girlfriend plopped down next to me. "How is Paula, by the way? Send her my regards."

"She's a grandmother."

"Don't tell me that. She can't be more than . . . "

"And a lesbian."

"*Vey iz mir!*"

"But that might be just a phase."

"And what about you and Harry here? Why are you sitting in a back booth at three in the morning, like Bolshevik conspirators?" Never missing a trick, Corwin caught me darting my eyes back and forth between Rabinowitz and the journal. "What have we got here, boys?"

I made a move to grab the journal, but Corwin beat me to it. Opening it, he read the first line aloud: "'*Ich bin ein Magiker.*' Uh-huh." He read a few more lines to himself then asked me: "How much does he know?"

"This is between Alvin and me," I muttered, unable to meet Corwin's penetrating gaze.

"Have you known Harris long, Alvin?"

"Actually, we only met yesterday. I'm translating this journal for him."

"Should I presume this volume has to do with your patient?"

"Don't do this, Marty!"

Corwin turned back to the Little Cantor: "Did he tell you about her, the JAP from New Jersey who is possessed by the soul of a girl from a little *shtetl* in Tsarist Russia? What's the name of that town again? Irmunsk?"

Rabinowitz's eyes looked as if they might pop out of his head. He clapped a hand to his mouth and gasped: "You've met Leah? She's still alive?"

Corwin stared at the Little Cantor in despair. "You're as crazy as he is. How the hell do you know about Leah?"

"It's all in there," blurted out Rabinowitz, pointing to the journal. "This is the libretto of my opera."

The noise we were making was starting to stir up the normally blasé Greek waiters. They were pointing to the curious quartet in the back booth, muttering in Greek, and making what were probably death threats.

"We'd best adjourn to my place and discuss this," said Corwin.

"I'm starving!" said Maureen.

"Double bacon cheeseburgers and fries—to go!" Corwin patted my mournful face affectionately and returned his gaze to the journal.

\* \* \*

The Pasha and the Little Cantor sat next to each other at Corwin's dining table. The two resembled Talmudic scholars in a medieval woodcut, as they pored over the Magiker Rebbe's journal. Of course, the double bacon cheeseburgers they were munching were far from kosher. They passionately argued the merits of their respective translations. I sat in impatient silence across from them, while Nurse Flanagan snored seductively on the couch in the living room.

"Must you guys quibble about every adjective?" I finally asked.

"There's a tradition of scholarship here," said Corwin, "which a Midwestern *demi-Juif* couldn't possibly appreciate."

"Half Jewish?" asked Rabinowitz, adding yet another sin of omission to his list of grievances against me.

"His mother."

"Ah! Halachically speaking, if the mother is Jewish, then he's also…"

"Guys, guys!" There was considerable irritation in my voice. "It's half past three and you've only translated two paragraphs. How about more speed and less accuracy?"

Corwin gave me a withering glance, picked up his bacon cheeseburger, and gestured for Rabinowitz to proceed.

"Okay. Where were we?" The Little Cantor ran his finger along the lines of Yiddish text. "Got it. 'I assured the boy that this great beauty would be his before long. That perhaps I could even persuade the girl's father to give them his blessing plus a handsome dowry. Shimon, of course, wanted no money from the fat merchant.'"

"No, no. '*Grosse*' doesn't translate as fat, Alvin. Not in this context. It's more of a sarcastic commentary on 'great' or even 'renowned.'"

"Marty, stop already!" I held my hand up. "'Fat' is good enough. We get the general idea. Please, Alvin! Go on with your translation."

"'My next challenge was to win Leah's confidence. Her absolute trust.'" The Little Cantor had definitely picked up the pace in his translation. "'She possessed a remarkable mind for a female, an intellect starving for nourishment. What puny, half-baked ideas her beloved Shimon had filled her lovely head with. I dreamt of the days and candle-lit nights when I might make her my special student.' What a scoundrel this Magiker was, huh! By the way, do you have a piano here? I've got a tune running through my head for his big solo."

"Later, Alvin, please!" I clutched my hands together in supplication.

"'I introduced the notion to Leah of bravely defying her father and eloping with Shimon. Her lovely face flushed with excitement and her hands—like hot coals—trembled in mine. She kissed and embraced me with deepest gratitude. I turned away abruptly, for fear she might feel my arousal. It was no longer possible for me to remain near Irmunsk. Yet I realized I could not leave without the beauteous Leah. But this would mean disposing of that irritant Shimon.

"'Concocting a brilliant but wholly false tale of intrigue against the Jews of Prague, I dispatched the all-trusting Shimon as my emissary on a fool's errand to that distant city. And all this on the eve of the elopement, which he—poor dolt—knew nothing about. Sworn to secrecy, Shimon told Leah nothing of his imminent departure. So she, faithful creature, went to meet him at their usual spot in the woods outside the town, a spot I told her he had expressly chosen. Needless to say, Shimon never appeared. Leah was heartbroken when her father finally found her. There were no longer any impediments for her marriage to Yochanan Levy. All was proceeding according to my plan.'"

"What a colossal prick!" Corwin said. "Not to mention a raving megalomaniac."

"Why do you say that?" I felt an illogical responsibility to defend my grandfather's honor.

"Do you think what he did was nice, Harry?"

"He was in love with her. He was obsessed."

"Oh! Are you identifying with this mystical Machiavelli? 'The Hitlers Are Coming to Dinner.'"

"What's that?"

"A syndrome peculiar to my second wife," said Corwin. "She totally lacked any sensor for dysfunctional behavior.

The woman would roll out the welcome mat to serial killers without thinking twice. 'Oh, sweetheart! Did I tell you the Hitlers, Adolf and Eva, are coming to dinner? Oh, I know they've gotten a bad rap, but you really ought to hear their side of the story. Nothing's black and white.' Why on earth are you justifying this monster's behavior, Harry?"

Ignoring Corwin's question, I turned to the Little Cantor and asked: "What happens next?"

"I don't know." Rabinowitz stared in bewilderment at the page and began flipping through the journal.

"Go on, Alvin."

"It doesn't make any sense." Rabinowitz scratched his bald pate. "What's going on here? Marty, have a look at this." The Little Cantor shoved the book across the table to Corwin, who was scratching his bald pate at the same moment. "Has he gone and switched dialects? Is this Aramaic? I...I can't understand a word of what he's written."

"It's in code."

"Code," repeated Rabinowitz. "Why?"

Corwin shrugged then lit up a cigar. "Maybe he didn't want anyone else to know what he'd done. It was probably something illegal."

"What makes you say that?" I asked testily.

"We're not in court, Harry. Your 'client' has been dead for many years. But having boasted and bragged for over a hundred pages of his great achievements, why else would he suddenly feel the need for subterfuge? Something must have gone wrong. Something really bad."

"Very interesting," said Rabinowitz, continuing to examine the pages. "The narrative resumes again in Yiddish, fifteen pages later. On a cattle boat to America."

"Probably on the lam," said Corwin. "'Give me your tired, your homeless, your sociopaths yearning to find new victims.'" He exhaled a thin skein of cigar smoke. "Well, Dr. Strider, you finally solved the mystery of Barbara Warren."

"Why do you say that?"

"All those previously inexplicable details about Irmunsk, Leah, and the Magiker Rebbe. How did she know what she knew? Somehow, she got her hands on this journal and read it."

"Impossible."

"Why? Maybe this journal was published once upon a time, possibly even translated. Were there Jewish vanity presses back then? Gelbschein was certainly vain enough to want his legend perpetuated."

"It was never published, Marty. Okay?"

"How can you be so certain? Where the hell do you come off being an expert on Yiddish texts? Or Yiddish anything?"

"Don't take that supercilious tone to me, you dropout Hasid. My credentials are just as—"

"Credentials?"

"Pedigree."

"What the hell are you talking about, Harry? You can't even read this book. Why would you—"

"Because my grandfather wrote it! Okay?" I had lost my cool completely.

Corwin and Rabinowitz stared at me in astonishment.

"Is this true?" asked Rabinowitz. "Meyer Gelbschein was your grandfather?"

"Yes, he was."

"So you've been stringing me along like a prize sucker, right from the get-go." The Little Cantor's cheeks had grown flushed. "Feigning ignorance..."

"How long have you known?" Corwin asked.

"What relevance does—"

"Stop the Perry Mason horseshit! Okay? When did you find out about your connection to the Magiker Rebbe?"

"Friday night. My mother brought me the journal from Chicago."

"Why?"

I hesitated, to consider my response and to reconsider my mother's motives. Why had she brought me the journal? I nervously began fingering the apricot-colored envelope on which I had scribbled the address of the Greek diner.

"Why?" Corwin repeated the question testily.

Stalling for time, I stared at the front of the envelope. It was addressed in oversized gold calligraphy to "Dr. and Mrs. Harris Strider." And it was postmarked Tenafly, New Jersey. I tore it open and read the engraved invitation.

*JEFFREY AND MARSHA WARREN*
*INVITE YOU TO ATTEND THE WEDDING*
*OF THEIR DAUGHTER*
*BARBARA JOY*
*TO*
*GORDON JACOBS*

Clearly the wedding planner had not been told to scratch my name off the guest list, or she'd slipped up. The invitation went on to say the marriage ceremony was scheduled for five o'clock that afternoon at the Primrose Club in Tenafly, New Jersey. The Primrose Club, the six hundred guests, the day that I had been dreading for weeks had finally arrived. Barbara—Leah, my beloved Leah—was about to make a disastrous mistake. And only I could prevent it from happening. Snatching the journal away from the Little Cantor, I fled the apartment, oblivious to my collaborators as they shouted obscenities at my unexplained departure.

# THE PRIMROSE CLUB

THERE WERE NO CABS at five in the morning, so I walked across the Park. I was hacking violently by the time I reached home. Fortunately there was a year-old, half-empty bottle of prescription cough syrup in the bathroom. Would it still be potent? My question was answered when I passed out ten minutes later. When I finally awoke, it was four in the afternoon.

Could I possibly get to Tenafly in an hour? I struggled to get off the bed and on my feet. Still dizzy from the medicine, my coughing fit resumed. The label on the bottle carried a warning not to attempt driving a vehicle or to use heavy machinery, not even to contemplate it. But what choice did I have? I grabbed the bottle of cough syrup and took a deep drink. Moving as briskly as possible through my medicated stupor, I changed into my formal wear—no time to shave or shower—and dragged myself to the car-rental place around the corner. Would anything be left on a Saturday afternoon? Miraculously, they had one car.

Driving away from the lot, the attendant shouted something at me I couldn't hear over the din of traffic. Traversing the park at Ninety-Sixth Street, I caught the Henry Hudson Parkway and continued north to the George Washington Bridge.

Traffic was worse than usual on the bridge, but the cough medicine had made me woozy enough not to mind. It was freezing, so I switched on the car heater. Nothing happened. That's what the rental attendant was trying to tell me. The car's heater was broken, thus the miracle of the unrented vehicle.

It was five before I finally got to the Jersey side of the bridge, and I prayed through chattering teeth that the wedding hadn't started on time.

Getting on to the Palisades Parkway, I sped north toward Tenafly—clueless as to how I would handle the situation once I arrived.

My patent-leather shoes sank into the falling snow that blanketed the Primrose Club parking lot as I raced toward the entrance. The time was twenty minutes past five. The first two doors I tried were locked. Finally I found one that was open, went in, and was greeted by the orchestra booming "I Will Always Love You."

The marriage service had concluded and the reception was in full swing. I was too late. But I wasn't prepared to give up that easily. So what if Barbara and Gordon had exchanged vows in the sight of God and a cross section of New Jersey fat cats? It didn't mean Leah had gone along with the arrangement. No, my business was not with the newly married Mrs. Gordon Jacobs. It was with Moishe Littman's daughter Leah.

A beaming waiter thrust a flute of champagne into my hand as I entered the packed ballroom. The throng of guests resembled delegates to the Republican National Convention and was not what my brief experience of Jewish weddings had led me to expect. Against my better judgment, I tossed back the bubbly in one go and began prowling the room in search of Leah.

Sherman Rosenbaum was standing in a clutch of Dick Cheney and Donald Rumsfeld look-alikes wearing apricot-colored yarmulkes. The Chevalier was holding them hostage as he recounted one of his innumerable self-aggrandizing stories. Pausing to catch a breath, he looked up, saw me, and did a double take. A Hamas assassin wearing a dynamite-studded cummerbund would have been a more welcome sight. Murmuring apologies to his fellow guests, an apoplectic Rosenbaum made a beeline in my direction.

"My nephew has an order of protection against you."

"Sorry I missed the service, Sherman." I beamed and held up my printed invitation. "One likes to be on time but traffic was murder on the—"

"Leave this instant or I will call the police." Rosenbaum whipped out a cell phone from his tuxedo to indicate he meant business. "As a matter of fact, the Deputy Chief of Homeland Security is sitting right over —"

"C'mon, Sherm. Lighten up." The combination of cough syrup and champagne was clearly contributing to my behavior, as I waved my embossed invitation playfully in the irate Chevalier du Tastevin's face. "I was invited to this *simcha*."

"If Gordon sees you, he will break your neck. And I will gleefully not raise a finger to stop him."

"The groom shouldn't waste his strength on his wedding night. Hmmm. Is that from the Talmud or the Kama Sutra?"

Before the Chevalier could go nuclear, I caught sight of Gordon and Barbara, on the dance floor in each other's arms. She looked positively radiant, but poor Gordon seemed perplexed, almost mystified. She was laughing at him, and he abruptly and angrily deserted her in the middle of their dance and marched determinedly towards us.

"Get out there!" snarled Rosenbaum. "How do you think it looks, you abandoning her like that? Do you want to cause a scene?"

"Me? She's the one—" Gordon stopped midsentence and registered my unwanted presence for the first time. "What the hell is he doing here? Are you the one responsible for this obscene behavior, Strider?" Gordon appeared on the verge of tears. "She's doing it again. She…she doesn't recognize me and keeps calling me Yochanan."

Squeezing Gordon's arm with all the false sympathy at my command, I murmured: "Perhaps I could be of some small assistance."

"Is that a good idea, Uncle Sherm?" Gordon's voice had lost all its usual confidence, and he sounded like a forlorn adolescent, who'd just lost all the money he'd saved from his paper route. "After all this lunatic's put her through. Put us through."

"What have we got to lose?" The Chevalier du Tastevin shrugged his shoulders helplessly. "She's obviously having one of her episodes again. Please, do what you can…Harris."

Wow! He was really desperate if we were back to buddy-buddy first names again. Trying to maintain a straight if not grim face, I marched purposefully onto the dance floor. My heart was pounding. Leah's eyes lit up when she saw me.

"Hello, Rebbe. I knew you'd come."

"You had me worried for a while, Leah." I took her in my arms and began dancing with her. "There was no way for me to contact you."

"Barbara and I quarreled," explained Leah, gazing up at me with those twinkling, mesmerizing eyes. "But in the end, I made her bend to my will. I can't marry the wrong man again, Rebbe."

"Don't worry, my darling. It won't happen." Bringing my lips down to hers, I kissed her tenderly. My soul was soaring. I was back on the toboggan once again with my *bashert*. All my previous conceptions of love were shattered with that one blissful kiss. Every lyric of every romantic ballad ever written was caroming off the walls of my brain. I continued to kiss my beloved, oblivious to the outraged gasps from the wedding guests nearby.

Leah pressed her head against my chest and asked: "What can we do, Rebbe? All these guests!"

I whispered something in her ear. She shivered at the idea and nodded, giggling all the while like a mischievous child.

Five minutes later, we ran from the reception and were fastening our seat belts as we sped out of the Primrose Club parking lot. Snow continued to fall, seemingly in league with us as it instantly covered our tracks. In the rearview mirror, I could see Sherman Rosenbaum and Gordon Jacobs shaking their fists and chasing after the rental car. The last thing I saw before I jacked the car hard to the left and onto the street was the esteemed Chevalier going airborne on a patch of ice, executing an awkward grand jeté in midflight, and landing face first in the snow.

Leah squeezed my arm with a mix of gratitude and adoration. "Barbara's mother thinks I've gone to the ladies' room. Where are we going?"

"Do you trust me?"

"Of course."

"Then be patient until we get there."

I knew that I did not want either to live with or love two women. If I was to have a life with Leah, I had to free her from Barbara's meddling, controlling presence. If, as Molly had suggested, their two souls had collided in Vermont, then taking Leah back to the scene of that existential encounter might somehow reverse their tragic consanguinity. A snowstorm is a snowstorm is a snowstorm. *Aleva!* God willing! Leah could come to me—at long last—as her own, sweet loving self. And Barbara? Callous as it must sound, she was no longer my problem.

As if reading my mind, Leah took my hand in hers and squeezed it. "Thank you, Rebbe." She raised my fingers to her soft lips and kissed them. "I thought I would never love again. But you kept your promise, as you said you would."

What promise was that? What did it matter? The beloved Leah was mine at last. The touch of those soft lips on my fingertips made all questions irrelevant. I struggled to overcome my libidinous urge to pull the car over and make love to her on the spot. Oh, no, I wouldn't yield to that temptation. Not with Gordon and the police hot on our tail. Leah's chattering teeth brought me out of my reverie.

"Are you cold?" What a ridiculous question! The beautiful young bride was clad only in her wedding gown, and the car's heater was broken.

"It's all right," she whispered in a voice I could barely hear.

Pulling the car over to the side of the highway, I removed my overcoat and draped it around her shoulders. She curled up like a kitten and was fast asleep by the time we crossed back into New York. It was almost seven, and there were still many miles to be traveled through Connecticut and Massachusetts before we reached our final destination.

At half past one on Sunday morning, we arrived at the Vermont inn where she and Gordon had stayed months earlier. If the cadaverous night clerk, whose name, fittingly, was

Graves, had found our wedding attire slightly suspect—apparently most honeymooners change into more comfortable traveling clothes after the nuptials have been performed—then his visage was transformed into a mask of Yankee condemnation after I informed him that we had no luggage. Nevertheless, he gave us a key and we proceeded to our room.

By that time, Leah was extremely pale and shivering hard enough to alarm me. I ran a hot bath, phoned downstairs, and asked Graves to send some extra blankets to our room. When they finally arrived, Leah was in the bathroom. My cough had resumed full force; I pulled the bottle of cough syrup from my coat pocket and swallowed what meager drops were left. Placing the blankets on a nearby chair, I stretched out on the bed and shut my eyes for a brief second.

The next thing I knew, dawn was breaking and Leah was gone. I ran to the window, but the snow swirling around outside made visibility impossible. Dashing downstairs, I found Graves half-asleep at the front desk. A roaring fire was blazing in the lobby's stone fireplace, warming a smattering of guests in fashionable skiwear. They were sitting and reading the local paper as they waited for the breakfast buffet to be laid out and the snow to let up before taking the lift to the summit.

Trying to conceal the panic in my voice, I asked the cadaverous clerk, in a barely audible voice, if he'd seen "my wife."

"Bit skittish, is she?" Graves showed me no mercy, as he looked me up and down, then down and up, taking in my wrinkled formal wear, my uncombed hair, and two days of unshaven whiskers.

"We…eloped." Even I realized the excuse sounded lame.

"Uh-huh." Clearly Graves thought so, too. "Well...I'll keep an eye out for her. Don't think she could have gone far in this kinda blizzard."

A woman's voice seemed to echo in the distance. Could Leah foolishly have ventured outside?

"Did you hear that...that voice?" I asked Graves.

"Nope."

"That was my wife calling. Didn't you hear a woman's voice calling out just now?"

"Kitchen'll be opening soon, sir. Mebbe you'd like some coffee and breakfast. World has a different complexion, so they say, on a full stomach."

"No, thank you. I've got to find her!"

"Suit yerself."

I raced out the front door and into the blinding snow. Following the voice, I managed with difficulty to walk about two hundred yards. With my snow-blurred vision, I was barely able to make out what I took to be Leah's silhouette walking slowly towards the woods. She was crying out: "Shimon! Shimon!"

Oblivious to the merciless wind and bitter cold, I trudged through the snow to catch up with her. As I approached the tree line, I caught hold of her arm and spun her around to face me.

"Please, Rebbe, let go! Shimon is waiting for me. Release me, I beg of you."

Release her? Release me! Or whatever spirit or neurosis had engulfed my life these past winter months. Why hadn't I gone to Tahiti when I had had the chance and escaped from the frozen demons that had turned my life upside down? Before I could reason with Leah, she pulled herself loose from my grasp and trudged through the snow into the woods.

"Stop! Stop, Leah!" I shouted after her until my voice was hoarse. "There's no one to go to. Shimon is dead—years ago and far away from here."

She vanished from sight, and I stumbled after her into the deep woods. My patent-leather-clad feet were completely frozen by this time. Ten minutes later, I was hopelessly lost, as the ferocious roar of the wind echoed in my frostbitten ears and the snow continued to fall relentlessly.

"Leah! Barbara! Where are you? Can you hear me, Leah? Barbara!"

Just as I was about to give up and make my way back to the inn, I saw Leah stumbling in the snow toward me, her arms outstretched. Tears of joy filled her eyes.

"My darling!" she sobbed. "I thought I had lost you forever."

"Don't be silly," I cried. Tears were streaming down my face, as well. Why had I given up hope so soon? Wasn't it obvious at last? She did love me. "Everything's fine now, Leah. Promise you won't ever run away from me again. I was so worried about you."

"My beloved. Take me in your arms."

I held out my arms but suddenly realized that she wasn't looking at me. Leah walked right past me and flung herself into the arms of a man, who seemed to have materialized from nowhere. Tall, bearded, in his late twenties, he swept her off her feet and spun her round and round.

"Shimon! Shimon! Shimon!" She repeated the young man's name deliriously. "What happened to you, my love? Where did you disappear to?"

"The Rebbe lied to me," replied Shimon. "He purposely deceived me so he could—"

Leah shook her head repeatedly. "No, no, no. That's not true. He's brought me here to you, Shimon. The Rebbe is our friend."

I stared at the two young lovers clutching each other and felt certain I had taken complete leave of my senses. The potent hate reflected in Shimon's eyes burned through me like a laser. Then, just as quickly, a warm smile crossed his face, and the young man held his hand out to me.

"I must believe my beloved. Thank you, Rebbe. Clearly, there was a misunderstanding."

As I stepped forward to clasp Shimon's hand, a huge gust of wind came between us creating a thick wall of snow. When the wind finally subsided, Leah and Shimon had vanished from sight.

I wandered hopelessly in the deep woods for another hour, futilely calling out their names and begging them to answer me. By the time I emerged, the blizzard had ended and state troopers waited outside the inn…with their guns trained on me.

# THE CODE REVEALED

ALL THAT WAS two years ago. A great deal has happened to the world since then and, of much less importance, to me.

The state troopers drove me to Stowe and grilled me at the local jail for hours. Later, two FBI agents, who made it clear that kidnapping and murder was both a capital and Federal offense, joined them. They ran the show from that point on, and the endless grilling began all over. Where was Barbara's body? What had I done with her? Graves, the night clerk at the inn, had already told them in detail how I had followed Barbara, whom he suspected all along wasn't really my wife, into the woods. Whoa! I never went into the woods with Barbara. In fact, I denied being with Barbara at all. What the hell was I talking about, asked the lead FBI agent? What about all the witnesses, who had sat up bleary eyed through the night in Tenafly, giving sworn testimony? The guests were mistaken, I said. And, as a topper, I challenged the Feds to give me a polygraph.

The results of the test confirmed that I wasn't lying, which left the FBI utterly baffled. How could I have fooled their infallible machine? It wasn't difficult. I merely told the truth. I had gone nowhere with Barbara Warren on the night in question. The companion with whom I had left the wedding at the Primrose Club was Leah Littman. That was the truth. But no one bothered to ask me about Leah. Why would they? And I saw no reason to volunteer her name and go through another polygraph test.

The next day the New York tabloids reveled in my sad story:

## THE SHRINK WHO SHRUNK HIS PATIENT
### Kidnapped Bride Vanishes in Vermont Woods

## STALKER STRIDER SLIPS UP IN STOWE
### Parents' Plea: Where is Barbara?

The media swooped down on my office and bombarded poor Evelyn with questions, for which she had no answers. Jeffrey and Marsha Warren and their daughter Judy became familiar, tearful figures on the cable news shows. They begged me to show some humanity and reveal what I had done with Barbara. Where was I hiding her? To my amazement, the ever-faithful Claire came back from Iowa and began screening criminal lawyers to handle my case. My parents selflessly offered to take out a second mortgage on their home to help pay for my defense. Molly Friedman, that toughest of tough cookies, who miraculously had survived the fall in her apartment, signed a blank check to cover any and all of my legal expenses.

"Tell them the truth," Molly begged me, squeezing my hand with her bony fist on her visit to my cell in Newark (where I had been transferred after an ambitious New Jersey

district attorney won jurisdiction over Vermont for my case).
"They've got to believe you."

"The only one who believes me is you. And if I were
you, Molly, I wouldn't tell anyone."

"But it makes perfect sense. All Leah ever wanted was to
be with Shimon. No matter how long it took."

My attorney was Abner Greenglass, a clever and flam-
boyant trial lawyer with a well-deserved reputation for mesmerizing juries and bending them to his will. All he asked
from me was the truth, no matter what. When I finally finished my lengthy tale, Greenglass smiled warmly, pinched my
cheek, and said he'd see me in court.

I was visited later that day by a distraught Marty Corwin,
who, with tears streaming down his face, grabbed me in a
bear hug and said: "Don't worry, kid. It's gonna be okay. I've
spoken to Greenglass. There's nothing to worry about."

"Who's worried? I didn't do anything, Pasha. There was
no kidnapping. She came willingly."

Corwin stared into my eyes and sighed. "Just stick to
your story, Harry, and you'll live to a ripe old age."

The courtroom was packed throughout the trial. My
mother and father attended every day. Claire did as well, escorted by Edwin, who had survived his auto accident and
now sported two artificial kneecaps. Donna Schuman appeared occasionally and offered moral support to my parents
and me. Dalton Lafferty showed up once but reverted to his
old behavior. He was banned from the courtroom after vocal-
ly protesting "the shameless Stalinist purge" to which the authorities were subjecting me. And, every once in a while, I
noticed the solid presence of Detective Fletcher Jones, seated
on the aisle scratching his snowy white head in amazement
and amusement at the proceedings.

Miranda Cho, an ambitious, take-no-prisoners assistant district attorney from Hoboken was big on show and tell. She played several videos in an attempt to convince the jury of my pathological obsession with Barbara. Those stolid twelve citizens watched shaky, grainy video—blown up from Gilles's cell phone—of me dragging the lamented victim out of his salon. Also there was the passing pedestrian's footage of me, slightly inebriated, having words with the foul-mouthed truck driver outside Molly Friedman's apartment building. Ms. Cho attempted to create a portrait of me as a drunken reprobate, whose license should have been revoked years before. Gordon bounded athletically up to the witness stand and eloquently denounced me. Then he broke into racking sobs, which caused several female members of the jury to follow suit. Sherman Rosenbaum had one helluva tough act to follow after his nephew's lachrymose performance on the stand but came close with his portrait of me as a modern day Svengali, who had wrapped everyone around his fingers and made them dance to his evil tunes. Not content to stop there, the shameless Miranda Cho summoned the despised Robert Ortega—much beefier and shorter than I had ever imagined him—to explain under oath how I had fraudulently manipulated my insurance claims for years. "Are you an Axis One or an Axis Two?" became a media catch phrase for days afterwards.

I was taken aback when Abner Greenglass summoned the Pasha as a defense witness; I had to listen painfully as Corwin described my mental health in less than flattering terms. At one point, I was on the verge of taking Professor Lafferty's lead and shouting out a vocal protest, when Claire, seated directly behind me, squeezed my shoulders and hissed: "Keep quiet."

Needless to say, Greenglass refused to let me take the stand in my own defense, despite my recurrent requests to "set the record straight."

After three hours of deliberation, the jury found me not guilty. The jurors explained to the media afterward that the absence of a body and the lack of sufficient circumstantial evidence to convict me beyond a reasonable doubt had led to their verdict.

When I showed no remorse for my "crime" and continued to insist on my "demented" version of what had occurred, Claire and the Warrens joined forces, petitioned the court, and had me committed, as "a real and present danger" to both the community and myself.

\* \* \*

I was admitted to Pinehurst, a venerable upstate loony bin perched high on a hill, with a beautiful view of the Hudson.

The doctors at Pinehurst didn't like me much at first. I constantly criticized their treatment and diagnoses of my fellow patients. Despite considerable overcrowding and an insufficient number of quality therapists, they rejected my initial offers to help alleviate their professional load. Only after the Church of the Christian Brotherhood incinerated two thousand copies of the Koran on a public bonfire in Dallas did the administrator of the understaffed hospital reluctantly consent to my counseling some of the more paranoid patients, who feared imminent nuclear reprisals by various Al Qaeda sleeper cells scattered throughout the land.

Tilly McIntire and Molly Friedman both died peacefully in their sleep on the same weekend six months after the trial. Their brief obituaries appeared side by side in the *New York Times*. Tilly was described as "an eccentric figure in Gotham music circles and a one-time secretary to Leonard Bernstein."

Her adopted son (news to me), composer Edwin Sheffield, was writing a requiem for her that he said would be his masterwork. Molly was "a noted philanthropist, who had kept a very low profile throughout her long life until the recent trial of Dr. Harris Strider, whose champion she had mysteriously become."

By an odd coincidence, a third death occurred a week later. The body of Sherman Rosenbaum, the Long Island property developer and longtime Republican fundraiser, was discovered under mysterious circumstances in a Chinatown hotel. Police would not comment on the possibility of foul play.

My curiosity about the Chevalier's death was rewarded by the unexpected appearance of Fletcher Jones in Pinehurst's visitors' lounge the following Sunday.

"I wouldn't have paid it no mind," said the detective, sitting across from me in the visitors lounge and flashing a big smile, "except I remembered his name from the trial. He had some pretty harsh words to say about you on the stand. So I called up an old buddy of mine who handles homicide in that precinct. He told me that the old Jew was a regular at the Chinese whorehouse on Mott Street where they found him. He was with two hookers! Had a little black attaché case with him, and some fine wine inside it."

"He was a Chevalier du Tastevin."

"Say what?"

"He was a knight in a Burgundian wine-tasting order...in France."

"Well, he sure went with a smile on his face. I'm telling you the truth."

"Thank you for coming to the trial, Fletcher. For a while there, I was afraid the prosecution was going to call you as a witness."

"Wouldn't do them no good. 'Cause I know you ain't guilty."

"What makes you so sure, Fletcher?"

"Me and Dr. Freud." Jones flashed that big smile of his again.

"Same birthday, right?"

Jones nodded: "And the caul."

"Your sixth sense?"

"That girl ain't dead."

"How do you know that?" A chill ran down my spine.

"I think old Lucifer made you tussle with your id and your superego for a while. But you ain't no killer, Doc, no way, no how. And there ain't no body."

"Then where the hell is she, Fletcher?"

"Tell you what, if I hear from her, I'll let you know." Jones roared with laughter, slapped a huge paw down on my knee, and got to his feet. "Maybe I'll come by and see you again some time."

"I'd like that."

Not long after Fletcher Jones's visit, Alvin Rabinowitz arrived with a pink box of his mother's homemade rugelach. The Little Cantor had come to visit in the hope of persuading me to collaborate with him on his magnum opus, *The Magiker's Spell*. I agreed to the partnership for my own reason: slowly and patiently, Alvin taught me to read Hebrew. This, in turn, became my gateway to Yiddish, the Book of Zohar, and my grandfather's infamous journal, which my WASP colleagues, in their ignorance, thought a harmless enough volume to bring with me to Pinehurst.

But what was the key to unlocking the code? I had scoured the Internet for hours, reading up on spies, ciphers, cryptographs, anagrams, and rebuses–anything that might be the "open sesame" to Meyer Gelbschein's obsession with

Leah Littman. Then one day, I said her name to myself, and it came to me. Leah! Could it be? No, this was too easy. But try it! Try it! Leah, in Hebrew, is spelled lamed, aleph, he. Lamed is thirty. Aleph is one. He is five. The total is thirty-six. And three plus six is nine. I added nine onto the number for every letter in the journal, took that new number and matched it to its corresponding letter, and—frustrating and laborious as it was—the code was broken!

Thus, a month ago, I was finally able to decipher my grandfather's journal, right under the noses of my keepers. Oh, if they only knew the magnitude of the Magiker's crimes!

I haven't taken the Little Cantor into my confidence yet. My discovery would make the perfect climax for his opera. Unquestionably, it rivals *Rigoletto* for sheer power and irony. The problem is that, in the current climate, with Sean Hannity and his Fox cronies still clamoring for me to get the death penalty—habeas corpus be damned—no one would buy a ticket to see this obscene and twisted tale set to music, no matter how beautiful and melodic. No, it is better to let the Little Cantor dream of the glory that might be his than share the nightmare of my purgatory.

So, you ask, what did those missing pages reveal? Nothing that surprising, once you realize what a devious mind my grandfather possessed. Having dispatched Shimon on a wild goose chase to distant Prague, the Magiker took the next step in his twisted plan to make Leah his own.

But first, he had to contact the newly married Leah. As a pariah in the *shtetl*, though, how could he do that? The answer lay in the festival of Purim, the most joyous and nonreligious of all the Jewish holidays. It celebrates the triumph of Queen Esther, a Jewess married to the King of Persia, over his evil wazir Haman, who wanted to exterminate all the Jews in the land. Falling on the fourteenth of Adar in the Hebrew calendar, Purim usually corresponds to late February on the Western calendar. It is marked by celebrations that include great feasting, drinking to excess, wearing masks, and burning an effigy of Haman.

As the most beautiful girl in Irmunsk, the newly married Leah had been chosen to play Queen Esther at the *shtetl*'s Purim pageant. As she walked through the crowd of masked revelers, dispensing freshly baked hamantaschen—the triangular stuffed pastries served only on Purim—the Magiker, wearing a mask and a hooded cloak, approached Leah. He whispered that he had news of Shimon, described the location of a secret spot in the forest, and told Leah to meet him there the next day.

At her meeting with the Magiker the day after Purim, Leah learned Shimon was staying in the gentile's town with him and was so heartsick that, ever since the news of her wedding, he had not stirred from his bed. The Magiker was afraid, or so he said, that Shimon was dying.

Oh, had Leah only known that Shimon was still in Prague. She would have seen my wily grandfather for what he was, and run from the forest. Instead, she threw herself sobbing into his arms. Between hating her life with Yochanan and longing for a life with Shimon, she told him she felt as if she too were dying. She begged the Magiker to help save them both. Which was exactly why he was there, he said…and he already had a plan. And with that, the Magiker Rebbe became the *haymishe* Friar Laurence to my beloved Leah's unsuspecting Juliet.

He reached inside his cloak and pulled out a vial filled with a strange oily liquid. He told Leah that a kabbalist in Galicia had given him the formula to concoct the magic potion he now held in his hand. If taken in steadily larger doses over a week, it would simulate the appearance of death. Then, he told Leah the details of what he had in mind.

It didn't take much effort for the Magiker to persuade the guileless Leah that his plan would work and his "harmless elixir" would be her passport out of Irmunsk and to a joyous reunion with her adored Shimon.

To the puzzlement of her family and her new husband, Leah's health started to degenerate. To their abject horror, a week after Purim, the young bride was pronounced dead and, as is the Jewish custom, buried immediately. The Magiker's plan was to dig her up that night, bring her around with smelling salts, tell her Shimon had disappeared, and spirit her away to a new life in France or England.

But my grandfather failed to take into account the un-predictable nature of the Russian winter, particularly that February, when an unprecedented freeze after Leah's funeral had turned the cemetery ground as hard as concrete. The Magiker's attempt to dig up Leah in the dead of night only resulted in a broken shovel. Frantic, he clawed at the snow-covered dirt with his nails and stabbed it with his knife. But nothing could penetrate the frozen ground where Leah lay buried alive, six feet below. The Magiker hurled his anguished body across her grave, wailing her name.

Wait! Wait! Catching himself, he paused. What if some-one had heard him, and people started to ask questions? He could do nothing for Leah now. Maybe the Angel of Death had already taken her. Perhaps the potion had not simulated death but truly caused it. If that was the case, he must flee immediately. He would go to England as planned. No, no, that would not be far enough. He would cross the sea to America! They would never find him there.

And so, Meyer Gelbschein came to New York City, where, as the Magiker Rebbe, he found fame and a following in the borough of Brooklyn. He lived to a ripe old age and had a wonderful daughter. Seemingly his crime went undetected and unpunished. But the dead's cries for justice do not go unanswered.

The souls of those star-crossed lovers, Leah and Shimon, demanded *tikkun olam*. Amends. And I, Harris Strider, had to pay for my grandfather's capital crime. After all, was I not prepared to follow the Magiker Rebbe's same scenario? Was I not his *gilgul*? Was Gordon Jacobs any different in his relationship to me as Shimon had been to my grandfather? And, even before that, hadn't some evil Gelbschein gene whispered in my brain and dared me to steal Claire away from Edwin? And hadn't I—out of hubris, not love—done that solely to exercise my power?

\* \* \*

The Sunday after I had decoded all this, I was told I had a visitor in the lounge downstairs.

Professor Lafferty rose from the sofa and greeted me with outstretched arms. He was wearing a smart Brooks Brothers suit and a button-down shirt, and his shoulder-length hair had been cut conservatively short.

We embraced with great gusto. He laughed, stood back, and, as if reading my thoughts, explained: "I met a woman."

"Professor!" I was thrilled.

"Call me Dalton. We've known each other long enough to abandon formality."

"Tell me about her."

"Her name is Wanda. She's Polish, in her midfifties, and a former actress—a legendary Desdemona in her native Warsaw. And her Cleopatra! Ho-ho-ho! You haven't lived until you've heard her say 'give me to drink mandragora' in Polish. She's read all my books in translation. She adores me. Look, Harris! My clothes match. The woman has given me a makeover. And—annus mirabilis—she has me talking to my grandchildren on Skype. 'Is not this love, indeed?'"

"You don't need a therapist anymore, Dalton."

"That's what Corwin keeps telling me."

"Martin Corwin?"

"Yes, the Pasha. He sees some of your patients now; the ones who felt abandoned after your incarceration. He's trying to wean me off slowly."

"Are you paying him?"

"Certainly not. We bartered for a signed first edition of *Tropic of Cancer*."

"Sounds like Marty. He could quote Henry Miller verbatim. How's he doing? I haven't heard a word from him in months."

"He has joined the ranks of Benedick."

"Sorry, Dalton. I don't…"

"*Much Ado About Nothing*. Beatrice and Benedick. The Pasha married a gorgeous colleen."

"No! Nurse Flanagan? When?"

"Three months ago. She is with child. Though I'm not sure whether that occurred before or after the wedding. She also went to the *mikveh*. Did I pronounce that word correctly?"

"Ritual baths," I translated the word for Lafferty and explained: "She must have converted to Judaism."

"Yes."

"But his first two wives were Episcopalians."

"Apparently it was Maureen's idea. She wants the child to be raised Jewish."

"And Marty told you all this?" I asked.

"No. She told Wanda. They've become great friends."

"Extraordinary."

"Do they get the *Times* here, Harris?"

"Yes. But I never read it."

"Ah! Then you don't keep up with wedding announce-
ments and the like."

"Marty and Maureen were in the *Times*?"

"No. Your ex-wife was."

"Claire?"

"She married a composer, who has his own virtual orchestra. I have no idea what that means."

"Skype."

"Ah!"

Lafferty and I sank into a long thoughtful silence. I was
happy for Claire. She had been happily heading down the
matrimonial track with Edwin until the Magiker *gilgul* devious-
ly derailed what had previously been *bashert*.

Again, Lafferty must have read my thoughts, for he
cleared his throat and said: "I keep thinking about Leah."

"It must be Wanda's Eastern European chi."

"I saw that girl, Harris. The one you described, not that
bejeweled narcissist whose photograph was all over the air-
waves and the Internet. Leah was not of this earth."

"Please, Dalton, don't get yourself agitated. I've made
my peace with the situation."

"But it's so unfair, Harris. You're a young man—
brilliant, vital. To be locked away like this…"

Lafferty took my hand and squeezed it in comradely affection. "I'm organizing a petition for your release."

"No, no. Don't!"

"It's what I do best, Harris. Wanda marched for Solidari-
ty. She can't wait to storm the barricades again:

*Once more unto the breach, dear friends, once more;*
*Or close the wall up with our half-Jewish dead.*

"Oh! Perhaps I shouldn't have said that. Leapt before I
looked. Story of my life."

274

Lafferty embraced me again and promised he would bring Wanda the next time.

"She will recite for you, Harris. Your soul will be liberated—even if you aren't."

The next day I had an even more surprising visitor. An orderly came to my door just after lunch and presented me with a business card, which read: Diane Mazzeo, Ph.D.—Spiritual Investigations.

I had no idea who Dr. Mazzeo could be, but my curiosity was piqued. Waiting for me in the visitors' lounge was a woman wearing a pastel-colored Armani power suit. Her cropped gray hair was obviously a salon cut, and the care lines on her face established her as a contemporary of my mother. Oh, no! Had something happened to Mitzi?

"Hello," said Dr. Mazzeo, holding out her hand. "Do you remember me?"

I shook her hand. "There have been a lot of doctors examining me in the last two years. Forgive me if…"

"I wasn't a doctor when we met."

She smiled, and I recognized those unforgettable blue eyes for the first time.

"Sister Aurelia!"

"Hello, Harry." She burst out laughing. "Sorry, but you had that exact same look on your face in the library. Remember, the poster?"

"What happened, Sister? Have you left the order?"

"First Audrey Hepburn, then me. It just didn't make sense anymore."

"Do you want to sit down, Sister?"

"I've been on a train for hours. Is there someplace we can walk?"

We stepped into the garden, and she took my arm as we walked around the grounds. I was startled at first, but she seemed so relaxed by the physical contact that I relaxed as well. And it had been some time since I had touched a woman, even as casually and platonically as this.

"Sister…"

"Diane. That's my real name."

"What happened, Diane? Tell me." After two years, I was back in my shrink mode again.

"You're partly responsible, Harry."

"Me?"

"Your trial. I watched the recaps every night. The Sisters were really pissed off at me for hogging the TV. They're all Home Shopping Network junkies, even if they can't buy the stuff. The trial was a very disturbing experience for me. It took all my willpower to keep from contacting the defense as an expert witness. But then I'd have ended up in here with you. How's the food, by the way?"

"Awful. Too much salt and no garlic."

"American cuisine. Not this girl! At least I taught them to cook Italian at the convent."

"Diane?"

"Yes?"

"The trial? You, leaving the order?"

"Right, sorry…little acid flashbacks once in a while. I can talk about them now that I've left the order. The thing is, Harry, I just couldn't do it anymore, the Vatican and me. All the nuns and the Vatican…we're falling away from the Church. That's the big 'C' church, not the little 'c.' Know what I mean? But I have all this knowledge, and it's stuff the Church doesn't want to know about. Certainly the law doesn't want to know about it; look at the way you were treated. You had to sit there like a mute."

"My lawyer wouldn't let me talk."

"Of course he wouldn't. But the bottom line is, you did it! You actually did it!"

"What? What did I do?"

"The exorcism."

"No, I didn't. I never found a *tzadik*."

"Yes, you did. It was you, Harry. You were the *tzadik*. You were the Magiker. You released the *ibbur*."

"No! My motives were entirely selfish. I was in love with Leah. You recognized that, Diane, and warned me against it. Besides I didn't just love her. This was not a teenage crush. I lusted after her."

"But was it really you doing the lusting, Harry? Or your grandfather's *gilgul*?"

"Please, don't!"

"Why are you running away from it? *Tikkun olam*. You made amends for all the evil the Magiker Rebbe perpetrated."

"You're as crazy as I am!"

"How many other people are there like you, Harry? Like Leah? Suffering for the sins of others, ancient sins going back generations, centuries even. We could help them. We have a duty, Harry."

I unwrapped Diane's arm from mine and stared defiantly into her piercing blue eyes. "I don't pretend to understand what happened in those woods. Maybe all this talk of *ibburs* and *gilgulim* has some substance. But it doesn't answer the question everyone wants to know: What happened to Barbara's body? Where did it go? That unanswered question is what is keeping me in here."

"Barbara was a vessel…Don't look at me like that, Harry. Her physical body was a vessel for migrant souls. *Ibburim*! Leah's soul was finally free. Another *ibbur* is probably inside Barbara now. Who knows? Maybe she's an Inuit woman in

Labrador. Wait until she finds herself wanting to hang Laura Ashley curtains in the igloo!"

"It's not funny, Diane. I feel a degree of responsibility. My obsession has led to this transmigration. Where has her new soul taken her?"

"Want to find out?"

"What are you talking about?"

"Become my partner. We can help people."

"How, by forming the Department of Missing Souls?"

"There are people suffering, Harry, all over the world. Not just Jews, but Catholics, Protestants, Muslims. We are experts. We possess certain gifts. Knowledge that mustn't be wasted."

"Diane, I think you should leave now."

"Don't you believe anymore, Harry? Why did you have to go through everything you experienced? It was your Burning Bush."

"Look, I don't know what I believe, Diane. But I'm in here and you're out there. Way out there!"

"You could leave anytime you want."

"How?"

"Recant. Tell them it was all a delusion, brought on by overwork and the Great Recession. Dr. Corwin will write you a note, I'm sure. He has a very nice face. Just go to bed, wake up in the morning, and say it just occurred to you that the whole Leah thing had been a dream. They'll be glad to see you go. They would probably like the bed for someone who really needs it. You're not crazy, Harry."

"I know that, Diane. So, you're telling me that in order to be discharged as sane, I have to pretend to have been crazy. It's like *Catch-22*."

"Exactly. Think about it, Harry. It would be a *mitzvah*. You have my card, right? Keep in touch."

\* \* \*

*That was last week, and I haven't had a decent night's sleep since. I dread dreaming. Strange voices and stranger faces plead with me to help them. Sometimes they call me Doctor. Other times they call me Rebbe.*

*Could I possibly tread the path Diane proposes? Certainly through my recent experiences, I have learned that there is a higher order, a stronger power, than that recognized by the Supreme Court or Cambridge Medical. Could I really explain the concepts of* ibbur *and* bashert *to the police, the FBI, or even someone as sympathetic as Fletcher Jones, without having them ship me back to Pinehurst posthaste? Could I possibly make them believe that love does not really die, that there are more things in heaven and on earth, and that Leah and Shimon are finally together? And, that I—a jaded and cynical doctor of the mind—finally helped, truly helped, one of my patients? How could I make them understand, as I know you now do?*

# ACKNOWLEDGMENTS

First the therapists: Myra Pomerantz, who explained the mysteries of Axis One and Axis Two to me; Matthew Seidman, who assured me in my moments of despair that this book would be published; Melvyn Iscove, who shares the family secret behind this story.

To the people who knowingly and unknowingly aided in the writing of this book: Kenneth Welsh, Elliott Gould, Ed Asner, Macey Dennis, Gene Mack, Kim Eveleth, Jason Kravits, Fred Melamed, Patty McCormack, Josh Mostel, Bailey and Bert Bloom, Daniel Brewbaker, Michael Laskin, Ron Orbach, Rebecca and Steven Dennis, Laila Robins, Serena Dessen, Michael Dennis, Lenore Feldman, Geoffrey Holder, Lyn Frankel, Earl Pomerantz, Colleen Camp, Mark Rydell, David Iscove, Adam Iscove, Miranda Dennis, Joe Liss, Lorne Weil, and Theodore Bikel.

To those who are no longer with us but whose influence can be felt throughout this book: Sam Dennis, Sade Dennis, Mike Okun, Eva Dessen, Mary Wolfe, George Bloomfield, Sol Dennis, Jerry Iscove, Henry Ramer, Lew Weitzman, August Schellenberg, Herschel Bernardi and Lou Jacobi. And to all the Eisikowitch clan and their descendants who left Apt a century ago.

To the incomparable Margot Frankel for her inspired cover design. And to Califia Suntree, the most intrepid of copy editors, who astonished me with her ability. Finally to my steadfast friend Holly Palance, who introduced me to her husband, Robert Wallace, who in turn enthusiastically made me part of his new publishing venture.

# ABOUT THE AUTHOR

Photograph by Ed Begley Jr.

Charles Dennis lives in Los Angeles. *The Magiker* is his twelfth novel. His other books include *Given the Crime, Shar-Li, The Dealmakers,* and *Bonfire.* He wrote the screenplay for Richard Lester's film *Finders Keepers,* which was based on Dennis's novel *The Next-to-Last Train Ride.* His play *Going On* has been produced in New York, London and Los Angeles. He played Sunad on *Star Trek: The Next Generation* and was the voice of Rico in Disney's *Home on the Range.* He won the Samuel Fuller Guerrilla Filmmaker Award for *Atwill.* He wrote and directed *Chicanery,* the first feature film shot on an iPad. He is hard at work on his next novel: *Hollywood Raj.*

**A-W**

*Asahina & Wallace*
*Los Angeles*
*2013*
www.asahinaandwallace.com